MEGAN FRAMPTON

FOUR WEEKS *of* SCANDAL

AVONBOOKS

An Imprint of HarperCollins*Publishers*

FOUR WEEKS OF SCANDAL. Copyright © 2022 by Megan Frampton. All rights reserved. Printed in the United States of America. No part of this book may be used or reproduced in any manner whatsoever without written permission except in the case of brief quotations embodied in critical articles and reviews. For information, address HarperCollins Publishers, 195 Broadway, New York, NY 10007.

First Avon Books mass market printing: June 2022

Print Edition ISBN: 978-0-06-302312-3
Digital Edition ISBN: 978-0-06-301104-5

Cover design by Amy Halperin
Cover illustration by Victor Gadino
Cover image by chuckhsu © 123RF.COM

Avon, Avon & logo, and Avon Books & logo are registered trademarks of HarperCollins Publishers in the United States of America and other countries.

HarperCollins is a registered trademark of HarperCollins Publishers in the United States of America and other countries.

FIRST EDITION

22 23 24 25 26 BVGM 10 9 8 7 6 5 4 3 2 1

To Scott

Chapter One

$\mathcal{I}$t's very simple," Octavia explained, taking a deep breath. The carriage chose that moment to hit a rut, and so she fell against the side, grasping the edge of the velvet-covered seat. "I'll take care of everything." She spoke with her usual confidence, though she did not *feel* her usual confidence. But perhaps that was just due to the shaking carriage. "I'll arrange the selling of the house, and its contents. We should be able to get a substantial amount of money."

No response from her companion. To be expected, she supposed.

"The money will go toward paying what I owe Mr. Higgins." She scowled as she thought about him; she'd done research when she was considering borrowing money, and he did offer relatively reasonable interest rates (for a money-lender), but he also offered extremely prompt retribution if his funds were not paid in full on time.

She'd already received two visits from the gentleman himself, assuring her he would break all her limbs and ruin her life if she didn't make up for the payment she'd already missed.

Or perhaps it was the other way around—ruin her life and *then* break all her limbs.

"And which of my limbs will he break first?" she asked. Again, no response. "If he means to break one of my arms, then that would be difficult, but not impossible. The leg, now, that would be trickier. I can learn to write with the opposite hand, if need be," she explained. "But moving about on only one leg could prove problematic." She gave an annoyed huff. "What was I to do?" she asked, holding her hands out in supplication. "I believed I saw an opportunity, and if I see an opportunity, I should take it. Despite the risk."

Since Octavia was part owner of and ran a gambling house, it stood to reason she would take a risk—a gamble, if she was being coy—when she was so certain the reward would be worth it. Hence the debt.

"It should be simple," she repeated, lifting her chin defiantly. Which made her bonnet hit the back of the carriage, sending it tilting over her eye. She straightened it with a fierce gesture. "Father left a will, and with a little searching, I should be able to find it."

It was at this point that Ivy, Octavia's sister, would usually point out some flaw in Octavia's plan.

For instance, she would point out that they hadn't seen or communicated with their father for over five years, so they had no idea what the house and its contents might look like; that Octavia shouldn't bother about their father's holdings since the sisters were doing all right on their own; that they knew their father had died only because Ivy had chanced to see a paper from their village in Somerset sharing the news.

If Octavia was currently speaking to her sister, that is.

But she wasn't. And it wasn't that there was a disagreement between them; Ivy and Octavia got along exceedingly well, remarkable considering that both women had strong opinions.

No, it was because Ivy was not there. Instead of being in London, where the sisters had lived for the past six or seven years, Octavia was sitting in a well-appointed carriage bouncing on the road to Greensett, a place she hadn't been to since she was fourteen years old.

"You are a much better listener," she said in a soothing voice to her companion. If Ivy had been there, Octavia would not have been able to speak at length for such a long time. Ivy was presumably safe at home with her husband, unaware of Octavia's departure. Ivy and Octavia were close, but Ivy was generally too busy to check on Octavia's whereabouts more than once a month, so she might never know.

Her companion was Cerberus, her Italian mastiff, who slept on the opposite seat, a distinct circle of drool marking the velvet upholstery. Theoretically, she was speaking to him, but since he was asleep as well as being canine, she couldn't expect a response. Though she would have welcomed one.

She *had* spoken to Ivy earlier that day, but she had not said anything she was saying now. Her sister had arrived early that morning to share the news about their father's death—discovered by accident in a newspaper Ivy had intended to use for her and her own family's dogs—and Octavia had listened, which was rare.

Usually, Octavia spoke and Ivy tried to interrupt.

The sisters had cried together, remembering a time when their father hadn't put his own passion for gambling ahead of his family. Long before the estrangement. When Father promised them he'd always have a home for them, even when his fortunes were low.

They'd cried because of what they had lost, and would never have now: a father who loved them. Who cared for them.

And then they'd wiped their tears, and a plan had begun to unfurl in Octavia's mind. *He'd promised them he'd always have a home for them.* That had to still be true.

Mr. Holton had died just a month before. Although he and his daughters were estranged, Octavia's fellow gambling club owners and workers kept her apprised of her father's activities. Just a few months earlier, she'd heard he'd bet on a race between a cow and a frog—she hadn't heard who'd won, but the very nature of the wager made her appreciate her older sister Ivy's taking Octavia away from their father's household. But perhaps his luck had changed; there was no telling what might be in the house. Never mind that the house itself was also valuable.

What if, by his death, he was finally able to do something good for his daughters?

What if she were to go to Greensett herself and see what he'd left to her and Ivy? It would remove her from London, out of Mr. Higgins's reach, and it would definitely yield some money, hopefully enough that Ivy might never know of Octavia's risky venture. She'd pay Mr. Higgins back without anyone being the wiser.

Octavia had originally wanted the money to make improvements to the gambling club she and Ivy co-owned. The club was making money, true, but Octavia believed it could make so much more, given proper investment. And at first the new tables, expanded playing rooms, and additional personnel had increased revenue.

But then the business faltered thanks to a combination of horrible weather and a distracting political crisis, and Octavia was staring at the possibility of being broken-limbed and ruined.

Or the other way around. She wasn't certain.

"It will be fine," she assured her still-sleeping dog. "Father left a will. And we will inherit everything. I'll be able to scrape up enough to pay Mr. Higgins. Just the house itself should take care of it. Ivy never has to hear of this." She spoke with a confidence she told herself she felt.

Cerberus opened his eyes, looked at her, and promptly went back to sleep.

"I would have thought feeding you would count for some loyalty," she said with a smile, leaning forward to pat Cerberus's head. He only made a low woof and shifted on the seat.

She leaned back against the seat cushion and gazed out the window, wishing she could be there right now rather than in five hours.

Patience was not her strong suit. Nor was caution. Nor, for that matter, doing anything but being her obstinate self.

A benefit when it came to being a woman in a field usually reserved for men, but not so much when it came to navigating life in a rural village.

Thank goodness she had been able to get out of London so quickly—she had recalled that her frequent, and frequently losing, customer Lady Montague was sending her carriage to fetch her niece from school. It was only a matter of asking the good-natured lady to have her carriage make a tiny detour to drop Octavia off before picking the niece up. And since this carriage was Lady Montague's second best—the best was with the lady herself—it wouldn't inconvenience her client at all.

Which meant she had no way of returning if she needed to get back just as fast.

But she didn't anticipate any trouble once she arrived.

She never did.

GABRIEL RAKED HIS hands through his hair as he surveyed the chaos that was his new house.

Mr. Holton had died close to a month ago, but

Gabriel had been busy sorting out the details of his own father's estate, who had died only a few days before Mr. Holton.

Like Mr. Holton, Gabriel's father, Mr. Fallon, was a gambler. Unlike Mr. Holton, however, Mr. Fallon was very, very lucky. He'd transformed his modest holdings into a vast network of property, liquid assets, shares in a variety of companies, and several items that couldn't be assessed properly because they were unique.

Something brushed against his calf, and Gabriel looked down and smiled. "I know you're hungry," he said to Nyx, one of the unique items. She yipped in reply, then trotted off to sniff the leg of a chair whose upholstery had faded to an unpleasant brownish-gray color.

A tiny, fluffy Pomeranian, Nyx had been part of a parcel his father had won four years earlier. Mr. Fallon hadn't wanted to keep the dog, but Gabriel had hidden her in his satchel and brought her back to school. By the time Mr. Fallon discovered his son's duplicity, it was too late—Nyx was already a favorite at Gabriel's boarding school, and Mr. Fallon valued his access to Gabriel's schoolmates' parents, so he couldn't just get rid of her.

"Those lords are always easy to fleece," he'd confided to Gabriel during one of the rare occasions he'd spoken to his son. "Think they will win just because of who they are." He snorted. "When it's what they do and how they play that makes all the difference."

As parental advice it wasn't much to go on, but

Gabriel had embraced it, determined to make himself into someone who would succeed by his actions, even though his origins were merely respectable, at best, and infamous, at worst, thanks to his father's machinations.

And the final machination before he'd died had been to win Mr. Holton's house. He'd tried for years to best the other man, at one time even winning his daughter in a bet, but losing to that very same daughter only a few hours later.

Gabriel's father had been so triumphant about finally winning the house that he'd grown careless over the next few days, until one night he'd drunk more than usual and tripped over a candle, setting his house ablaze with him in it.

Thankfully, no one else was in residence at the time; Gabriel had gone to inquire about a rare manuscript, and Mr. Fallon's servants didn't live in the house because Mr. Fallon didn't trust anybody. Not even his son.

Gabriel had mourned his father, as anyone would, but he had been most sorrowful of what the elder Mr. Fallon had missed out on—his father had been so busy playing cards, he'd never played with his son. Hadn't risked opening his heart to another person because he was risking pounds and pence in stakes.

Gabriel had been happily surprised when he'd gone through his late father's papers—miraculously untouched by the fire—to find the scrawled piece of paper declaring Mr. Fallon was now the owner of Mr. Holton's house.

And since Mr. Fallon's own house had burned down, Gabriel didn't have anywhere to live. He'd taken rooms in the village, but three weeks of the innkeeper's meat stew was an exquisite torture he thought Prometheus would have refused in favor of the whole "bird pecking out an organ" torture.

He'd arrived that morning, dropping the satchel containing his books, linen, and other items of clothing in the main hallway. It sent a cloud of dust into the air, making him and Nyx sneeze.

It was clear that if Mr. Holton had had any servants, they hadn't spent any time cleaning.

But Gabriel wasn't afraid of hard work—he liked manual labor. It kept his hands occupied as his brain sorted through his research.

"This place would make Hades flinch," he told Nyx, who had given up on food and was lying on a crumpled piece of fabric in the corner of the room.

Gabriel had walked through the entire house, assessing what needed to be done.

Everything.

In addition to the dust, it seemed a robust family of mice had taken residence in the library. The bottom shelves' books were uniformly marked by teeth, and when he'd entered, he'd heard a frantic scrabbling indicating the mice were retreating to wherever they lived.

There was a hole in the roof in at least one of the attic rooms, and the upstairs bedrooms were competing with one another as to which one was the worst.

The kitchen was an equally disgusting mess, streaks of grease on the walls and a dubious-looking stove.

But unless he wanted to endure more of Mrs. Packham's beef stew, this was where he would be living.

Having a house to himself, turning that house into a home, would be deeply satisfying. His father had sent him to school, then hadn't cared when Gabriel wanted to continue his studies. Gabriel had lived in rented rooms near the British Museum in London, poring over ancient texts as he worked to create a more lively, more modern version of a slew of Greek myths.

He saw the promise of the house, of what it had been when Mr. Holton's wife had been alive and their two daughters had lived there as well.

Their father had staked his oldest daughter in a wager against Gabriel's father, and lost. Ivy, the oldest, had then had the audacity to challenge Mr. Fallon to a wager, using her younger sister as a stake.

Gabriel's father had wanted the sister, Octavia, to marry Gabriel, even though nobody had consulted either one of them. Why his father had wanted him to marry the younger Holton girl was a mystery, but then again, most of what his father had done was a mystery to Gabriel.

Thank God Ivy had won.

And promptly left that very night for London, taking her younger sister with her.

"Enough of that, though," Gabriel said to Nyx

as he strode from the kitchen back to the main entrance. He undid the buttons of his shirt as he walked outside into the early evening air, yanking it up and over his head.

The day had been warm, and he hadn't been able to resist moving a few pieces of furniture, making him sweat.

He'd spied a small pond in the back of the house when he'd looked out a smoke-smeared window.

"We're going for a swim, girl," he told Nyx as he circled around to the back. He dropped to the grass, slid his boots and socks off, then stood back up to remove his trousers and his smallclothes.

Nobody was here, nobody would come here, and he'd be damned if he'd walk around in damp underclothes.

He plunged into the water, a blessedly cool relief on his heated skin. Nyx followed, her little head bobbing up and down in the water as she paddled.

It was peaceful. He was alone, which he relished. He had a purpose, which he craved. And he now had plenty of time, funds, and a house, all of which would further his work.

He wanted and needed nothing else. He wanted and needed nobody else.

He floated on his back, stretching his arms out to his sides, when he heard an enormous splash. He lifted his head to see a gigantic black dog barreling into the water, and a woman running behind, yelling at the dog to come back.

"Cerberus!" she shouted, her attention focused

on her dog. Gabriel jerked upright and grabbed Nyx, holding the tiny dog to his side as the other dog—Cerberus—continued his quest toward them. He instinctively thrust Nyx nearly behind him, protecting her.

And then the woman saw him.

Her eyes widened, her mouth dropped open, and she yelped, making an *eep!* sound. As though *he* was the interloper, and not she.

Gabriel gritted his teeth, keeping a wary eye on her enormous dog, who could have swallowed Nyx as a snack.

"I don't know who the hell you are," he said in a fierce tone, "or what you are doing here, but you need to control your dog."

Her eyes narrowed. "Cerberus wouldn't want to have anything to do with your dog. Would you, Cerberus?" she said to her dog, who was steadfastly ignoring her. He'd emerged from the water, and was now sniffing at its edge, thankfully far away from Nyx.

She turned her gaze back to Gabriel. "*You* are the trespasser," she said in a firm, righteous tone. "What are you doing here?" she demanded. "And who are you?"

"I could ask the very same of you," Gabriel replied. "Since you are on my property."

"Your property!" she echoed. "It is most certainly not." She raised her chin. "This is my house."

Chapter Two

The carriage deposited Octavia and Cerberus at the front gates, then quickly departed, leaving Octavia feeling—for nearly the first time in her life—almost unsure.

Likely that was because she had been in the carriage for six hours, and had forgotten to do more than snatch a stale roll before she left. She was probably just hungry.

And why hadn't she brought food?

Because I acted on impulse. As usual. Trusting that things would be all right if she just continued on her own course.

It was late afternoon, and the sun shone brightly above, making her squint as she gazed ahead. It was early summer, but it was already hot. At least for England. And for a lady who was dressed in the full requirement of crinoline, corset, and traveling outfit.

The house was as she recalled: large, but not ostentatious. It appeared to be more dilapidated than before, with a few broken windows on the upper floors and a general air of being unoccupied. The lawn was overgrown, and the fountain that had been their mother's pride and joy was dry.

She pushed the rusty gate, hearing its hinges protest as it creaked open. If she were a more fanciful sort, she would have imagined this was what one of the houses in a Gothic novel would look like. But she wasn't fanciful, and she wasn't a damsel in distress hoping for a rescue from a tall, handsome stranger. If there was rescuing to be done, she would do it herself, thank you very much.

She picked her way through the grass toward the front, Cerberus trotting behind. She held her satchel in one hand, leaning over to the other side to help her carry it. It was heavy, not only filled with her clothing and other personal items, but also containing a few of those Gothic novels, including the latest by Percy Wittlesford, her favorite.

It would be a relief to get inside and put it down. Judging by the quiet stillness of the house, there wasn't anyone in residence now, which would make sense. Her father had died a month ago. Nobody would have stayed on even if he had left money to pay the staff, which she doubted.

"When was the last time I was alone?" she said aloud. Immediately she answered her own question with the very act of speaking, because if she was accustomed to being alone, she probably wouldn't have spoken at all. She glanced back at Cerberus. "Well, not entirely alone," she amended. "I don't want to dismiss your presence."

Cerberus ignored her, too busy sticking his snout in the long grass.

The front door was shabbier than she recalled, its bronze knocker now turning a distinct shade of green. She held her breath as she twisted the knob—what if it was locked? What if she would have to tromp to the village to find someone to help her? Why hadn't she planned?

Right. She never planned.

The door swung open, and she stumbled inside, blinking at the sudden darkness. *See?* she thought triumphantly. *Things do work out.*

She dropped her satchel on the floor as Cerberus immediately began to sniff the corners of the room. She untied her bonnet and dropped that on top of the satchel, noting with curiosity that there was another satchel also resting inside. Had her father been traveling and then returned home, dying so quickly nobody had a chance to put his things away?

She pushed that horrible thought away, where all her other bad memories resided. There would be plenty of time to sort everything out. To understand what had happened since she and Ivy had left. She would be here until everything was inventoried and sold, at which point she would be able to return to London with all of Mr. Higgins's money. Hopefully.

It was warm inside the house, warmer even

than outside. She unbuttoned her pelisse and let it slide off her arms, then picked up her bonnet and placed the garment underneath it.

Enormous whorls of dust sprung up wherever she walked, and she felt it tickling her nose. "It will take a lot of work to make this house presentable again," she said, glancing at the worn wallpaper and the scuffed floor. But that thought didn't daunt her; if anything, it made her more enthusiastic to be there. If she could—and she would—transform this house into a sparkling home again, she would be certain to get the most amount of money for it when she sold. It just needed a little elbow grease, which she had plenty of. And there was no need for her to rush back to London. Mr. Higgins was there, and her clients were not; most decamped to their own country houses in the summer, and her business was slow. Her staff could handle a few months without her anyway.

And it would take a few months to bring the house to rights. The bones of it were fine. It was just that her father had let everything slide into disrepair.

She didn't notice until he was halfway through the library that Cerberus had decided to take his exploring to another room. "Wait!" she said, scampering after him. Cerberus paid no attention to her, instead bounding through the room to the glass door that led to the back of the house. There was a pond there, she remembered, with some trepidation.

Cerberus loved to swim.

But the door would be shut since nobody was in residence, she reasoned.

Unfortunately, reason did not carry the day. Both doors were flung wide, allowing Cerberus to burst through toward the body of water he must have smelled.

"Cerberus!" she shouted, running after him. She emerged outside again, her eyes wincing at the return of light. She couldn't see for a few moments, just long enough for Cerberus to wade into the water.

It wasn't that she begrudged him a swim; it was that he was bound to be smelly after, and her nose was already irritated from all the dust inside.

She heard him splashing as her eyes adjusted.

And then she froze, wondering if the dust had done something to her brain.

Because in addition to Cerberus, there was a person in the water. A man. A wet, dripping, shirtless man who was even now standing up so she could see his neck, his shoulders, his broad chest, and then—thank goodness the water was deep enough not to allow her to see any further. He'd wrapped his arm protectively around a tiny dog that looked even tinier next to his size.

She heard an odd noise, and realized it was her. She'd made some sort of inarticulate squeal, not at all in line with the sophisticated lady she knew herself to be.

But sophisticated ladies—even *very* sophisticated ones—seldom encountered naked gentlemen in ponds.

"I don't know who the hell you are," the naked gentleman said angrily, "or what you are doing here, but you need to control your dog."

His tone and words snapped her out of whatever reverie his shirtlessness had threatened to cast her into. "Cerberus wouldn't want to have anything to do with your dog. Would you, Cerberus?"

Cerberus, as usual, did not reply.

"*You* are the trespasser," she declared. "What are you doing here? And who are you?"

"I could ask the very same of you," the naked man said. He didn't sound as though he was insane, but his behavior most definitely was—sneaking into other people's homes to take themselves and their dog for a swim. Definitely not what a normal person would do. "Since you are on my property."

"Your property!" she echoed. "It is most certainly not. This is my house." He was delusional. That was the only explanation. But how was she to remove a deluded naked man from her home with only herself and her dog who wouldn't listen to anything she said?

Before she could come up with anything, he gestured toward where she stood with the hand not cradling his dog. "Perhaps I should come out and we could discuss this on dry ground?"

"Fine," she replied, folding her arms over her chest and glaring at him.

His expression was mild. "You might want to turn around, lest I offend your maidenly sensibilities." He spoke in a dry tone, as though he was offering her refreshment rather than offering her a glimpse of—

She spun around so quickly, her skirts whirled up and she felt dizzy.

The only sound she heard now was a snort of amusement, followed by the distinct sound of a person walking through water.

As if that wasn't bad enough, Cerberus returned to her, shaking himself vigorously, sending water all over her. The man must have let his dog go, since it was scampering after Cerberus. The two wrestled in front of her—still splashing water—with Cerberus clearly allowing the much, much smaller dog to play. She made a grumpy noise as she realized she was miffed at Cerberus for succumbing to the other dog's cuteness so quickly. They were both dogs. It stood to reason they would want to play. Or do . . . other things to one another, depending on the dogs' respective genders.

"I'm decent," the man called. "You can turn back around."

She took a deep breath, then twisted back, at which point she got a better look at him.

Her first thought was *He's tall*.

The second thought was *Really tall*.

The third was *And so, so handsome*.

His hair was darkened by the water, but it looked as though it would be a goldish-brown color when dry. His eyes were whisky-colored, nearly amber in the sunlight. His nose was strong, his lips full.

His chest was broad, his shirt clinging damply

to his outlined muscles. He didn't wear a neck-cloth, and Octavia could see the length of his neck.

His legs appeared to be powerful, his trousers also damp and clinging to his muscles.

She had never seen a gentleman so close to unclothed before.

It caused a distinct reaction inside her belly, making her shift as though she was uncomfortable. Though she wasn't; it was another reaction entirely, something unfamiliar that made her breath come a bit more rapidly.

He tilted his head as he regarded her. As though he was searching out her secrets. "I am Gabriel Fallon. Mr. Gabriel Fallon," he amended. He gestured to the house. "As I said, this is my house, and you are on my property."

Octavia forgot all about his attractiveness when he spoke, reminding her of what he'd said before.

She felt a surge of fierce anger, her words pouring out of her before she even realized she was speaking.

"This is not your house." She planted her fists on her hips. "I beg your pardon. This is *my* house." Was there an insane asylum nearby from which he had escaped?

His eyes narrowed. "And who might you be?" he asked in a deceptively soft tone. She could see the reciprocated anger in his gaze.

She straightened. "Miss Octavia Holton."

His expression shifted to one of understanding, and she wondered just what he was understanding. Maybe he was insane only intermittently, and now he knew the truth of the situation?

In which case, she wouldn't mind his trespassing. If he'd leave quietly.

After all, he *was* remarkably good-looking, and she wasn't above being entertained by the sight of a handsome gentleman. She could be accommodating.

As long as he left. And soon.

"I am sorry to be the bearer of bad news, Miss Holton," Mr. Fallon said with a twist of that full mouth, "but this house does not belong to you. It is mine."

He spoke so authoritatively that if Octavia was a different sort of woman, a more amenable, more compliant woman, she might have accepted his premise.

But she was not.

She raised her eyebrow. "Why?"

His lips tightened.

"Your late father—my condolences on his passing—lost the house to my father." He spread his hands out as though that explained everything. "So you see, this is my house."

Mr. Fallon. She should have remembered his name. He was the one Ivy had gambled against before they'd left. He'd wanted Octavia for his son—this man?

But that didn't matter. She couldn't allow the house to slip through her fingers, not when it would mean so much to her. Owning the house would mean her father had been able to do some good after all. It would mean her father would not have gone back on the one thing he had promised, no matter what the circumstances.

She regretted it wasn't as simple as this remarkably attractive man having lost his senses. That would have been an easy solution, at least in relation to what he was saying now.

She frowned. "Where is your father?"

At that, his jaw clenched, and she thought she saw a passing look of grief in his eyes. "He is likewise dead." He huffed out a breath. "It appears we have much in common: Both of us have lost our fathers. Both of our fathers were gamblers." Now his expression didn't reveal anything. "And we both insist we own this house. Unfortunately, only one of us is correct. And that person is me."

Just as she was about to retort, her stomach decided it had something to say. Namely, that she hadn't eaten in hours, and she was starving.

He looked as though he wanted to laugh. "I brought some food with me. How about we go inside and eat?" He glanced up at the sky. "It will be dark soon. But you can eat before you leave."

"Leave?" she replied, frowning. "I'm not leaving."

He looked as though he was about to argue, but she kept speaking.

"I can't leave. I don't have anywhere to go, nor do I have a way to get there."

Chapter Three

*G*oddamn it.

Gabriel stared at her, neither his mind nor his mouth able to make words. He was acutely aware of how she regarded him, of how damp and uncomfortable he was. He wished she hadn't shown up to interrupt his swim, and now he wished it even more fervently.

"You can't leave?" he said at last.

She shook her head decisively. "No. I cannot." She took a deep breath, looking as though she was trying to calm herself. As though *she* was the injured party here. "But I am quite hungry," she continued in a more reasonable tone. "Perhaps we can discuss what to do next while we have some food?" She didn't wait for him to answer, just turned on her heel, whistling for her dog.

Which did not follow.

But Gabriel did, watching the shift of her skirts as she strode back to the house.

This was Octavia Holton. The younger daughter of Mr. Holton, the lady he might have been married to if her sister had not prevailed against his father.

She was of average height, but the force of her personality made it look as though she was taller. Her hair was a dark red, while her nose had a pert tilt to it, and her mouth looked—when she wasn't frowning—as though she liked to laugh, and often.

She wore a gown that Gabriel could tell was in the height of fashion, mostly because he'd never seen its like in the village. It was voluminous in the skirt, with layers and layers of fabric, one on top of the other. A light blue, the color likely meant the gown would need to be washed after each wearing. The bodice of the gown was cut snugly to her figure, with a row of what appeared to be entirely impractical buttons marching vertically from her waist to her neck. The sleeves were nearly as wide as her skirt, ending three-quarters of the way down her arm, allowing her hands freedom of movement.

She looked like what Gabriel presumed she was: a fashionable lady who made her home in London and had no idea what country living was like.

In other words, a lady he should be able to easily persuade to return to her accustomed life.

Though even as he thought that, Miss Holton turned back to face him, her arms folded over her chest as though she was preparing for a battle. "You said there is food?" she said in a combative voice, even as her stomach growled again.

"Follow me," he said in a brusque voice, walking past her and back to the hallway.

Gabriel found his satchel, noticing hers was also in the hallway, her bonnet and a jacket lying on top of it. He withdrew the hunk of cheese and loaf of bread he'd brought—sufficient for him for a day, at least, as he reviewed what would need to be done—and gestured toward the dining room. "We'll be more comfortable in there."

She gave a brief nod, heading to the room, both of the dogs now staring at the food Gabriel was carrying. He hoped she had something for—Cerberus?—because he imagined that what he'd brought for Nyx would be just a snack for this enormous dog.

The sun had truly begun to set now, and Gabriel placed the food on the dining room table directly in front of Miss Holton. "Keep your hands on that until I'm back." He nodded to Nyx and Cerberus. "They don't care how hungry you are."

She immediately cupped her hands around the food in a proprietary gesture, and he returned to the hallway, finding his flint in his satchel and, thankfully, locating two candlesticks. He lit one, then the other, and returned to the dining room, setting the candlesticks on the table. The room was dark and dreary, the light of the candlesticks doing little to dispel the gloom. The table was worn, and when he pulled out one of the chairs, it wobbled ominously. He held his breath as he sat down across from her.

And then realized. "Wait—you don't have any-one with you?" he asked.

She threw him a look. "No, of course not. I was planning—I *am* planning—to stay here to work on the house. I came as soon as I heard about my father's death. I didn't have time to arrange a party." She spoke in a scornful tone.

"I thought all young ladies had to travel with an entourage to protect their—"

She cut him off. "Maidenly sensibilities?" she said with a snort, repeating his words from earlier. "I assure you, Mr. Fallon, I am not one of those la-dies." She tore off a hunk of bread and took a bite, speaking as she chewed. "I am a lady who gets things done. By herself."

He held his hands up in a gesture of surren-der. "My apologies. I didn't realize you were a veritable Amazon." He leaned back in his chair. "Although Greensett is hardly Themiscyra."

"I don't know what you're talking about," she muttered, reaching for the cheese. "Nor do I care to," she continued.

"Let me," he replied, taking the cheese from her hand. He pulled the small knife he used to sharpen his pens from his trouser pocket, un-folded it, hacked off a slice of cheese, and handed the piece to her.

"Thank you," she said, raising her chin as though in challenge as she spoke.

"You are welcome," he replied, ignoring her combative expression. "Tell me, how precisely did you get here? You say you cannot leave, so how did you arrive?"

She shrugged. "A client let me borrow her carriage as she was sending it close by." She met his gaze. "But the carriage didn't have time to waste, and the coachman dropped me and then left." That chin went up again.

"Your client?" he asked.

She gestured for him to cut another piece, and ate it quickly before replying.

"I run a gambling house in London. Lady Montague is one of my best customers." Her mouth curled into a smile. "Which is to say she loses a lot."

His spine froze. "You—you're a gambler?"

She stiffened. "I run a gambling house. I am not a gambler. There is a difference, as you well know."

"But you encourage gambling. As you well know," he repeated. He gave her a measured look. "So you encourage the behavior that caused you and your sister to flee your home when you were what—twelve? Thirteen?"

"Fourteen," she replied. He could see her cheeks had flared red, visible even in the candlelight. "Our club is unusual in that we do not allow people to gamble who do not have the funds to afford it. Debts are paid the same night, and if we believe someone is gambling beyond their means, we deny them entry."

"So your gambling club is compassionate," he

said in a dry tone, emphasizing the last word. He'd known his own feelings toward gambling, and how it had affected his life, but he hadn't been prepared for the visceral punch her words had given him.

"It is," she replied shortly. "But it is also none of your business what I do. I don't even know why I bothered to tell you. You can disapprove of me all you want. I don't care." She waved a hand to indicate the house. "My father left the house, its contents, and any monies to me and my sister. Which is why I am here. What you do, and how you feel, is none of my business," she finished. "I suggest you leave. Now, before it is too dark. I presume you still live in Greensett?"

He felt another surge of anger. How had this woman managed to rile him so much in the short time since he'd met her? He was usually so calm, nothing rattled him. Except, it seemed, her. He half rose from his chair, planting his palms on the table between them.

"I live here," he said, pinning her with a harsh stare.

OCTAVIA HAD NEVER been challenged more in her life than in the past hour. This man—this interloper—had the audacity to declare he owned this house, the house that belonged to her family, and was so bold as to go *swimming* in the *pond* with his *dog*. Entirely unclothed.

She didn't know why it added insult to injury, but it did.

And now he was refusing to leave.

"It will be proved that this house is mine." His words were like a splash of the coldest water on her face. "Your father signed it over to mine just a bit over a month ago." His mouth tightened. "I know because my father celebrated, making him too inebriated to notice when his own house was on fire."

Her eyes widened in shock.

"He died a few days later."

She reached her hand out to touch his across the table. "Oh, my goodness, that is terrible. I am so sorry." Her whole body ached with a sympathetic response, forgetting entirely that this man was her newest enemy. "Were the two of you close?" she asked. And then immediately shook her head. "I'm sorry. That is none of my business."

"We weren't," he said in a clipped tone. "I didn't understand his choices, and he never made the effort to understand mine."

"I'm sorry," she said again. She squeezed his hand, running her thumb over his skin. He was looking down at where she held him, a somber expression on his face. "Which of your choices did he not understand?"

Dear God, she hoped one of his choices hadn't been that he had married. Because if his wife, or anyone else, heard that he had shared a meal with her, let alone spent any time in the house together with her, it might ruin whatever trust he and his wife shared. Unless she was a remarkably understanding woman, in which case it would only be that everyone else who knew them would always harbor suspicion about his true feelings.

He exhaled. "I'm a scholar. I plan on taking care of my father's interests now that he is gone because it is the right thing to do, but I don't wish to make it my vocation. I cannot." He glanced up at her, and she was caught by the intensity of his gaze. "My father sent me to school because he wanted his son to rub elbows with important families. Fathers who might wish to gamble with him." He snorted. "And lose."

"That's terrible," she replied. She was still holding his hand. She didn't want to let go, but would he think her forward?

Though given that she was an unmarried woman in a house alone with him, probably that opinion had already been decided.

Besides which, it felt nice. As though she was able to be comforting even as they disagreed about everything else.

Another snort. "No worse than having your parent use you as a stake. And I did receive an excellent education." His mouth curled up ruefully. "So we've both been used by our respective fathers." He slid his fingers over hers, now squeezing her hand. "I do hope your father took care of you. It would be a shame for you to come all this way and leave with nothing."

She snatched her hand back and straightened in her seat. "Mr. Fallon," she said in a forceful tone of voice, "I will leave with everything, I promise you."

GABRIEL FELT THE loss of her hand immediately. He hadn't registered her touch at first, but once he did, it was nearly all he could think about. She'd reacted so honestly and simply, reaching out to make a connection, and he had felt that through his entire body.

But then she had thrown the gauntlet down even more forcefully, if such a thing were possible. Still, he couldn't find it in himself to see her as his opponent, even though she was clearly on the other side of the battle; they had each found means to survive, despite their respective parents' neglect.

Goddamn it.

"I am certain we can reach a compromise," he began, stopping when he saw her face—both weary and wary, her eyes shadowed. "Unless you want to wait until the morning? There is an inn—"

"I will not be leaving this house," she snapped. "What compromise do you have in mind?" she said, her words dripping with disdain.

He leaned back in his chair, meeting her gaze. "I have a piece of paper, signed and dated by your father, that proves he lost the house to my father."

"You say that, but the two of them have been wagering against one another for years. Long before *your* father lost a bet to *my* sister," she said pointedly. "How am I to know that there isn't another piece of paper indicating your father lost the house back to mine?" She folded her arms over her chest in a defiant pose before continuing. "Or that your father didn't sign something else over to mine as they continued to try to prove themselves by a roll of the dice or a play of the cards?" She shook her head in disgust. "Really, it's a shame they outlawed dueling. It would have saved the rest of us a lot of difficulty."

"How could there be another piece of paper?" Gabriel asked, trying to keep himself from shouting at this stubborn, stubborn woman. "My father died soon after."

Her gaze softened, and she was opening her mouth to speak when he shook his head in resignation. "Though it was a few days, and I was not here to say it didn't happen. Perhaps they gambled again, and my father lost it all back to yours." He took a deep breath, knowing he'd have to be open-minded, even though it would cause more complications. "The only fair thing to do is for both of us to present whatever proof we have to one another." He held up his hand as she looked ready to object. "I know that you don't have any proof yet, but you are here, and this is where your father would have kept whatever papers he had. Let's say—let's say at the end of a week—"

"Two months," she shot back.

"Two weeks," he rejoined.

"A month," she declared.

"Fine," he said, exasperated. "One month, at which time we will present our proof to one another. And whoever has the most recently dated piece of paper will own the house. Does that seem fair?"

Her mouth twisted as she thought. "I suppose it does," she agreed.

He stuck his hand out. "So, it is a deal?" he asked.

She put her hand in his, meeting his gaze. "It's a deal," she agreed, shaking his hand.

And then she removed her hand, putting it up to her mouth as she stifled an enormous yawn.

"Now that that's settled," he said, running his hand through his hair, still damp from his swim, "we'll need to find bedding and rooms that aren't too mouse-infested."

She squeaked, appropriately, at the mention of mice.

He raised an eyebrow. "Your dog—Cerberus?— he should be able to take care of any mouse intruders."

Now her eyebrow rose. "Mouse intruders?" she echoed, her voice amused. Apparently the lady didn't hold any ill will toward him, now that they had reached an agreement. "Your talents are wasted as a scholar, Mr. Fallon. You should be writing children's stories."

He shook his head in reply, though he chuckled. "The stories I research should not be shared with children."

She put her elbow on the table, resting her face in her palm. It was shockingly rude, and he had to imagine she was being deliberate in the action.

"Now you have me intrigued," she said, her eyes sparkling with interest. Her moods were mercurial; just moments ago she was entirely adversarial, and now here she was, engaging him in conversation. "What kind of stories do you research?"

Few people asked him about his work. Even fewer appeared actually interested—usually, the inquiries came from young ladies who wished to appear to take an interest, hoping he would take an interest in *them*. He'd engaged with some of them early on, before realizing that none of them actually listened to what he was saying.

"It's boring, honestly," he replied, his usual response when anyone tried to speak to him about it.

She rolled her eyes. "I asked you a question, Mr. Fallon. You can't just tell me something isn't appropriate for children and then say it's boring. Unless it's about complicated maths, which I will agree with you about."

"It's not maths," he said, huffing out a laugh.

She straightened again, putting her hands to her waist. Nyx leaped up to sit on her lap, and she startled, but then began to pat the dog's head.

"What's your dog's name?" she asked.

"Nyx," he said.

"Nix as in nothing?" she said, a puzzled look on her face. She looked down into Nyx's face.

"You're not nothing, sweetheart," she crooned. "Don't listen to the mean man."

Now it was Gabriel's turn to roll his eyes. "Nyx as in the goddess of the night. N-Y-X."

"Ah!" she exclaimed. "And you've met Cerberus, who is the—"

"The three-headed dog of the Underworld," Gabriel cut in. "Yes, I know. That's what I study—Greek mythology."

"Ah," she said again. "No wonder you say your stories are not for children. All those gods and goddesses running around falling in love with inappropriate people."

He opened his mouth to argue, then shrugged. "A reductive way of putting it, but you're not wrong."

"Of course I'm not," she said breezily, waving her hand in dismissal. And confidence. "You can tell me some of your stories later on. I'll agree with you on one point only, which is that I am quite tired, and I would like to find a room to sleep in."

"And avoid the mouse intruders," he couldn't help but add.

She grimaced as she rose, Cerberus getting up from where he'd flopped on the floor.

"We'll discover who the real intruder is in a month," she said with significant emphasis.

OCTAVIA WOKE THE next morning in a state of confusion. She stared up at a peeling ceiling that was a completely unfamiliar site. Cerberus lay warm against her back, fed last night on the remnants of bread and cheese, and the sun streamed in through a grimy window. She'd slept deeply, not interrupted as she usually was by the night watchmen, or drunken revelers, or early vendors calling out their wares.

"Where am—oh!" she said, sitting up. Cerberus glared at her, then lay back down. "The house! *My* house," she corrected herself. She would not allow for any doubt to enter her mind. It was her house, it would be her house, and if it wasn't? Well. She would deal with that later.

If Ivy was here, she'd make a face at Octavia and remind her that she needed to plan for all eventualities. But Ivy wasn't here, and Octavia had never planned, and she didn't see a need to start now.

She swung her feet out of bed and onto the floor, then got up to look out the window, yawning.

She saw him in the front yard swinging a scythe, of all things, hacking at the overgrown grass as his dog lay nearby. For all that he insisted he was a scholar, he didn't look like any scholar she'd ever met. Not that she had met that many, but every so often some determined young man would come to her club with a mathematical formula he was confident would win him everything.

And would leave, skulking out of the club as luck, not maths, triumphed.

This man's body was strong, his shoulders broad, and it was apparent he was clearing the grass with a significant amount of force. She smirked at the thought he had her in his mind as he whacked at the grass. She couldn't have been a welcome arrival, what with insisting she owned the house, not he.

But he had been remarkably polite about all of it. He'd admitted he couldn't know for certain that he owned the house, and then had fetched bedding for her, ensuring she knew he would be sleeping at the opposite end of the house, and that she should lock herself in if she felt in danger.

She hadn't. First of all, the lock—like everything else in the house—was old, and he was obviously strong enough to break the door down if he wished. Second, if he had wanted to harm her, he would have done it before bedtime, and third, she had Cerberus.

Cerberus was up, leaning against her legs, and she put her hand down to pat his head. "We're so close to getting the money we owe," she said. "I just need to prove it. And I will," she vowed. She turned away from the window and went to fetch one of the gowns she'd packed—her most worn ones, gowns she wore in the club when no one was there. She'd left so hurriedly she hadn't changed, so her traveling costume was the very height of fashion, but the clothes she'd brought were far more suitable to a small village like Greensett. What had he called it last night? Themis-something? Had they changed the name?

But she didn't have time to wonder about any of that. She would discover it soon enough.

After dressing, she twisted her hair up into a loose knot on top of her head and straightened her skirts. It wouldn't be possible to bathe today; perhaps she would take a dip in the pond herself to get clean. There was no telling how long she would be here, and she didn't want Mr. Fallon to toss her out because of poor hygiene. "Not that he could toss me out," she said quickly. "We have a deal." This time she didn't pretend she was talking to Cerberus.

Reasonably attired, she marched out of her room and down the stairs, Cerberus trotting alongside, likely eager to get outside for doggy reasons.

The hallway was as dusty as it had been yesterday, but there was a mop, a broom, and a bucket against the wall. Apparently Mr. Fallon had the same thought she had—to clean the house himself, though she didn't think he was planning to sell it, as she was. What did he want with it anyway? Not that she would ask. She didn't care at all, especially since the house wasn't his in the first place.

The front door stood open, and Mr. Fallon was framed by it, his back to her, sweat making his shirt cling to his broad back.

The sight made her knees wobble. And she wasn't even looking at his remarkably handsome face.

He was not a distraction she needed. Though she had to admit she wanted.

Just then, he turned around, and her breath hitched.

His expression was focused and intense, as though he had been considering some great philosophical—or perhaps mythological—question, not where to shear the lawn next. His eyes shifted up to meet hers, and they were so beautiful, like those of a fearsome tiger on the hunt, all topaz and whisky-colored and compelling.

She reminded herself to breathe, and walked toward him, assuming a nonchalance she didn't feel. Not in the presence of all that beauty.

"I do not believe you are a scholar, Mr. Fallon." She gestured to the neatly cut grass. The lawn looked nearly presentable now, though something would have to be done about the shrubbery.

He set the scythe in the ground, the dangerous edge in the dirt, and placed both hands on top of the handle, leaning his chin on them. "And why not, Miss Holton?"

His tone was amused.

She arched an eyebrow. "Because scholars have their noses in books, not their hands on scythes." She gestured to the lawn. "Because most scholars can't see what is in front of them, only what is in their minds." The corner of his mouth curled up into a smirk. "Because scholars certainly do not look like you do."

"So your objection to me is my observational powers and my appearance?"

Put that way, it did sound ridiculous.

He raised his head off the scythe to jerk his chin toward her. "What is wrong with my appearance?" he asked.

Nothing.

She swallowed.

"Because," he continued, thankfully relieving her of the need to speak, "I would have to point out that you look nothing like what a gambling house proprietor usually looks like." He spread his hand out, palm up. "Neither of us is what we seem to be. And what is wrong with that?"

For once, Octavia had no answer.

Chapter Four

Gabriel reminded himself, as he'd done throughout a night of fretful tossing, that she was his opponent in the game, not his companion. That she would like nothing more than for him to remove himself from the property and leave it to her to do with what she would.

Open a gambling den. Paint all the walls scarlet red. Insist that anyone who enters own a dog that reaches their knees.

But that was difficult to remember when he was finding her so intriguing to speak to. Not enjoyable, per se; it was painful, for example, for him to speak about his father, who'd neglected him in life and left him suddenly in death. But he had never met anyone who could empathize with his unique upbringing. Until her.

"Do you plan on starting your search for your proof today?" he asked. "Who knows, perhaps your father left you a secret fortune."

She rolled her eyes. "I doubt it," she replied. "If he had, do you think he would have gambled away his daughter?" She held her hand up. "Before you answer that, bear in mind it was my sister, Ivy, he gambled away, not me."

"Ah, then no. If it had been you . . ." he said, trailing off, allowing a cheeky smile to appear on his face.

"Never mind that," she snapped back. "But I was thinking, no matter who ends up the owner, that person will want a house in much better shape than it is now. That is something upon which we can agree. I propose we work together to make it livable again."

"That is a very pragmatic approach to the problem," he said admiringly.

"I don't know what that means." She spoke in a tone that indicated her lack of comprehension was his problem, not hers. "It just seems that we might as well be productive while we settle this," she continued. "And I will look for the proof, or a will, while we clean."

"What if I find the proof? And then destroy it?" he asked.

She gave him a clear, assessing look. "Because you asked the question in the first place, you are obviously too honorable to do something so underhanded."

It wasn't a compliment, not delivered in such a matter-of-fact way, but it warmed him nonetheless. And not just because he was standing out in the sun doing yardwork.

He considered her cleaning proposal, wishing he wasn't so intrigued by the thought of spending more time with her.

"Fine," he said shortly. "We'll work together to set the house to rights."

At that, they both turned to look at the house in question.

And both exhaled at seeing all the work facing them.

"Before we tear the house apart, however, I will need to go to town," she said, turning back to him. "In my haste to get here, I neglected to bring some essential items. Like food, and tooth powder, and food for Cerberus."

"I can take you," Gabriel replied quickly.

"I can find my own way," she shot back. "I haven't lived here for years, but I do know that that way," she said, pointing to the road, "leads to the village. Greensett." She frowned. "It hasn't changed its name, has it?" She shook her head. "That's not important. As I said, I can find my own way."

"I have a horse," he said. "You won't be able to carry everything back on your own, you know."

She harrumphed. "Fine. Don't look smug."

"Too late." He grinned.

It took about half an hour to get into town, Miss Holton riding astride since, of course, Gabriel didn't own a sidesaddle. He held the reins and guided Pegasus since it was immediately clear that Miss Holton didn't know how to ride.

The dogs trotted alongside, Nyx getting distracted by interesting scents on the route with Cerberus nudging her back to the road.

Miss Holton stiffened as the first buildings of the village came into view.

"You haven't been here since then, have you?" Gabriel asked in a low voice. A few people were walking the other way down the road, giving them curious glances, but besides acknowledging them with a wave, Gabriel didn't stop to talk, as was his usual custom.

"No." Her reply was curt. Almost rude, but he guessed she was more uncomfortable than wishing to give offense.

He imagined she was like him, accustomed to fitting in wherever she found herself. Even though inside he never felt as though he belonged.

With a house, with a *home*, however, he saw the chance to finally be at peace. Not waiting for his father to return with respectably won, but still dishonorable, gains; not at school, where he was one of the few students who couldn't claim an aristocratic heritage. Not working his father's lands, where he was a worker to himself but an owner to everyone else.

"I missed this when we first left," she said. He glanced up at her, noting her strained expression. It couldn't be her awkwardness riding a horse. "I was so homesick. I was furious that Ivy had made me leave." He saw her swallow. "But then she explained what had happened—well, not all of what had happened, that came many years later—but she told me what our father had done, how he had literally gambled with our lives."

Her voice was choked. He reached up to touch her hand, squeezing it as it held Pegasus's pommel. It was odd, that they were on either side of a battle, but they could still offer one another comfort. The result of such similar experiences, he supposed.

"Which is when I decided not to look back," she continued in a much different tone. "I never wanted to feel that loss again. My home is where I am, where my sister is. And Cerberus," she said, glancing toward her dog.

"So, why do you want the house so badly? If it's not where you want to live."

"I'm going to sell it," she announced. "Sell it, and use the money to improve my club."

Her words stung. Not because she was so confident she owned the house, but because she was renouncing the chance to make a home for herself here, where she and her family had once belonged.

He was altogether too softhearted. Why should it matter that she was denying herself? That she was on her own except for her dog and her sister?

"Mr. Fallon!" a voice greeted him as he was mentally shaking himself.

"Mrs. Hall," he replied, noting the lady's avid curiosity as she looked at Miss Holton. "May I introduce you to—" He paused, then took a deep breath as he continued, "To my fiancée, Miss Holton?"

He tightened his grip on her hand, willing her not to contradict him. He heard her inhale sharply, and he squeezed more. *Don't say anything. This is the only way.*

"Oh, my goodness!" Mrs. Hall replied. "Miss Holton as in Mr. Holton's daughter?" Mrs. Hall's gaze took everything in about Miss Holton's appearance, from her shocking seat upon the horse to Gabriel's holding her hand to the dogs.

"I am," she said tightly.

Gabriel exhaled.

Mrs. Hall was the biggest gossip in Greensett, and he hadn't even thought before he'd spoken. He'd just known that in order to preserve some reputation for either one of them, he'd have to come up with a believable lie.

He couldn't say they were related, since everyone in the village would know better, and he didn't want to pass her off as a distant cousin under a false name, since it was probable that someone here would recognize her.

Claiming her as his fiancée was the only thing he could possibly do.

If she thought about it at all, she'd recognize his brilliant quick-wittedness.

He didn't hold out much hope for that, however.

"That is such excellent news!" Mrs. Hall exclaimed. "Though many of Greensett's young ladies are going to be heartbroken, Mr. Fallon," she said, wagging her finger at him. "You cause quite the stir when you come to town to go to the library."

"The library," Miss Holton echoed. "Of course, the library."

Why did her obvious disdain bother him so much?

"As you know, Mrs. Hall," Gabriel said, thinking furiously, "Miss Holton's father and mine were well-acquainted. It was their lifelong wish that we marry." He glanced up at her, donning a fond expression. "And then, when we met again after so long, it seemed as though it was fate."

"Fate," Miss Holton said, her eyes glaring down at him. "There must be a Greek word for that, isn't there?" she added, her tone sharp.

Mrs. Hall thankfully did not notice the tension between them. She clasped her hands to her bosom, looking skyward. "Out of the flames rises the phoenix of love!" she declared. "Your father, Mr. Fallon, must be looking down on you so pleased."

"Or up," Gabriel murmured. He heard Octavia smother a snort of laughter. She couldn't be that angry with him if she was able to laugh so quickly.

"We'll have a wedding in Greensett!" Mrs. Hall continued. "Miss Holton, you must allow me to assist you. I know everyone in the village. You won't have to lift a finger!"

"Uh . . ." Miss Holton began, only for Gabriel to interrupt.

"We plan on having a very small wedding, Mrs. Hall. At—" He gestured in back of them, not wanting to call it the Holton house. "Miss Holton has only just arrived. Her carriage had to go—" he said, faltering. Knowing they'd have to explain Miss Holton's lack of—well, anything—so they wouldn't know the truth.

"To the Duke of Hasford's for books," Miss Holton supplied. "The Duchess of Hasford is a friend of mine, and she confided that her husband isn't certain what to do with the books at his estate in the country. I knew Mr. Fallon here, a renowned scholar."

Was it his imagination, or was her tone somewhat sarcastic? Once again, he offered up a silent thanks to Mrs. Hall's obliviousness.

"A duke!" the lady said with such obvious delight, it was as if her previous exclamations were monotoned comments on the weather.

"A duke, yes," Miss Holton said dryly.

"And if you will excuse me, Mrs. Hall, my fiancée needs some things in town. We will bid you good day." Gabriel didn't wait for Mrs. Hall's inevitable continuation of the conversation; he'd found the best way to stop her talking was simply to walk away, even if she was in the middle of a sentence.

"What," Miss Holton began in a fierce whisper when they were safely out of earshot, "was the meaning of that?"

OCTAVIA SHOOK WITH anger, frustrated at being pinned inside a lie with no chance to make her own decision about it.

"How dare you?" she continued, her chest tightening.

It wasn't that she was against lying in general; she saw the benefit of the occasional falsehood, a misrepresentation of facts, if it meant she got what she wanted in the end.

It was how, for example, she'd subdued the occasional miscreant. If she intimated that there were several enormous men lurking in the back rather than just Sam and Henry, the two men who'd worked for Ivy since the club opened, then she would be able to eject the troublemaker with no bloodshed.

But he had just *said* it, without even asking her.

"I dare," he began, his tone direct and clear with none of his previous good humor, "because if we do not come up with some sort of story to explain the next thirty days, your reputation will be ruined."

"I don't care about my reputation!" she exploded.

"And mine would be ruined as well," he retorted. "If the inhabitants of Greensett believe I am the type of blackguard to be alone with a lady who is neither related nor engaged to him, they will assume I have evil intentions. They will make my home a living hell. And not a gaming hell," he added with a rueful snort.

"Oh," she replied in a soft voice. She hadn't thought about what her presence, unaccompanied and without explanation, might mean for him. She'd forgotten, if she'd even known it in the first place, how everyone knew everyone else's business in a town like this.

Even if—even *when*—the house was declared rightfully hers, he would still live here, she presumed. This was where he had grown up. Where the young lady he might eventually actually marry likely lived.

Which raised more problems, things he hadn't even thought of when he'd blurted the news to that woman.

"And how do you propose, so to speak, we get out of our fake engagement?" she asked tartly. "Will you tell everyone I've died? Or perhaps you can let them know I ran away with a ship captain or something. That way your reputation will remain spotless. I will be the fallen woman who jilted a scholar." She accompanied her words with a theatrical gesture.

He gave her a startled look. "A ship captain? You have an active imagination, Miss Holton."

She shrugged. "You're the one who thought of mouse intruders, Mr. Fallon. It seems I should be able to have a ship captain."

He chuckled, then released her hand. She hadn't realized he'd still been holding it.

She felt the loss immediately.

"This is going to cause far more trouble than just having the village think I am a scandal and you are a blackguard," she warned, unable to let the argument go.

She did have to admit to feeling a bit smug that

someone other than herself had behaved impetuously without thinking everything through. Though that didn't excuse what he'd done. She did not want to arrive in town already affianced, for goodness' sake.

But here they were. She would have to accommodate his lie in order not to make everything worse. Perhaps this exercise would give her a better understanding of Ivy. Or not.

By now, they were in the center of town, and he led her toward a store that looked familiar—it was smaller than she'd remembered, but it was the same place. Some things never changed.

But you are very different. She needed to remember that.

She swung her leg over the horse and hopped down without waiting for his help.

Which meant she stumbled into him, putting her hand on his chest to steady herself.

Her face was buried in his chest, and she inhaled, smelling his clean, warm scent. Of course he smelled clean—he had taken a dip in the pond not twenty-four hours earlier. She just hoped she smelled as good.

He had his hands at her waist, making certain she didn't fall, and she couldn't help but melt a little bit into him. Just a little bit. It wasn't as though he would notice. Or if he did, he would assume she was more unsteady than she was.

His chest was firm and strong under her fingers, and she recalled how he'd looked when he emerged from the water—water streaming off his hair and down his body, rivulets on his muscular upper body, glistening in the sun.

Octavia wasn't anything close to a fallen woman, but this wasn't the first time she had stumbled, so to speak. She had had flirtations, some caressing, more kissing, and so she knew just what it would be like if she were to succumb to Mr. Fallon's undeniable attraction. To have the right to touch that skin with her bare hand, to find out just how strong and powerful he was. To have that power focused on her.

"Miss Holton," he said in an urgent tone. "Octavia. Are you—are you all right?"

I am most definitely not all right. You are making me think of things I should not be thinking of about the man who is hoping to upend my plans.

She exhaled, pushing off his chest and meeting his gaze. Plastering a benign smile on her face, which made his eyes narrow.

Drat.

"I'm fine, thank you. I am not accustomed to dismounting."

The words, innocuous though they were, managed to sound lurid, and she blushed, hoping he wouldn't guess what she was thinking of.

She'd been on the receiving end of enough lustful thoughts to know how unwelcome they were. She did not want to put him into an awkward—or even more awkward—situation.

But he was just so damned handsome.

"Do you feel up to venturing to the shop?" he

asked, gesturing toward the store after securing his horse. The sign read HALL'S ELABORATE EMPORIUM. Ah. Mrs. Hall must be related somehow to this shop.

The news about their engagement, therefore, would be spread to anyone who came in. Which, since it was a small town and this was the biggest store, would likely be everyone.

She couldn't help but groan.

"You're not all right," he said, guiding her to a bench in front of the store. "Sit down for a moment." He knelt down beside her, his hand on the back of the bench.

"I'm fine," she replied, swatting at him. "I'm just annoyed that I have to be your fiancée."

He grimaced. "I'm not pleased about it either," he said. "But I don't see what other choice we have."

"Yes, you said that," she bit out.

"Gabriel!"

They both turned toward the sound of the voice, which came from behind where Gabriel crouched. He leaped up immediately, and Octavia tried not to look at his firm backside.

And failed.

It was a remarkable specimen. And she did appreciate a nice firm backside. His was one of the best; his trousers were worn and snug, and she had never been so grateful a gentleman hadn't tossed away an item of clothing because it was a little bit old.

"Mrs. Jennings," he said, a warm tone in his

voice. She leaned past him to see who he was speaking to.

An older woman with gray hair stood just beyond him, a wide, bright smile on her face. Her eyes were piercing blue, and her cheeks were a soft pink. If a fairy tale had come to life, this woman would have served as the model for the kindly grandmother in every one.

"Miss Holton," he said, turning back around to her, "may I introduce you to Mrs. Jennings? She taught me before I went away to school."

"Such a smart boy. Though I should call you Mr. Fallon now, not Gabriel," Mrs. Jennings said. "And I hear, Miss Holton, that the two of you are engaged!"

Word certainly traveled quickly. It had been, what, ten minutes at most?

"Mrs. Hall says that your carriage had to leave to fetch something or another," Mrs. Jennings continued.

"Books," they said in unison.

"Do you know," Mrs. Jennings said to Octavia, "I worked at your father's house when I was young? It was your grandfather's house then. But your father was living there as a young man, before he met and married your mother." Her tone was reminiscent. "He was constantly losing things, and I'd find them in the oddest places— penknives stuck into the dirt of potted plants, papers in books and in his hatbands. One time he'd put a flask inside the flour bin!" She shook her head. "I didn't see him in town often once I'd left. I am so sorry for your loss." She reached up to take Octavia's hand.

"Papers inside of books, you say?" Octavia asked, trying not to sound too eager.

She saw him stiffen out of the corner of her eye.

"Yes, not that I knew wha—"

"Mrs. Jennings," Octavia said, cutting the older lady off as her mind raced, "I am here entirely without a chaperone or any servants at all. My lady's maid took ill on the journey here, and I sent her along with the carriage that went to the Duke of Hasford's house." She was certain Mrs. Hall had not forgotten to mention that there was a duke involved in her story. Mrs. Jennings nodded, as though she knew that part. "I could ask my sister to come, but she is in London, and I am wondering if—since you know the house and everything—if you would agree to come stay at the house? Just for a bit, perhaps a month?"

This time, she couldn't resist a quick glance at him. His lips were pressed into a thin line, and he looked as though he wanted to argue. But he couldn't, not without giving the game away. Not without damaging both of their reputations and putting their deal in jeopardy.

"No servants!" Mrs. Jennings said. "But how is that possible?" She looked at Mr. Fallon, her expression aghast. "And I heard that you removed from the Packhams' inn. Don't tell me you are staying at the house as well!"

Octavia held her breath, waiting for him to deny everything she'd just said.

He did not.

"Well, of course you cannot stay there alone together, especially if you are engaged!" Mrs. Jennings shook her head. "There is nothing for it. My daughter and I will come stay with you. You'll need a housekeeper and a maid, after all. And my grandchild can run errands. He reminds me of you at that age, dear Gabriel."

Octavia shot another pointed glance toward Gabriel, who appeared dumbfounded.

You could have made up something else, she wanted to scream. *That you were returning to stay at that inn, or wherever you had been. You didn't need to announce that we were betrothed, for goodness' sake. Of course they were going to notice I arrived with no servants.*

But the damage was done.

"That would be wonderful, Mrs. Jennings," Octavia said smoothly. "You are right. We will need servants." Gabriel, meanwhile, was having difficulty closing his mouth. "How kind of you to be concerned about my reputation. Though I know my Gabriel"—she fluttered her lashes toward him—"is a gentleman."

"Of course he is, my dear. I didn't mean to imply anything else. I'll just go pack up and be there in two hours. Oh, and make sure to purchase additional foodstuffs—little Charlie is a bottomless pit! I swear, I don't know where he puts it!"

Mrs. Jennings walked briskly away, leaving them alone.

"Well," Octavia said brightly, "now we'll have

someone else to help with the search. She must know where my father might've put his important papers."

"The flour bin," Mr. Fallon replied in a dry tone of voice. He turned toward her, his whisky eyes lit up with anger. "Did you think of the consequences of inviting Mrs. Jennings—and apparently her entire family—to come stay at the house? We'll have to maintain the engagement charade, and we'll have to pretend we're planning a wedding."

Octavia wrinkled her nose. "No, I didn't think about that. I was too concerned with finding proof that I own the house. So we have to pretend to be engaged. That was *your* invention, if you recall."

"I do," he said.

"You're not supposed to say that until we are in front of a clergyman and our dearest friends and family," she said in a falsely sweet tone.

He glared, and she gave him an impertinent look, daring him to do or say something else.

When he didn't, she slid her arm through his. "Let's go purchase my things. The sooner we're back at the house, the sooner we can begin to search and clean."

"Clean and search," he said through gritted teeth.

Chapter Five

A few days later, Gabriel felt as though they had invited the entire village to live with them. Or Miss Holton had, since it was her idea to begin with.

Not only had Mrs. Jennings arrived with her daughter and grandson, but Mrs. Hall sent her cousin Mary along, a woman who was hoping to land a position as a cook, and Mrs. Hall knew that the Holton house would be the perfect place to practice her skills. Everyone else knew not to argue with Mrs. Hall.

And then there was Old Joe, who'd been Old Joe for as long as Gabriel had lived in Greensett, which is to say he'd been Old Joe forever.

Old Joe made a meager living running errands and turning sod and whatever odd jobs anybody had. But he was getting older, and he'd arrived on the doorstep with his few belongings in a pack, offering to help out however he could in exchange for room and board.

He'd insisted on sleeping in the stable with Pegasus, and Gabriel had given him the task of taking care of the horse, since Gabriel was too occupied with figuring out what needed to be done inside the house.

He hadn't seen Miss Holton that much the past few days, however. It seemed as though she was set on avoiding him, or she just happened to be where he was not.

He'd caught sight of her a few times, just enough to remind him that she was there. He wished she was friendlier; he'd enjoyed speaking with her that first night, but it seemed she was trying to keep some distance between them.

Awkward, perhaps, to be pursuing one's ownership of a house when the other person who claimed ownership was also in residence. Also awkward, however, to be so conspicuously separate when they were supposed to be engaged.

Their dogs, however, were determined to spend every waking minute—and many sleeping minutes—together.

"Mr. Gabriel?" a voice said at his elbow. No, not at his elbow; slightly below. It was Mrs. Jennings's grandson Charlie, a shy, curious young boy who did seem a lot like Gabriel when he was his age.

"Good morning, Charlie. You've had your breakfast, I see." Gabriel took his handkerchief out of his pocket and wiped Charlie's face, which bore the remnants of buttered toast.

"I did. It wasn't *that* burnt," Charlie replied.

Gabriel winced. Mary seemed to have gotten her cooking skills from Mrs. Packham, whose beef stew still loomed large in Gabriel's night-mares.

"I wanted to ask if I could help Old Joe with your horse." Charlie's face glowed when he mentioned Pegasus. "He said I had to ask you first." The boy looked at Gabriel with a pleading expression.

"Of course," Gabriel replied. "Ask Miss Mary if she has any carrots you can bring to Pegasus. I happen to know she likes them."

Charlie was already halfway toward the kitchen by the time Gabriel finished speaking.

"Mr. Fallon."

Gabriel turned to see Octavia standing at the bottom of the staircase. A spiderweb clung to her hair, and the bottom of her gown was smudged with dust. He stepped forward, removing the web as he spoke. She batted at his hand in irritation, then faltered when she saw what he'd removed.

"Miss Holton, good morning."

She glowered at the spiderweb, then looked up into his face. "Good morning," she said in a grouchy voice.

"No luck?" he said, raising his eyebrows.

She scowled. "Mrs. Jennings has been helping me search. I won't give up, you know," she said fiercely.

He held his hands up in mock surrender. "I know full well that you will not, Miss Holton. Not until it's been thirty days." He lowered his hands to his sides. "But then you will have to admit defeat."

She glared up at him, her nose wrinkled. She looked fearsomely cute.

He resisted the urge to lower his mouth to hers and press a kiss to her lips. *That* would certainly surprise her. And would be what he had been thinking about ever since he'd met her.

"You'll have to help me search," she said. "Mrs. Jennings has revealed all the hiding places she knew of, and I've found two brass paperweights, a pair of earrings, and a lady's shoe, but no papers of import yet."

"A lady's shoe?" Gabriel said. "Just the one?"

"That doesn't matter," she said dismissively. "The point is, I need you to help me search."

"Oh," he said, moving a fraction closer. "You need me."

She rolled her eyes. "Yes. And don't get all puffed up about it. You're taller than I am. You can reach high places. That is all there is to that."

"It's not because you wish to spend more time with me?" Gabriel asked, knowing the suggestion would infuriate her. Which only made him want to do it more, oddly enough.

She opened her mouth, but he held his hand up. "I will help you search. Mrs. Jennings remarked just yesterday that she finds it odd we do not spend more time together, what with our being so passionately in love." He gave her an impudent grin.

Her cheeks turned pink, and he had to suppress a laugh.

"Fine. And Mrs. Jennings has also mentioned our upcoming nuptials, and what we will want for it—flowers, decorations, music, food, invitations—so we'll need to decide those things as well. And set a date, of course."

She tilted her head to look up at him, batting her eyelashes exaggeratedly.

He huffed out a dry laugh. "You don't have to flirt with me, Miss Holton. Remember, we're already engaged. You can treat me as you would any fiancé."

She smiled in response. "Oh, I will, Mr. Fallon. *Gabriel*. I will."

Her words, her smile, the way she regarded him, all made him uneasy, but not in an unpleasant way. More in a way that she had something planned he was not at all expecting.

Perhaps he should start expecting the unexpected.

OCTAVIA SUPPRESSED A delighted chuckle at unsettling him so. He'd been unsettling *her* from the moment she'd seen his naked, dripping form rising out of the pond, so it was a relief to know she could do the same to him.

She'd been ashamed to admit it to herself, but she'd been avoiding him since they'd returned after the visit to Greensett. And then all of Greensett's inhabitants came to live with them, or so it seemed. It was easy to stay out of his way.

Instead, she'd enlisted Mrs. Jennings to help her search, but that lady found it difficult to stay on task. It had been frustrating to uncover so little in the way of proof.

She was keenly aware of the days slipping by—she now had only twenty-seven days to find proof she owned the house, since she had no doubt Mr. Fallon—*Gabriel*—had the paper he claimed to. It was inevitable that her father would eventually wager the house, even though he had wagered everything else before resorting to that—including his own daughter.

She couldn't succumb to bitterness now, though. She had too much to do if she wanted to achieve something out of this country sojourn.

"Well?" Mr. Fallon said impatiently, stirring her out of her thoughts. Apparently this was not the first time he'd said something to her.

He should stop being so distracting if he wanted her to pay attention to what he was saying.

It was totally unfair that he be so stupidly good-looking. Like most days, he wore a simple, threadbare shirt open at the neck to reveal his strong throat. The sleeves were rolled up, exposing equally strong forearms covered with a light dusting of golden-brown hair.

His trousers were also worn, lighter bits of fabric at the knees showing where he'd knelt to do some work. Perhaps grunting from the strain.

And now she was fantasizing about him. Of all the things not to be doing right now.

"Pardon?" she said brightly.

He looked heavenward, as though begging for patience. "I was asking you where you'd like to search."

"Well," she said at last, trying hard not to think about him kneeling in front of her, "the library, I think. Mrs. Jennings did mention he put papers in books, and it feels as though I've looked everywhere else." She wrinkled her nose. "I found the lady's shoe in a trunk with the initials M.R. on it. No idea who that might have been."

"Have you looked everywhere, though?" he asked. "I'm occupying his bedroom. I don't think you've searched there." One side of his mouth curled up. "Unless you snuck in while I was out?"

Her cheeks flushed. "I would not presume to do anything so duplicitous!" she exclaimed.

"Oh, of course," he replied dryly. "I'd forgotten gamblers are such an honorable lot."

"I don't gamble," she bit out. "I told you. I run a gambling house. That is quite different."

"And yet," he continued, his whisky-brown eyes narrowing, "you arrived here with no accompaniment, no means of leaving, and as far as I can tell, no plans beyond finding a dubious piece of paper while cleaning the house to make it presentable for sale. I'd say that is a gamble, wouldn't you?"

She clamped her lips together in frustration. Frustrated because he was right, curse him.

"I hadn't planned on having to hunt for proof that I own my family's house," she said haughtily. "Besides, that's different."

"Oh, of course. *Different.*" The last word was skeptical.

"Anyway, I believe we should rule out the library before going to your bedroom."

Both eyebrows rose at her words.

"That is not what I meant to say." Her words came out in a rush. "I—I—" When had she ever been at a loss for words? When had she ever not known what to say, no matter the situation?

Apparently her weakness was ridiculously handsome strong-armed men challenging her. Her Achilles' heel, so to speak.

If she was ever able to speak to him like a normal human being, she might share the observation with him. Though then she would have to admit just what her weakness was.

And she would never do that.

"To the library, then?" she said, hating that she sounded uncertain.

He swept his hand out in invitation. "After you, Miss Holton."

She lifted her chin as she strode forward, keenly aware of him following behind. Of his long legs encased in that worn fabric, how expressive his eyes were. Narrowing in suspicion, or warm with appreciation as he spoke with any of the house's other inhabitants.

Thank goodness he hadn't looked at her like that. She would melt into a puddle on the floor.

Though why hadn't he?

She couldn't help but glance down at herself. She wasn't the most beautiful woman, but she knew she was attractive. She wasn't missing any teeth, her figure was appropriately curved, and she'd been told she had a nice smile.

Hmph.

"Are you all right?" he asked as they entered the library, him right after her.

She spun around, nearly falling into his chest. Again.

"What?"

He gestured toward her. "You made an odd noise."

Oh that. Merely wondering why you haven't regarded me with appreciation.

"I'm fine. Just preoccupied. I don't claim to know much about my father. I tried to forget all about him when we left. But I do recall he wasn't . . ." She hesitated, wondering if she should say the word again. ". . . duplicitous."

"Like father, like daughter," he remarked. Only now he didn't sound suspicious, but more as though he was teasing her.

That was perhaps more dangerous than when it seemed he didn't trust her.

Chapter Six

Gabriel bit back a laugh as she clearly bristled, then settled herself, presenting him with a deceptively bland expression.

It was easier to be amused by her than be aggravated by her, after all. Since his aggravation was tinged by a prickling awareness of her as a woman, as the woman he'd claimed was his fiancée.

The first day they'd met, she'd worn something preposterously fashionable, making her look so far removed from him and his daily life that he hadn't thought about her being approachable.

But since that day, she'd worn gowns that were clearly meant to be worked in, whether she was searching for gamblers' chits, scrubbing greasy kitchen walls, or dusting furniture.

Not that he'd tell her she was adorable. He could only imagine what kind of reaction *that* would engender.

But she was; her pert little nose wiggled when she sneezed, like a kitten's, her eyes were impossibly huge in her face, and her hair always seemed to be on the verge of escaping whatever style she'd put it into.

And like an adorable kitten, she demonstrated her claws frequently when she felt under attack. The response was doubtless because she had been without a parent and been forced to rely only on herself and her sister for protection. Just the thought of those two young ladies arriving in London over six years ago, alone, with only their wits to guide them, made his fists clench, wishing he could go back in time and retroactively pummel anybody who made them feel unsafe.

"Mr. Fallon?"

Her voice made him shake his head. "Sorry, what?"

"Now you're the one I need to ask if you're all right. You were making a growling noise, and you had the most fearsome expression." Her mouth quirked up at one corner. "Thinking of how angry you'll be when I prove your father ultimately lost to mine?"

He snorted. "You know the truth, Miss Holton. I own this house." He met her gaze. "You've got twenty-seven days left, correct?"

A panicked expression flitted across her face, and he wanted to take his words back, even though he spoke the truth. But then he saw a steel resolve in her eyes, and he resisted the impulse to cheer her on. He should not be encouraging an opponent, for goodness' sake.

Even if she was the most adorable opponent

ever. And he wanted to kiss her, not triumph over her.

"But," she said airily, "even if you prove he gambled away the house, it would be my understanding that the bet would not include the contents." She gave him a smug smile. Adjusting the wager, as any true gambler would.

She was more like her father than she would probably care to admit.

"Speaking of the house's contents," Gabriel said, determined to get back on track, whatever *on track* meant, "where do you want to start?"

They both turned to survey the room.

The library was a mess. The mouse intruders had ruined nearly all of the books on the bottom shelves of the bookcases, while the rug was more threadbare than not, and the enormous desk was pitted with scrapes and burn marks, as though someone had literally tried to start a fire on it.

The books on the shelves higher up were less eaten, but no less ancient. Most of the lettering on the spines had worn away, and so it would be impossible to catalog the books without removing each one and looking at the title page.

There were blank spaces on the walls where paintings clearly used to hang, while the wallpaper was peeling in a few places.

The two of them stood just inside the doorway, directly opposite the doors that led into the backyard and the notorious pond. A faint light trickled in through the grimy windows, illuminating the dust motes that had flown up into the air at their entrance.

Gabriel put his hands on his hips as he assessed the entirety of the room.

"It's a lot of work," she said, following his train of thought. "I remember when Ivy first secured the club, it required at least this much effort to make it presentable." He glanced at her, watching how her gaze traveled around the room, documenting each task.

"How old were you?" She'd said, but he didn't recall.

She turned to regard him. "Fourteen." She jerked her chin at him. "Apparently old enough for your father to want me for your bride."

He felt a wave of disgust for his father at the thought.

"And here we are, engaged so many years later," she said. Those batting lashes again. "Truly, it is a story found in torrid novels, not in real life."

He didn't like it when she was mocking. As though she was far more cynical than anyone else, as though she was impervious to human pain and suffering. Even though of course she wasn't. It was just that she'd had to develop a thick skin to endure what her father and her subsequent life had dealt out. Being wagered at fourteen years old would do something to a person, after all.

"Do you read torrid novels?" He kept his tone mildly neutral, not wanting to engage her in whatever argument she was spoiling for.

A wicked grin lit up her face. Making him want her to read one of those torrid novels aloud to him. "As often as I can. I have the new Percy Wittlesford. His books are the most lurid I've read. Which means, of course, they are my favorites."

"You should make it a point to read some Greek mythology, then," he replied.

She gave him an inquisitive look. "I'm surprised you are a scholar of such ramshackle people. Gods. Whatever."

"Why?" he asked, puzzled.

"I would think you would be far too staid to tolerate such miscreant behavior," she replied. "You certainly seem as though you do everything properly. Never duplicitous, never lying. Unless it is to preserve a lady's reputation," she added hastily.

An intrigued sort of anger curled low in his belly. She thought him staid?

He advanced toward her, an unfamiliar emotion taking hold of his body. Her eyes widened, and she flung her head back as though in challenge.

He took hold of her arm, drawing her into the room, then grabbed hold of the door with his other hand and swung it shut behind them.

His hand still held her arm, and they were mere inches apart, their eyes locked on each other's, both of them breathing more rapidly than before. He hesitated, his body frozen in place, since if he moved, it would be to gather her into his arms and kiss her senseless until she was forced to admit he was anything but staid.

But he couldn't allow himself to succumb. She'd made it clear what she thought of him, what she thought of their having to pretend to be engaged, to be in love, and she would likely be appalled at the behavior. As would he.

But he also couldn't move. His feet felt rooted to the spot, his entire focus on her, and her mobile, expressive face, the way she packed all of her personality into her small frame.

How her chest rose and fell with her breathing.

"I am so—" he began as she spoke.

"Goddamn it," she said, startling him with her language.

Only to forget all about it when she startled him even more by lifting herself up on tiptoe, taking his hand, and placing it at her waist.

"Goddamn it," she repeated in a whisper before putting her mouth on his.

SHE HADN'T MEANT to kiss him.

Then again, she never *meant* to do anything— borrow money from an unscrupulous man, get a dog, lie to her sister, dash off to the country to see about a possible inheritance.

But all of her decisions made sense at the time, even if later she questioned whether she had made the right one.

Perhaps later, when she was able to reflect on it, she'd realize she should not have, after all, kissed Mr. Fallon.

But when he was looking so fiercely ruffled by her words, and she was imagining him in one of the Wittlesford novels, perhaps as the intense hero who sent the heroine into a state of confusion because she couldn't tell whether she should kiss him or kill him?

She absolutely knew she should kiss Mr. Fallon.

His mouth was soft, and warm, and for a moment she just pressed her lips against his. Settled herself into the feeling of him, of his large hand at her waist. Of the hardness of his chest pressed against hers.

She hesitated, waiting to see if he would recoil from her, appalled at her behavior.

After all, she had surprised him. And if the situation was reversed, and he had been the one to instigate the kissing, she would have wanted the opportunity to refuse.

But he did not.

Instead, his fingers gripped her waist, dug into her side as he clutched her tightly. His other hand held her arm, drawing her closer to him.

He nipped at her mouth, and she relished the sharp feel of his teeth. And then his tongue licked her lips. She opened her mouth to allow him entry, a luxurious pleasure suffusing her bones as his tongue found hers.

His other hand was also at her waist now, holding her against him. He nudged her backward, and her arse hit the door as his body crowded hers.

No, not crowded. Enveloped. *Overwhelmed.*

The feel of the long length of him pressed against her was delicious. He planted one hand on the door to brace himself, the other still at her waist.

She eagerly gave herself up to the sensation of kissing him, of the sensual feeling that there was only him, and her, and his mouth, his tongue, his hands. She stroked her hands down his strong arms, her thumbs brushing along his biceps. He grunted as he pressed his body more into hers, and she felt his erection against her, just achingly away from that spot she knew would bring her pleasure.

This was far from her first kiss. She'd decided, when she was old enough, to go ahead and kiss anyone who wanted to kiss her that she wanted to kiss back.

But this was the first kiss that felt as though it swathed her in passion, made her forget their surroundings, or who they were, or why they should not be doing this.

And then he suddenly leaped away from her, his expression shocked, his eyes wide.

His mouth moist from their kiss.

"I shouldn't have—" he began.

She huffed out a breath, still leaning against the door. "You didn't. I did." She pushed herself off to step toward him.

He stepped back.

Because he thought she was a predator? Because he didn't think he could trust her not to leap on him?

Or because he was tempted, too?

"I am sorry if I took advantage—" she said, keeping her tone neutral.

Now it was his turn to snort. "You didn't do anything I didn't want to. Do you truly think you were taking advantage of me?"

His tone was skeptical.

"I am close to a foot taller than you, and I outweigh you by a substantial amount," he said, raking his gaze over her body. She didn't miss that his eyes lingered at her bosom, her waist, and then her hips.

It felt like a caress, and she couldn't help her involuntary shiver.

"Then why not?" she said with a shrug.

He crossed his arms over his chest—that firm, muscular, spectacular chest—and gave her an exasperated look.

"Because we are on opposite sides of the argument. Because you will be leaving as soon as we resolve this situation. Because we have no intention of—of—" he said, shaking his head in frustration.

"But we are engaged, Mr. Fallon. *You* saw to that," she said pointedly. "And if we decide we wish to dally, as many engaged couples do, why shouldn't we? Unless there is someone—" She froze, stricken. Was it possible he was interested in someone, and she had just stomped right in and presented herself to be kissed?

"There is no one, I assure you," he replied, before she could continue. "I would not toy with someone's affections like that. I would not have announced our engagement if I thought it would hurt anyone."

"Thank goodness," she said in relief. She moved past him to look out the glass doors leading to the pond. It was mostly cloudy, but the day was warm, and the water looked deliciously refreshing. If only she could assuage the heat inside her with a plunge into the pond.

But it was not that simple.

She turned around. He still had his back to her, and she saw his fists open and close at his sides. As though he was tormented by what had just happened.

"I am truly sorry," she said as she exhaled. "I don't want to upset you. I just—"

He shifted so she could see his face. She couldn't read his expression. Not only because they were in the dim light of the library, but also because his face was guarded.

"You just didn't think," he finished. She saw his chest rise as he took a deep breath. "What if I was the kind of man who would—"

"But you're not." She walked toward him, propelled by her frustration. "If you had been, you would have ravished me on our first night." She flung her hands up in the air. "No, I don't think, but does that mean I am not a good judge of character?" She moved even closer to him, looking up into his handsome face, regret tingeing her words. "You are obviously an honorable man, and I am sorry to have insulted you." Her throat felt tight, and the only thing she wanted to do was run away and try not to have her sister's voice in her head telling her she'd made yet another impulsive mistake. "We can search another time. If you will excuse me?"

She brushed past him to open the door, yanking it wide through the tears that had sprung to her eyes. She dashed them away angrily, then ran through the hallway and up the stairs to her room, slamming the door behind her as she flung herself onto the bed.

Yes, she was being ridiculous. She knew that. But she also knew that if she indulged herself now, she could present a calm mien later on. Otherwise, she would just stew in her emotions, and she wouldn't be able to focus on what needed to be done.

She'd have to adjust her expectations of what might be possible between them, ignore the sparks of attraction she knew both of them felt, and concentrate on proving the house belonged to her. That was her only task, and she needed to focus on it.

If only she didn't wish to toss all that away to focus on him.

Chapter Seven

What the hell had just happened?

Gabriel ran a hand through his hair as he gazed, unseeing, at the library.

Her scent still lingered in the air, warring against the stale smell of the books. Or perhaps that was his imagination—maybe her scent had imprinted on his skin, and he only thought he could smell her.

He touched his mouth, running his fingers from side to side. She had kissed him. And he— well, he had definitely kissed her back.

If he hadn't remembered he was a gentleman, he would have rucked her skirts up and had her against the door. Slid his palms over all that smooth skin. Not that he knew it was smooth, but that was his presumption.

Even now, his cock throbbed, aching, and it was taking all of his willpower not to follow after her and finish what she'd started.

But it would be the dangerous thing to do. The *risky* thing to do, and if there was one thing Gabriel had learned from his father, it was that risky behavior seldom resulted in anything good. Yes, you might win the bet, but at what cost?

And since she would be leaving, he didn't dare do anything that might mean when she left she'd be taking his heart.

Because she would be so easy to fall in love with.

He took a deep breath, shaking his head to clear it. They were here, in this house together, for the next twenty-seven days. Cleaning and searching, as they'd agreed.

Alone together. In dark, quiet rooms filled with dust and mice.

Possibly upstairs in his bedroom, formerly her father's bedroom.

Which had a conveniently placed bed.

"Argh," he groaned, running his hand over his face.

"You speaking, sir?"

The cook, Mrs. Hall's cousin Mary, had popped into the room so quietly, he hadn't heard her enter.

Or perhaps he was too distracted by what had just happened to notice a herd of elephants tromping inside.

"No, Mary, sorry." He shifted his attention to her. "Is there something I can help you with?"

Mary nodded. "Yes, sir. You see, I am going to make something very special, a new recipe, and I want to make certain you'll be there. And the lady, too."

"You'll have to check with Miss Holton," Gabriel

replied, "but I will be there." He forced a smile onto his lips. He didn't want to discourage her, but her cooking was . . . not good.

"Thank you," she replied. "I am so grateful to you and Miss Holton for giving me the opportunity. It's been my dream to be a cook, but nobody would hire me without experience."

Or cooking talent, Gabriel supposed.

But she was working for free; he just had to pay for the supplies, which he'd offered to do when it became clear so many people would be living at the house. He suspected Miss Holton didn't have the funds to do so, not when she'd arrived with a satchel filled with just old gowns and books. And when it was finally established he owned the house free and clear, he would need a cook. It might as well be Mrs. Hall's cousin. She'd have to improve eventually—right?

Meanwhile, having all these people in the house lent a patina of respectability to the very shocking reality that he and his fiancée were underneath the same roof. He did have to commend her on that, even though there were several more people than she'd originally intended.

"Can you ask Miss Holton about dinner, sir?" Mary asked. "She has that big dog. I don't like to get near it." She did look nervous. Wonderful. Now he would have to go find Miss Holton and make certain she would be attending a meal when both of them would be thinking about—

Unless she wasn't thinking about it. Unless she

did things like that all the time, and he was just another passing fancy.

That thought made him want to stomp upstairs and show her just how not a passing fancy he was.

Not the response either of them wanted. But the response his body craved.

What had she said?

"Goddamn it," he muttered.

"Pardon?" Mary asked.

"Yes," he said in a louder tone. "I'll remind Miss Holton about dinner."

Mary's expression relaxed. "Thank you so much, sir. You can tell Miss Holton I've got a few bones from last night's supper for her dog. If she doesn't mind fetching them."

"I will tell her that as well," Gabriel replied, trying not to sound aggrieved.

Mary nodded again. Then she eased out of the room, shutting the door behind her.

Things were much simpler when he just had a ramshackle house to make habitable.

Now he had to navigate a pretend engagement with a woman who'd kissed him, share a house with random villagers from town who believed the pretense, and eat the inedible food prepared by a cook who was afraid of dogs. All while battling for ownership of a house he yearned to make into a home.

He wondered if Hercules would be willing to trade labors with him. Taking care of a few man-eating horses would be a lot easier than what he had to do.

OCTAVIA GOT UP from her bed to pace the bedroom, worrying at her fingernail with her teeth. She hadn't *meant* to kiss him. But he was so stupidly handsome, and tall, and strong, and he had an adorable dog.

Not that Nyx was at all responsible. It just made it seem as though he was more worth kissing if he had an adorable dog.

If Ivy was here—which, thank God, she was not—she would be rolling her eyes and chiding Octavia for her impulsive ways. But would agree with her on the adorable dog.

Good thing she could practically hear Ivy's voice in her head.

Why did you do that, Octavia? He is your opponent in this venture. Were you trying to seduce him into giving up his claim to the house?

Hmm. She hadn't thought of that. But Ivy, her wise, businesslike sister, would have.

However, even if she had thought of it, and been low enough to attempt it, Mr. Fallon would not be swayed. He was scholarly, far more interested in his mythology than in dalliance.

Though the way he kissed . . .

Octavia allowed herself a brief recollection of how it felt. How firm and warm his mouth was, how assuredly he'd swept his tongue inside to tangle with hers. How he'd planted one hand above her head as though capturing her there to plunder with his mouth.

She *wanted* to be plundered. She *wanted* to feel as though he was absolutely in control, and he could do whatever he liked with her. Just imagining the heat of his body on hers, the strength and power in the muscles she couldn't help but noticing, made her shiver.

And she was not cold.

No, she was hot, burning up with what she strongly suspected was a fierce desire, the likes of which she'd never experienced.

Is this what it was like with Ivy and Sebastian, her brother-in-law?

She marched over to regard herself in the mirror.

"Curse it," she said as she met her own eyes in the glass.

Her face held the same expression she'd seen on Ivy's face after spending time alone with Sebastian, both before and after they were married. Her gaze was dreamy, her mouth was slightly parted, and her cheeks were flushed.

Well.

She'd have to figure out how to solve this problem, among all the others that she also had to solve, so that she didn't end up making an idiot of herself over a man who had made it absolutely clear that he did not want any part of her kisses.

Though he *had* said she hadn't taken advantage of him, at least.

A knock at the door startled her out of her musings.

"Come in," she called.

She turned toward the door, gasping only a little bit as she saw Mr. Fallon. He kept himself just at the threshold, one large hand grasping the door to hold it open. Cerberus was behind him, and walked into the room, flopping onto the floor. At least one—possibly two, counting Nyx—of the house's inhabitants didn't mind its dilapidated condition.

"Miss Holton," he began.

Octavia rolled her eyes, then stepped forward to tug on his arm. "For goodness' sake, come in."

He stumbled toward her, and she darted around him to shut the door, then turned back to regard him. "I promise, I am not going to leap on you for ravishing purposes," she said in an indignant voice.

Both eyebrows rose. "Ravishing pur—" He shook his head. "Never mind. I came to check that you would be at dinner this evening. Mary"—his face twisted as though he was pained—"is planning something special."

"Oh God." Octavia couldn't help but groan.

He nodded, his expression shifting to one of shared amusement. "Yes, I agree with you. But it would hurt her feelings if we didn't eat dinner this evening."

Octavia opened her mouth to announce that she didn't care, she wasn't going to choke down unpleasant food if she didn't have to, when she stopped herself. It would be too cruel not to show up, not to at least try Mary's cooking. She was often selfish—Ivy reminded her of that far more than Octavia would have liked—but she wasn't actively mean. And all the work she was doing made her hungrier than usual.

"Do you suppose she will learn eventually?" she asked in a hopeful voice.

Mr. Fallon shrugged. "I suppose?" he said, but he didn't sound optimistic.

"What will happen if she gets a real job cooking?" Octavia demanded. "She'll be fired! We can't allow that to happen," she continued, her mind working it through. "I wonder if I could send to London for one of the people who work for my chef at the club to train her." She frowned as she thought. "Mrs. Jennings is proving to be a reasonable housekeeper, if you can keep her focused. Perhaps we could implement a system of checklists. I have a few workers at the club who have difficulty focusing. Checklists have proved to be an extraordinary help." She nodded, a rush of excitement coursing through her as she thought. This felt like when she was back at the club managing everything. She had to admit she'd missed that. "And Old Joe, he is good with—"

"If you could send to London, then you could presumably go to London yourself. Surely you wouldn't balk at taking the Mail Coach," he interrupted, folding his arms over that impressive chest.

She jerked back in surprise. "And lose the days I might be looking for my father's papers?" She folded her arms as well, lifting her chin. "No, I will not. Most definitely not." She spoke in a defiant tone.

His mouth tightened, and she kept her eyes locked with his. Both of them regarded each other with a challenging gaze, as though daring the other to break first.

He looked away first, and she suppressed a small smile of triumph. Though she did allow the feeling to course through her.

Along with the other feelings currently coursing. Feelings like desire, and passion, and a hunger that was not related to food.

"I'll see you at dinner, then," he said in a clipped tone. "And Mary has bones for Cerberus," he added.

She couldn't resist teasing him. "Remember we are supposed to be engaged. We'll have to act like we are in love." She gave him a beatific—and patently false—smile. If she couldn't kiss him, at least she could aggravate him in other ways.

He growled, and for a second it looked as though he was going to kiss her, but instead he just inhaled sharply and walked past her, opening the door and leaving without another word.

She wished he had kissed her. But if he wasn't going to kiss her, she was glad she had annoyed him so much he might have kissed her just to shut her up.

"HAVE YOU TWO set a date for the wedding yet?" Mrs. Jennings asked, serving herself more of whatever it was that Mary had cooked. Gabriel couldn't tell just what it was. Something involving heat and brown sauce.

She spoke to Miss Holton, who sat to his right. Charlie sat to her right, while Mrs. Jennings was on his other side, followed by Old Joe and then Mrs. Jennings's daughter. Mrs. Jennings's daughter, Mrs. Wycoff, was a younger version of Mrs. Jennings, with the same piercing blue eyes and rosy cheeks. She was a doting mother, always fussing around Charlie, but skittish when she encountered Gabriel in the house. She'd kept herself busy assisting Mrs. Jennings with cleaning and organizing when she wasn't with her son.

"We have not," Miss Holton said smoothly, giving him a quick glance from under her lashes. "I need to make certain my sister will be available to attend."

"I remember Miss Ivy," Mrs. Jennings said, her eyes getting a faraway look. "She was so brave to wager against—oh!" she exclaimed, giving Gabriel a guilty look. "I forgot Miss Ivy wagered against your father." Her rosy cheeks turned a bright red.

Gabriel's chest tightened at the mention of the bet. If Octavia's sister had lost, he might very well be married to Octavia, with Miss Ivy herself married to his father.

"It is fine." He looked over at Octavia. "I don't know much about the bet. Do you?" Gabriel had been away at school when it all happened. He'd never even met the Holton sisters before the younger sister surprised him in the pond.

And had been surprising him ever since that day. Was it only a few days ago? It felt as though he'd been sparring with her for a lifetime.

Octavia's expression grew shuttered. "I only heard of it recently."

Gabriel could tell that whatever she'd learned had bothered her, and so he spoke before any of the curious villagers—led by the indefatigably curious Mrs. Jennings—could ask more about it.

"Mrs. Jennings," he began, leaning back in his chair to look at her, "are you instructing young Charlie here?" He gestured to Charlie, who seemed to be enjoying Mary's food.

Someone had to.

Charlie must have taken after his father more than his mother in appearance; his hair was dark, as were his eyes. He was all limbs, as awkward and uncertain as a puppy, with the promise of growing up much taller than either his mother or grandmother.

As Gabriel watched, Charlie finished up everything on his plate, even going so far as to run a finger on it to gather every last bit of sauce. He turned pleading eyes to his mother, who immediately heaped another pile of whatever it was on his plate.

"Charlie is a good student," Mrs. Jennings began in a keenly interested tone, the same voice Gabriel remembered from so many years ago before he went away to school, "but he doesn't like to read all that much, I'm sorry to say." She made a harrumphing noise. "At least not *good* books."

Charlie shrugged, then met Gabriel's eyes. "All the stories are about boring boys who do something wrong and get punished for it."

Gabriel let out an unexpected snort at Charlie's insightful analysis of what passed for children's literature.

"It can't all be fairies and witches and such," Mrs. Jennings replied in a reproving voice.

"But why not?"

The question, posed by Miss Holton, took him by surprise. He wouldn't have expected her to champion fantastical tales, given how businesslike she was. At least in her approach toward . . . business.

Though perhaps she had a romantic streak?

She did enjoy torrid novels, she'd said. And that would explain her behavior earlier that day, he thought, suppressing a smile.

Mrs. Jennings let out a sputter of dismay. "Please don't encourage him, Miss Holton. I am constantly finding him with his nose in a completely inappropriate book."

Miss Holton leaned forward as though sharing a secret. "I like inappropriate books, too, Charlie." She winked at him, and Charlie's eyes widened.

"Some of those stories—such as the ones in my studies, for example—are merely demonstrations of the best and worst of humanity," Gabriel said. "I think all reading is good reading, Mrs. Jennings. In fact," he said, "I believe it was you who first taught me that. And would you just look at me now."

"Yes, would you," Miss Holton murmured. Whether it was in admiration or disdain, he couldn't tell.

Probably both.

"Mr. Fallon," Charlie said slowly, "would you be able to let me read some of your books?"

Gabriel thought about all the activities the various gods and goddesses got up to and felt himself blanch.

"I have a better idea," Miss Holton said smoothly. "What if Mr. Fallon was to tell us stories in the evenings?" She glanced around the table. "Unless you all have other plans?"

For the first time since he'd met her, she sounded hesitant. Because she was unsure of committing him? Or because she was unaccustomed to congregating with a group of strangers when it wasn't her line of work?

Either way, it was endearing.

"And I didn't even ask you first, Mr. Fallon," she continued in a rush, sounding mortified.

He held his hand up. "It's fine. It's more than fine. Anybody who is interested enough to listen to me blather on about my favorite topic is welcome to hear it."

She smiled in relief. "Well, that is excellent. I know I am interested. What about you, Charlie?"

"May I?" the boy asked, casting a pleading look at his mother and grandmother.

Mrs. Wycoff nodded first, giving Gabriel a shy smile. It seemed Charlie got his shyness from her—certainly Mrs. Jennings had never hesitated to venture into any conversation.

"Tomorrow night, then?" Gabriel asked.

Everyone nodded, even Old Joe, who Gabriel had thought was asleep, judging by how his chin rested on his chest.

Perhaps there was something nice about living with so many people. He'd only ever lived with a bunch of other schoolboys and his father. Not quite the same convivial atmosphere as here. Miss Holton had initially invited Mrs. Jennings to assist with her search, and to lend her respectability, but it was clear she liked the company and enjoyed being sociable. This was her attempt to mold the situation into a better one for herself. That it would be better for everyone else was a nice side effect.

She was a nice side effect, actually. If she weren't so adamant that she owned the property, having her here would be splendid.

Of course, if she didn't think she owned the property, she wouldn't be here in the first place.

He tried not to think about how much better it was that she *did* think she owned the house.

OCTAVIA SPENT THE morning determinedly searching through the attic, dragging the dustiest boxes toward the candle she'd perched on the windowsill. The attic was spacious in width, but had a low ceiling and only one small window through which a meager light emerged. When she'd first come up, she'd heard the pitter-patter of tiny feet—*very* tiny feet—and squelched the urge to yelp or run away.

When it was proved she owned the house, she could contact someone to take care of the mouse intruder problem—she smiled thinking of Mr. Fallon's phrasing—and clean everything out, tossing away anything that couldn't be sold.

Octavia had never been sentimental. There had never been anything to be sentimental about; her childhood was overshadowed by the persistent worry of her father's erratic behavior, which had been confirmed when she was fourteen, and Ivy had taken them to London.

She'd been forced to grow up quickly, although she had to admit she herself had forced her maturity, insisting she work in the gambling club at a far earlier age than Ivy would have liked.

So when she opened a box of what appeared to be artwork from her and Ivy's childhood, she merely closed the box up again and moved on to another. Though she did feel an odd pang somewhere in the region of her heart. It must've been Mary's cooking from the night before.

"Miss Holton?"

She heard Mrs. Wycoff's hesitant voice from the opening that led to the floor below.

It must be something important for the shy woman to seek her out.

"Up here, Mrs. Wycoff," she called.

The woman continued up the ladder to the attic, glancing around the space with curiosity.

Neither Octavia nor Mr. Fallon had mentioned that there was a dispute about the ownership of the house, so of course it would seem odd if Octavia was merely fussing around the attic when there were so many other more compelling places to be.

"Miss Holton, if I may speak with you?"

Octavia brushed her hair away from her face, feeling a cobweb stick to her fingers. This time she didn't have Mr. Fallon's strong, capable hand to take care of it.

Enough of that, Octavia, she chided herself.

"How may I be of help?"

Mrs. Wycoff's hands twisted together. She was older than Octavia but still young, with light brown hair and a tentative but genuine smile. She wore an old but clean gown in a shade that complemented her blue eyes. "You and Mr. Fallon have both been so kind. I know my mother insisted Charlie and I come to stay here. I know we were not specifically invited—"

Octavia opened her mouth to object, but Mrs. Wycoff gave her a look of exasperation. "I know my mother," she said in a long-suffering tone, "and I also know you asked her to join you, but she brought us along as well. That is what she does." Mrs. Wycoff shook her head fondly. "She wants to be certain everyone is well taken care of," she added.

"And her concern is quite appreciated," Octavia replied. "I also appreciate the work you've added. This house needs a lot to make it habitable again."

"Thank you," Mrs. Wycoff said. She took a deep breath before speaking again. "Neither you nor Mr. Fallon have mentioned your plans for after you are married, but I was wondering—" She paused, twisting her hands together again. "I was wondering if you might be in need of a lady's maid?"

Octavia opened her mouth to speak, but Mrs. Wycoff continued before she could say a word.

"I will be honest with you," Mrs. Wycoff said. "I am not married. My Charlie is mine, but his father"—her face crumpled, and Octavia felt her chest tighten in sympathy—"was killed before we could wed." She swallowed. "I use his name, but we were not—we didn't—"

Mrs. Wycoff brushed her tears away with the back of her hand as she straightened. Thank goodness she wasn't tall, or her head would have hit the ceiling.

"So I understand if you don't wish to employ someone of such—"

"I'll hire you," Octavia blurted out before the woman could finish. "I can't afford to pay you until we've—until my fiancé and I have settled a few things—but I will find work for you, I promise."

Mrs. Wycoff's expression cleared, and she gave a relieved smile. "Oh, my goodness, thank you.

Yes, thank you. And I believe Charlie would want to work with the horses, when you have them."

Right now there was only Mr. Fallon's Pegasus in the stables, but it was natural, again, for Mrs. Wycoff to assume there would be more—this was a large house a reasonable distance from town, and she and Mr. Fallon were gentlepeople, even if not strict aristocracy.

"Yes, of course," Octavia replied.

Knowing, even as she spoke, that she had no idea how she was going to employ Mrs. Wycoff, train Charlie in horse care, and, oh yes, make a decent cook out of Mary, but that she would do it because she had promised.

At least Mrs. Jennings was reasonably competent.

It was at times like these she had to admit she agreed with her sister, Ivy, that she was far too impetuous and spoke without thinking.

But if she hadn't, Mrs. Wycoff wouldn't have hope for the future. And wasn't that far more important than planning?

"Thank you, Miss Holton," Mrs. Wycoff said in a grateful voice. "I'll just go help Mary with lunch preparations. I am so glad you are here."

She descended the ladder before Octavia could ask her to help Mary cook something edible.

Octavia stared at the space where she'd stood, swallowing hard as she realized just what she'd done. Hired a lady's maid, when she was supposed to already have one, one who had taken ill on the journey here. Hopefully nobody would remember that until she had figured out how to explain. Never mind that by asking Mrs. Jennings to stay at the house, she'd wound up with half the town in residence.

Now it was even more important to prove she owned the house so she would have the means to afford Mrs. Wycoff's pay, and get a horse for Charlie to groom.

Though that last part was, of course, ridiculous. And it meant returning to London with a lady's maid, a young child, and a horse. But she'd seen how the boy's eyes lit up when he was talking about fairies, and mythical creatures, and how he'd begun to follow Old Joe around like an eager puppy whenever that gentleman did anything in the stable.

If an older person had stepped in to encourage her and Ivy instead of literally gambling away their futures, how would their lives have changed? And was it fair that Charlie be made to suffer more because his father died before marrying his mother?

No. No, it was not.

Instead of freeing herself from responsibilities, it seemed she'd added them. And she still had to pay Mr. Higgins back.

"You'd best get to searching, Octavia," she reminded herself, dragging another box toward the window.

Because if she didn't find what she was looking for here, she'd have to look in her father's old bedchamber. Where Mr. Fallon was currently living.

She scrunched up her face in mortification as she recalled what she'd done the day before. Kissing him like that when she knew perfectly well he wasn't the type of man who would dally.

Though it seemed pretty obvious, from the way he kissed, that he had dallied before. He knew what to do, and he did it well.

Her entire body had reacted when he deepened the kiss, licking inside her mouth and biting her lip.

She shivered just thinking of it.

She shivered just thinking of *him*.

Chapter Eight

Gabriel had spent far more time than he truly had to choosing the first story he would tell. But he wanted to capture everyone's imaginations, perhaps show them some of what he loved so much about the ancient myths, stories that could inform and instruct modern people with lessons for how to live one's life.

Mostly by not making the same decisions the gods would make, but he presumed his audience would reach that conclusion without his having to say it. It was far more interesting to share moral tales through fascinating recounts rather than—as Charlie had put it—the stories about "boring boys who do something wrong and get punished for it."

It was just after supper, and everyone but him was downstairs in the kitchen helping Mary clean up. The food that evening was less inedible than before, so Gabriel had hopes that perhaps one day Mary would prepare something he might actually like.

They'd all agreed the best place for the evening's event would be the spacious salon, which was also spacious with dirt.

He'd been grateful at having to think of a story to tell, because it kept his mind from obsessing all the time about the kiss.

The kiss he couldn't get out of his mind.

How she'd instigated it, showing him precisely what he wanted. Not acting coy or disingenuous about any of it.

This wasn't his first kiss; that had been with one of his schoolmates' older sisters on a visit home with his friend. She was sixteen, eager to follow her older sisters into Society, and he had been fourteen. He'd reached the height he was now, but he hadn't yet put on the accompanying muscle—he was as thin as Charlie, and far more gawky.

The girl had yanked him from the hallway into her room, kissing him briefly before shoving him out the door again. Over so quickly it had barely registered.

It had taken him a few years after that to have his second kiss, one that was far more rewarding.

But none of his kissing experience had prepared him for how intensely his body reacted to *her* kiss. A reaction that seemed to infuse every part of his body—not just his cock, which had definitely reacted as cocks did when stimulated so profoundly. But his skin, which ached to be touched by her fingers.

"Mr. Fallon," Mrs. Jennings said, entering the room. Snapping Gabriel immediately out of his thoughts, because he refused to think about a passionate interlude and his former teacher at the same time. Perhaps he should start asking Mrs. Jennings to join them when he and Miss Holton would otherwise be alone—that would keep his thoughts from wandering to where they shouldn't go.

But then he wouldn't be alone with her.

"You've done wonders in here," she exclaimed. "I wouldn't have recognized it!"

Gabriel had scrubbed the walls, paying particular attention to the empty spots indicating where paintings had once been hung. He'd pushed the sofas outdoors and used a broom to pound on them, releasing all their dust into the air. Then he'd found a rag and a bucket and cleaned the floors, noting with pleasure that the floors themselves, underneath the grime, were beautiful. Wide wooden planks, the color of Octavia's eyes, looked far more elegant than he would have supposed.

He hadn't had time to clean all the windows, so he'd found some bright white linens and hung them up, taking down the dark fabric that made up the curtains. The effect was immediate—the dark wood of the floors gleamed, the sofas looked inviting, and the light that filtered through the sheer linen lit the whole room up.

The sun was starting to set, but because it was

summer, it wouldn't go down for another hour or so. Meanwhile, the room was bathed in a warm, golden light that meant they only needed a few candles.

"Goodness," Mrs. Jennings's daughter murmured as she and Charlie walked in.

Old Joe didn't say anything, just snuck over to a corner of the room and sat down on the floor, his attention focused on Gabriel.

Mary and Octavia were last to enter, Octavia freezing as she saw what Gabriel had done. Her eyes flew to his, her mouth an open O.

"This is perfection," she said, causing a rush of pride to flood Gabriel. She stepped toward him, her gaze traveling around the room.

He wished he didn't immediately assume she was assessing the environs as a seller would— appreciating the revealed beauty of the room for the potential profit, not for how it was improving the likelihood of this house becoming a home.

He needed to look past the next twenty-six days to when he would make his dream a reality. He just needed to keep calm, to keep his plans moving.

Though he wasn't entirely calm, given how much his mind kept wandering to that moment in the library. As though he truly was one of the heroines in a Gothic novel, venturing through the house alone only to be trapped in a room with a—with a completely charming and aggravating woman who was determined to upend his life.

"Mr. Fallon?" the woman in question said. "We are ready, if you please."

She sat on one of the newly dusted sofas, Charlie next to her, with Mrs. Jennings next to Charlie. Charlie's mother was on another sofa, while Mary sat down beside her. The dogs had joined the party as well, Cerberus and Nyx sitting directly in front of him.

"Yes, well, so this evening I want to tell you about Persephone and Hades," he began.

OCTAVIA THOUGHT SHE knew—vaguely—the story of Persephone and Hades, but when Mr. Fallon told it, it was another tale entirely. She was enraptured, along with the rest of the house's inhabitants.

He truly had worked wonders in this room. It looked joyful and full of promise, not stripped of all its treasures because of a person's carelessness. His fecklessness.

She wished she wasn't so bitter about her father, but if anything, the past few days had made her even more so. He had had this house, this family, and he had squandered it all in a fruitless pursuit. For what? To win? To win what? Nothing was worth more than the feeling of home.

Something she should not be even thinking about, given her home was, as she'd told Mr. Fallon, wherever her sister and Cerberus were, not an actual place.

But this house could be a home, given proper care.

And when she proved she owned it she would—sell it? To someone who would make it into a home where she wouldn't belong?

Thankfully, Mr. Fallon's words drew her out of her reverie.

"Persephone was kind and lovely, and she brought joy wherever she went. Hades was the god of the Underworld. There wasn't a lot of joy in that place. So when he saw Persephone, he knew he had to make her his wife."

Not quite what the god had likely said, but he was adjusting his story for his audience, after all.

"And so he persuaded her to go with him to his town"—his eyes flicked toward Octavia, startling her—"and she spent time with him in his home. Eventually she came to care for him." Was it her imagination, or was he now deliberately *not* looking at her?

"But her mother, Demeter, was distraught at her daughter's absence—"

"What does *distraught* mean?" Charlie interjected.

"Sad and upset," Mr. Fallon replied.

"Charlie, we can write down the words you don't know and look them up afterward." Mrs. Jennings nodded, then glanced to Gabriel, who was regarding her with a half smile. "Go on," she urged.

"And Demeter was the goddess of farming and the seasons. She's the reason we have spring and summer," he explained. "But when her daughter went away, she was so sad that nothing under her guidance would bloom. It was winter all the time."

All the members of the group groaned.

"Demeter went to the god who was in charge—rather like a manager—and he listened to her, and knew it wasn't fair that Persephone had to stay in Hades's town all the time, even if she had come to feel affection for him." Again a quick glance, and she felt his regard like he'd trailed his fingers on her skin.

"So, what did he do?"

Octavia was surprised to hear Mrs. Wycoff speak so quickly and urgently—she was usually so quiet. Everyone turned to look at her, and her cheeks promptly turned a vibrant shade of pink.

"Well, Charlie's mother," Mr. Fallon said with a grin, "Zeus—that is the name of the manager of the gods—Zeus told Hades he had to let Persephone go home to her mother."

"But?" Charlie said.

"But before she left, Hades gave Persephone a pomegranate."

"What's a—" Charlie began.

"A pomegranate is a kind of fruit," Mr. Fallon cut in. "It doesn't grow here, although it's been tried. It needs warmer weather—"

"Don't we all," Mrs. Jennings remarked. "We'll write that one down as well."

"And the seeds of the fruit are what you eat," Mr. Fallon continued. "Now, Persephone knew that she should not eat or drink anything while she was in Hades's town or she would have to stay there forever." Mr. Fallon held his hand up when Charlie opened his mouth again. "These are the rules of the gods. I don't understand either."

Charlie closed his mouth.

"And Persephone thought she could eat just a few seeds of the pomegranate and be safe."

"Oh no!" Mrs. Jennings exclaimed.

"'Oh no' is correct," he replied. "Persephone went to see her mother, but Hades said that because she'd eaten in his town, she could never leave. Never see her mother again. But that would mean—"

"Winter forever!" Charlie shouted.

"Yes, that is right. And Zeus knew that would make the people suffer, since they needed crops and farming to survive. So he worked out an arrangement with Hades—Persephone would stay with him a month for each of the pomegranate seeds she'd eaten, and she'd be with her mother the other months."

"How many seeds did she eat?" Mary asked.

Mr. Fallon looked at Charlie. "Can you guess?"

Charlie twisted his mouth in thought.

"It has something to do with the seasons," Mr. Fallon said, a gentle look on his face.

"Is she with Hades when it's winter?" Charlie asked.

"Yes, exactly. Very clever, Charlie." Mr. Fallon glanced around the room, his gaze finishing on Octavia. "When Persephone is with Hades, the world grows a little dimmer. When she is back among people, the world seems to brighten."

Oh.

Was he saying— Did he think that *she* made the world brighter somehow?

Or was she just imagining that because she'd found herself far more intrigued by him than she should have been?

She should not be wondering about any of that.

She should be focusing on finding the proof, selling the house for a fair profit, and paying Mr. Higgins so she could return to London and resume working. Her clientele would be returning to London about that time as well.

She snorted.

"What is it, Miss Holton?" Mrs. Jennings asked.

Octavia waved her hand. "I was just thinking that Society leaves London right when the weather turns most glorious. Perhaps they are the opposite of Persephone—the weather improves when they are all away."

Everyone laughed in response.

"Or maybe the weather is glorious because you are here, Miss Holton," Mr. Fallon said with a sly smile on his face.

"Oh, you lovebirds!" Mrs. Jennings said, glancing from one to the other. "Of course you would think that, Mr. Fallon."

To her vast annoyance, Octavia felt her cheeks grow hot at his words—yes, he was playing to the audience, reminding them what he and she were supposed to be to one another, but his comment after he'd looked at her during the recitation of his story felt real.

And then she snorted again, this time at herself.

At her own foolishness. She was just imagining it—after all, *he* had been the one to say they should not be kissing.

"Oh, I forgot the best part of the story!" Mr. Fallon said with a grin, tearing her away from her thoughts. He gestured toward the dogs, who had both fallen asleep. "The guardian of where Hades lived was named Cerberus."

"Like Miss Holton's dog," Charlie exclaimed.

"Yes, just like Miss Holton's dog," Mr. Fallon replied.

"And if you will excuse me," Octavia said, rising from her chair, "I will be heading to bed now, where Cerberus will guard me for the evening."

"We wouldn't want any mischievous gods sneaking in during the middle of the night, would we?" Mrs. Jennings said in a coy tone, shooting a look toward Mr. Fallon.

Who immediately blushed.

Aha! Octavia tried not to feel gleeful that perhaps he *was* affected by her.

But failed. Because she had never been successful at suppressing her feelings, which was all part of the problem.

"Cerberus," she said as she walked toward the door, "come."

Her dog snuffled and trotted after her. At least she had him for company.

"Gabriel," she heard Mrs. Jennings say as she left, "could we have more of these stories? They are so entertaining and educational."

"Yes, if you would like." Mr. Fallon sounded

genuinely flattered, and she was reminded that he'd said few people seldom actually wanted to hear him talk about his work.

But she did. That in itself was dangerously unsettling.

Not to mention how unsettled she was by just one kiss.

Drat. She was in so much unknown territory, and she did not like that feeling, not at all.

"MR. FALLON?"

Gabriel turned sharply at the sound of Octavia's voice.

He was in the library the day after recounting the Persephone story, going through Mr. Holton's collection of books and trying to make either rhyme or reason of them. He didn't think he could make both, given their state.

She was at the door, clad once again in one of her work gowns. Her hair was tumbled around her shoulders, not pulled back as it usually was. The dark red curls looked as rebellious and spirited as she did.

"Yes, Miss Holton?"

She glanced behind herself and slipped inside, closing the door behind her. Like the other day. He shifted, that prickling awareness of her growing more prickly now that they were alone together in a room—the same room—again.

She raised her chin in what he had come to recognize as an imperious gesture. "I did not get an opportunity to search here for my father's will. If you recall—" She tossed her head, as though daring him to say anything about it.

Gabriel cocked an eyebrow. "I do recall, Miss Holton." He spoke in a knowing tone. He shouldn't be stepping this close to the fire—*her* fire—but he couldn't seem to help himself.

"Yes," she said, lifting that chin again. "That." Her nose would be pointing straight up if she tilted it any higher. "As I was saying. I did not get an opportunity, and most of the books are too tall for me to reach, so you will need to help me."

She didn't move from in front of the door, however. Waiting for his reassurance he wouldn't touch her? Wanting him to touch her again?

He wished he knew.

"Yes, of course," he replied. "I am just going through the books myself. Your father had an interesting collection."

She made a rueful noise. "Interesting because it doesn't make any sense, I imagine." She strolled further into the room, glancing over at the book-shelves. "He would take whatever wager anyone offered, so if someone had a few books to stake, he'd accept." She shrugged, pulling a random volume from the shelf. "This, for example, is titled *A Few of My Favorite Fox Chases in East Sussex.*" She gave him a pointed glance. "I imagine the only person who might be interested in this book is"—she flipped to the title page—"the author, a Mr. John Kent."

"And the fox, I assume," Gabriel replied.

She laughed at that, sliding the book back onto the shelf.

"I know why I am looking here, but why are you?" she asked, turning to regard him.

His expression indicated that she should already know.

"Oh, of course, *books*!" she replied. "Have you even searched his desk for any papers yet?"

"I have the papers I need," he said, his eyebrows arching. "Unless you want *me* to find the proof that you own this house?" He spread his hands out, an exaggeratedly innocent expression on his face. "If you're not up to the task . . ." he said, his words trailing off as his mouth quirked into a smile.

Octavia let out a disgruntled noise, going past him to the desk. She yanked the top right-hand drawer open, her eyes widening as she saw that there were indeed papers inside.

"You didn't even look?" she said as she withdrew the stack and placed them on the desk.

"Why should I?"

She shook her head. "Natural curiosity? I know I wouldn't have been able to resist looking, even if there was nothing at stake."

"You're very curious."

"I like knowing things."

Like how your mouth felt against mine.

"I do as well," he said. "Something else we have in common."

"What do we have in common in the first place, Mr. Fallon?" she asked. The papers on the desk were entirely forgotten—there could be something that indicated she owned the entire town of Greensett, and he still couldn't care.

"Well, our fathers, for one thing," he said.

"Ah, so these are not *good* things," she said, her voice bitter.

"Your mother—what was she like?" he asked.

"So you can tell if our mothers are similar, too?" she said.

He shook his head. "No. My mother died when I was young. I have no recollection of her. I'm just . . . curious," he said with a slight smile.

"Curious," she repeated, biting her lip.

She sat down in the chair behind the desk. "She was much more like Ivy than me. She was generous and thoughtful, and she tried to keep us from seeing the worst in our father."

"You don't think you're generous and thoughtful?"

She gave a short laugh. "Ivy would say I am not." Her chin lifted. "But I am generous to the people I care about." A pause. "I am not sure I could say I am thoughtful. Usually I'm trying to get things done so quickly, I don't spend time on thoughtfulness."

She exhaled, as though finished with the conversation. Proving her point.

She listed the items as she sorted through the stack, her frustration obvious. "A receipt for a thresher, whatever that is—"

"It sorts grains into seeds and stalks. The wheat from the chaff, so to speak," he explained.

"Of course you would know," she said in a tone that was more amused than judgmental. She continued thumbing through the papers. "A few letters of correspondence, a promissory note that says my father will turn over a collection of bones if a debt is not paid." She shoved the papers away as she reached the bottom. "He doesn't seem to have kept anything remotely important."

"Not surprising," he said in a low voice. "He let his most valuable possessions slip out of his fingers."

She flushed, feeling awkward when she understood his meaning. "Ivy and I left. He didn't let us slip," she said in a brusque tone, as though it didn't matter.

But it did. It did matter.

He stepped toward her, still holding the book he'd been looking at when she entered the room. "I know what it's like." He felt his throat tighten. "To have a parent who cares more for something else than you."

She turned her head, but not before he glimpsed how her eyes were suddenly glistening.

"I had Ivy," she said in a low voice. "She took care of me. She is my family."

He watched her collect herself, then turn back to him. That chin rose.

"Who did you have, Gabriel?"

Chapter Nine

He didn't have an answer. In fact, he had nothing.

She had felled him with five words, left him hollowed and empty.

"I'm sorry," she said quickly, walking to him, putting her hand on his arm. "I didn't mean—" She bit her lip, her eyes assessing his face. "I didn't mean to—"

"It's fine," he said, covering her hand with his. He dropped the book he'd been holding to the floor. It had already been mouse food, and therefore worthless.

But even if it had been the most valuable item in the room, it would have slipped from his suddenly nerveless fingers.

Not that the question itself was so startling; it was one he had asked himself many times growing up.

It was that someone had thought to ask it. That *she* had thought to ask it, a woman who—as far as he could tell—thought only of herself and her own circumstances. Not out of selfishness, but out of necessity.

He knew that feeling.

"You didn't have anybody," she said at last, speaking in a tone of certainty. "If you did, that person would be here now supporting you after your father's death." She made an all-encompassing gesture. "That is why you are glad there are so many people here, even though I'm the one who invited them. Because the people of Greensett are your family." Her mouth curled into a lopsided smile. "Even though some of your family members are very inquisitive."

"And others cannot cook," Gabriel rejoined, sharing her smile.

She burst out laughing, covering her mouth with her hand. "Last night's dinner was somewhat better, but I have to say her food is terrible." She shook her head. "I think the best meal I've had here so far was that first night when you brought out the bread and cheese."

That first night. When she'd startled him in the pond, and insisted she owned the house, and he'd realized who she was, and that even if she was his opponent, they had things in common.

Like owning dogs, having feckless fathers, and wanting to maintain ownership of this house.

Though their eventual choices were very different. He should remind himself that at her core, she was a gambler, despite her protestations to the contrary. She had gambled on coming to this house, completely unprepared, not even bringing food for herself or her dog. She'd refused to leave, even when staying would risk her reputation. She'd offered a challenge over the course of a month with the ultimate prize being this house. Which could so easily turn into a home.

"What are you thinking about now?" she asked. "Your expression changed. As though you're angry."

He shook his head. He needed to remember all of that, no matter that he was enchanted by her wit, her perseverance, her beauty. She was a siren, luring him to his doom if he let her.

Though that wasn't fair—she didn't intend to be a siren. But everything about her called to him. Even, he should admit, her risk-taking. He admired her bravery, even though it was also foolhardy.

"I'm thinking about our differences. Your gambling establishment." His chest tightened. "I know, firsthand, what havoc your gambling brings. The pain it brings to forgotten children, the uncertainty of survival. A turn of a card can change your entire life."

"And if the only way to rescue the forgotten children is through gambling?" she shot back. "If you have to risk things, important things, in order to survive?" She gestured around them. "Do you think I wouldn't want to live here? To have a respite from London?" She shook her head slowly. "I cannot afford that. Literally," she added in a bitter tone.

He gave her a searching look. "What is it, Octavia?" Was it the first time he'd used her given name? "What is worth the risk?"

She gave a jerk of her head. "Nothing. It is not your concern," she said. "You've made your feelings quite clear on how I live my life."

He felt shut out. But he had brought it on himself. He wouldn't compromise, not when it meant something to him.

"Forget that," she said, dismissing the discussion. Dismissing him. "Let us see if we can find my father's will." She gave an airy gesture. "Surely there has to be something valuable in the house, something he didn't know was worth anything."

The matter-of-fact way she said that, as though if her father had thought anything was valuable he would have gambled it away—as he'd tried to do with his daughters—made his heart hurt.

Her flinty demeanor, her sharp remarks, her apparently pragmatic outlook on life. All of that was due to the trauma of having her father as a parent.

Who would she have been if her father hadn't been who he was?

He wished he could peel away the outer layers to find the core of her. But he'd foreclosed on that possibility with his own bitter perspective.

Who would he have been if his father hadn't been who he was?

Perhaps he should take a closer look at that. Perhaps there was a compromise somewhere.

"WELL," OCTAVIA SAID, after they'd worked together for over half an hour in silence.

His judgment hurt. She couldn't deny that. She also couldn't deny—because she was able to see beyond her own nose, never mind what Ivy might say—that he had valid reasons for thinking as he did. "I am baffled," she admitted. "But I think something has to be in one of these books."

She truly wished she didn't have to take this house away from him. She could see it meant something, that creating a home was important. But he'd just have to take his home creation elsewhere, because her need to keep her limbs was more pressing than his for a comfortable place to live.

"I've looked at this shelf," he said, gesturing to one of the many shelves lining the walls, "and you say your father was not much of a reader. What is your reasoning for thinking he would have put a document here?"

She appreciated that he was still assisting her, even though it was not in his best interests. If she could think of any other solution to the problem, she would. But she could not tell Ivy what she'd done, and she knew Ivy and Sebastian didn't have the money anyway.

If she wanted to survive with her arms and legs, she'd have to come up with something.

She twisted her mouth in thought. "I did have a reason. Hold on," she said, casting her mind back over the past few days. "It's precisely because he was not a reader. He'd assume that nobody else was either, so his papers would be safe tucked in books because nobody would find them."

He looked puzzled, opening his mouth to speak, but then shut it again.

Wise man.

"So," she said, marching toward the shelves on the opposite wall, "how about I take these, and you can finish those?"

She spun back to look at him for confirmation.

The expression he wore was a familiar one—it was similar to a look Ivy got, generally right after Octavia tried to tell everyone what to do.

But he didn't object, as Ivy would. Instead he shrugged and began to pull books out methodically, shaking each one briefly before moving on to the next one.

They worked in silence for another half an hour, Octavia following what Mr. Fallon was doing, pulling a book out, shaking it, then returning it to the shelf.

Mostly what she found was dust, and she kept sneezing, which made Mr. Fallon laugh each time. She had no idea why.

The books were as varied as she'd anticipated they would be—travel diaries from long-dead men were side by side with books on agricultural methods, poetry, and, surprisingly, children's primers. They didn't look familiar, so they weren't ones she and Ivy might have used.

What they all had in common, however, was their shabby state. Books were, as she knew, expensive when new, and few people of her father's status owned as many books as were here. She suspected that he had either purchased them thinking they would be worth something or had gotten them when he'd won a bet.

Either way, he had not been lucky in his choices.

She paused in shaking out *Capitola's Peril* by a Mrs. Southworth—the title of which snagged her interest—when she heard Mr. Fallon make an odd noise behind her.

The book forgotten, she spun around to see him facing her, his eyes wide, holding a book against his chest.

"What is it?" she asked.

He shook his head, as though he couldn't speak.

She stepped forward and pried the book away from his chest, flipping to the title page. "Natalis Comes?" she said, sounding the name out slowly.

"The *Mythologiae*," he replied, snatching the book back from her. "The first volume of it, at least. It's exceedingly rare. It's from the sixteenth century." He glanced up to the shelf. "And some of the rest of the volumes are there as well." He peered at the books, counting out loud. "Two, four, seven. My God. How on earth did your father get them?"

"From some sixteenth-century gambler?" she suggested.

"Don't be flippant. These books are worth a lot of money, even if the set isn't complete. But more than that, they are valuable research books."

"Worth how much?" she asked, interested.

He shrugged his shoulders, looking at the book with what Octavia could only describe as a lustful gaze.

Similar to how he'd looked after they'd kissed.

"Perhaps as much as fifty pounds. Each."

Her eyes widened. "That's—that's a lot of money," she said slowly.

He nodded, his gaze still on the book.

"But it seems to me that we can't possibly sell them until we find the rest of the set." She gave a casual gesture. "In the meantime, why don't you hold on to the books? For research."

He raised his head to look at her, his eyebrows drawing together. "You aren't planning to barter for them? Perhaps buy yourself more time than the twenty-five days you have left?"

She folded her arms over her chest and gave him a pointed glare. "What kind of person would I be if I took advantage of your clear desire for the books?"

"One who has made it very clear she needs a large amount of money, though she won't say what for." He narrowed his gaze. "You're not planning on opening a restaurant with Mary as the cook, are you?"

She snorted in response. "Certainly not. There are better ways to get rid of my enemies, I assure you." Though she wished that were true. Mr. Higgins was a danger to her person, but he wasn't precisely an enemy. She couldn't blame him for wanting his money; she'd entered into an agreement with him, and she was obligated to pay her debts. "Fifty pounds won't solve my problems anyway," she admitted. "You should keep them, at least until our deal is finished. Twenty-five days, I think." Twenty-five days for her to find something of value—a piece of paper declaring she owned everything, a will revealing a secret treasure trove. A gold bar buried in the flour bin, though she'd already looked there.

"When it comes time to sell the books," she continued, "I will ask for your help. If you're willing to give it. Because what do I know about selling valuable books anyway?"

"Of course I'll give it," he said without hesitation. His hands still held the book as they would a lover, with tenderness and a certain amount of desire. She found herself smiling at him, despite herself.

"I'll go back to looking if you want to go cavort with your find," she said, nodding toward the book.

One eyebrow rose. "Cavort? Just what do you think scholars do with books, Miss Holton?" He held a hand up. "Never mind. Don't answer that."

MR. HOLTON SOMEHOW owned a few volumes, at minimum, of Natalis Comes's *Mythologiae*. How on earth? But given the oddity of the books he'd seen thus far, Gabriel supposed it would be odd if there weren't a few treasures buried among the rubble. That they were books Gabriel had a particular interest in was merely a happy accident.

But what a happy accident.

He went to the old, scarred desk, placing the book reverently on its surface. It was in bad shape, though not as bad as most of the other books on the shelves—the collection was high enough off the floor to have avoided the mouse intruder treatment, and it seemed as though it might be a recent addition to the library since it didn't smell like mildew. He assumed volumes two through ten would be similar. If Mr. Holton had the complete set, that is.

He opened the book, noting with relief that while the pages were yellowed, they weren't crumbling. He read the frontispiece in a low voice, his rusty Latin emerging haltingly.

"Are you saying something, Mr. Fallon?" she asked.

He looked up from the book to answer her. "No, just wishing I had studied harder in Latin class."

"That's in Latin, then?" she asked in a curious voice.

"Yes," he replied. "Most of the texts written at this time are in Latin."

"And you can read it?"

"With a little bit of study, yes. It is said that John Milton used the *Mythologiae* as a source for his poem *Paradise Lost*."

"Once again, Mr. Fallon, I have no idea what you are talking about."

Instead of sounding impatient, as she had the last time she had said the same words, she sounded amused. As though she was now pleased he was talking about things she didn't understand.

"I don't have to explain—" he began.

"No, please do," she interrupted. She gestured around them. "I do like learning new things, and it is not as though there is anything occupying my attention otherwise." She exhaled, blowing a strand of hair away from her face. "And I have many books to go through." She gave a wry smile. "Besides, I've heard how you tell a story. Perhaps we can find your next evening tale?"

So he carefully turned the pages, looking for the story of Pandora and the box that Zeus gave her.

He reasoned they could both learn about the dangers of doing something one knew one was specifically not supposed to.

Though the more he thought about it, the more he wanted to kiss her.

Next time—not that there would be a next time, he assured himself, but if there was—next time, he would be the instigator.

"PANDORA WAS THE first woman," Gabriel explained. The inhabitants of the house were seated as they had been the night he'd told Persephone's story, Cerberus and Nyx lying in front of him. He stood in front of the fireplace, which was unlit, due to the heat of the day.

He'd cleaned the windows and drew back the curtains so the sun shone through, picking up the beauty of the wooden floors and the elegance of the furniture, despite the pieces being some-what shabby. This room must have been glorious at one time, and it retained some of that glory, augmented by the vibrancy of the room's current inhabitants.

Particularly her. She'd looked through nearly every book in the library, sneezing at the dust, which made him laugh each time. Not that he could tell her why he was laughing—Octavia the Brave Risk Taker did not wish to hear she was adorable when she sneezed.

"The first woman?" Octavia said. "Ever?"

"Well, the first human woman," he added. "There were goddesses, like Zeus's wife, Hera. But no living women. Pandora was created by Hephaestus, the god of fire."

"Of course woman was created by a man," she said, rolling her eyes. "Because men write the myths, don't they?"

"By a god," Gabriel corrected her. "Zeus asked Hephaestus to create her to send down as pun-ishment, retribution against Prometheus, who'd stolen fire and given it to the humans."

"Hmph," he heard her say.

"Let Mr. Fallon tell us the story, Miss Holton," Mrs. Jennings said gently. "It is not his fault mythology is skewed toward the male perspec-tive." She wrinkled her brow. "Come to think of it, Christianity is skewed that way as well. That doesn't seem right, now, does it?"

Octavia patted the seat next to her. "Come sit here, Mrs. Jennings. We can be radicals together."

She gave a gracious nod of her head. "Continue, Mr. Fallon."

Gabriel grinned, offering her an exaggerated bow before speaking again.

"So Pandora was sent down to earth with a jar."

"Not a box?" Mrs. Jennings asked.

"It's a jar in the original myths," Gabriel replied. "A box only appears later."

"What is in the jar?" Charlie asked.

"All sorts of bad things," Gabriel replied. "Misery and evil, mostly."

"Why would she have that?" Charlie asked. "Wouldn't it be dangerous?"

"A reasonable question," Gabriel said. "But that is why Zeus wanted her to have it—she was blessed with beauty, and intelligence, and curiosity. So when she arrived on earth, Prometheus's brother made her his wife, forgetting that Prometheus had warned him about her and about Zeus."

"And it was her curiosity that caused the trouble, wasn't it?" Octavia asked, wrinkling her nose. "Because she had to open the jar, which caused all the misery and evil to emerge on earth."

"Exactly, yes," Gabriel replied.

"But if she hadn't opened the jar, who's to say things would have been perfect? Humans can find a lot of creative ways to bring themselves misery and evil." Her eyes grew distant, and he knew she was thinking of her own situation. "What if opening the jar was the only way to find out if there was a solution to her problem?"

Gabriel wished she would confide in him. Even

more now that she was associating the world's evils with whatever was plaguing her.

"It wasn't her fault," Charlie said defensively. "She had to open the jar to know what was inside."

"Or she could have left it alone," Gabriel said. "She'd been warned what might happen."

"But sometimes," Octavia said, "sometimes the thing you know you absolutely should not do is the one thing you wish to do the most in this world." Her eyes were locked with his, and he knew just what she was talking about. A dangerous topic, given that they were not alone.

But if they were alone, he would absolutely open what he was not supposed to—kissing her until she revealed her secrets, or kissing her until neither of them could speak at all. Kissing her.

"I think it's good to be curious," Charlie said doggedly.

"Sometimes," Gabriel said on an exhale, "it is."

Her lips curled into a slight smile, one only he could see.

Chapter Ten

Some days later, and Gabriel hadn't stopped thinking about the jar that was Octavia. He'd tried to immerse himself in cleaning, but all that did was give him more time to think.

He was by far the tallest person in residence, so he'd begun washing the walls on the second floor, which were covered in smoke, dirt, and grime. Only a few of the rooms on the floor were in use—his bedroom, her bedroom, and the room Charlie and his mother used. The other inhabitants were scattered about, from Mary living in the cook's room next to the kitchen to Old Joe in the stable and Mrs. Jennings on the third floor, living in what was the old nursery.

The rooms that were not in use were mostly bare of furniture, and like the main floor, there were marks on the walls where paintings used to hang. There were assorted boxes piled up in a few of the rooms, and Gabriel's eye wandered to them as he worked, wondering if another volume of the *Mythologiae* was tucked there, but he knew that if he began to go through the boxes, he'd likely never finish washing the walls.

And since he wanted to live here, make a home here, his first priority was the house itself.

But right now, his thoughts were driving him mad. He needed to get out of this house, even if just for a few hours.

His eyes widened as he realized he had a perfectly valid reason to leave—he needed to fetch the paper, the proof that Octavia's father had lost the house to his father. Perhaps he'd ask Octavia if she wanted to come, though he wouldn't show her the paper—that could wait until the time was up, in nineteen days.

He dropped the cleaning rag into the bucket and strode down the hall, then down the stairs.

He found her, eventually, in the kitchen. She was removing everything from the various shelves. Looking for where her father might have hidden his valuables, he realized.

Mrs. Jennings, Mary, and Mrs. Wycoff were helping her, though she couldn't have told them what she was looking for—for all that they knew, the house did already belong to her. Not that anyone had discussed it, but they'd just assumed, since she'd arrived so soon after her father's death.

It occurred to him that he could just cede the house to her. Just walk away and let her have it.

But he knew, even as the thought crossed his mind, that that would anger her far more than discovering his paper was dated more recently than anything she could find. If she could find anything at all, that is.

"Miss Holton," he said, when she'd finished sliding a fire iron behind the range. "Would you like to come to town with me? I have some errands, and I thought we could get a list together of things we might need."

She drew her brows together, as if to demand why he was asking her, when Mrs. Jennings clucked her tongue. "You two needn't be so formal. You're engaged, after all. You can call each other Gabriel and Octavia. It will not bother any of us. It's wonderful to be surrounded by a couple so deeply in love."

She looked from one to the other, and Gabriel attempted to summon a smile to his face, as Octavia hastily smothered a grimace.

He wasn't that intolerable as a fiancé, was he?

Wait. It wasn't real. She would be going as soon as she sorted out the contents of the house and assured herself of its rightful ownership. Why did it matter that she didn't want to be engaged to him? She wasn't, so it didn't matter. At all.

Keep telling yourself that, Gabriel, he thought, as she gave a dazzling smile to Mrs. Jennings.

IT MADE HER uneasy, how much she wanted to agree with Mrs. Jennings when she talked about their love for each other. Not that she loved him, of course; but she was fascinated by him, and she didn't like that feeling at all. She couldn't imagine how much more painful it would be to actually have fallen in love with him.

She wasn't accustomed to caring about anyone but herself, her sister, her brother-in-law, and her dog. Not always in that order, depending on how annoyed Ivy was with her at any given time.

"I thought you might appreciate a little time away," he was saying. "And I do need some things in town." They were walking down the road toward Greensett, the sun at their backs. She'd gone through the kitchen again, looking for anything that might be of value.

She hadn't even found a lady's shoe this time.

"Has Mrs. Jennings said anything to you before?" she asked. "About us not spending time together? Because she has me. I was wondering if that was why you invited me."

He looked surprised. "No, this was the first time I'd heard about it. I invited you because I wanted to have your company. If you can believe such a thing." He continued, "And Mrs. Jennings is correct. We haven't spent much time together lately. I don't know if you'd noticed. Probably not."

She wished she *hadn't* noticed, but she had. She liked sparring with him. She doubted he'd ever had anyone challenge him on anything—he was handsome, he was intelligent, and he was so confoundingly *tall*—but it seemed as though anytime they were in the same room, they were arguing.

Or kissing.

Her heart beat a little faster as she recalled the kiss—how masterful he'd seemed, his strong hand planted above her head on the door. His other hand at her waist.

His tongue tangling with hers.

Perhaps that was why she was so prickly around him—she found him infuriatingly attractive, and she couldn't do anything about it, so she had to argue with him to release some of her tension.

"I have noticed," she admitted. "We are going to have to break our engagement eventually. When I prove the house is mine." Even though that possibility seemed to be receding with every passing day. She had been here for a week and a half, and she was still no closer to finding any proof.

Though that just made her more determined.

"But until that day, we are going to have to at least pretend to get along." She glanced over at him, wishing her eyes didn't immediately notice his full mouth, his topaz gaze, and his strong features. "In fact," she said, unable to keep herself from saying the words, "we might want to have an affair while we're at it."

He froze, his eyes wide. "Have—" He closed his eyes and began to slowly shake his head. Then his eyes reopened, staring at her. "What are you saying?"

Well, she'd said it now, hadn't she? She might as well keep speaking. It wasn't as though she could take her words back.

"Since it seems that we cannot be in the same

room without bickering, we should find another way to release our tensions." She nodded, more convinced by her argument. "And having a physical relationship will spill over into our daily interactions, and we'll be able to persuade everyone we are madly in love." She folded her arms over her chest. "Really, it is the most elegant solution to our problems."

And it would mean she would get to press her mouth against his again. Something that, if she was honest, had occupied her thoughts far more than she would have liked.

"Octavia," he began, his tone holding a note of warning, "you should not be saying such things to me."

She bristled. "And why not?" She flung her hands out to indicate the space between them. "It's obvious there is something here. And I already know you would not take advantage of me, as we discussed after that first night. Whatever we do together would be our business alone. There would be no obligation afterward, I promise you. In twenty days—"

"Nineteen," he murmured.

"—nineteen days, one of us will have to leave. But why not enjoy ourselves during that time?"

"In nineteen days," he said slowly, "you will either have the money you seem to desperately need to acquire, or you will not. Though you won't tell me anything about it."

"I will not," she replied quickly.

He folded his arms over his chest and regarded

her with a pointed expression. "So you are saying you are willing to enter into a scandalous physical relationship with me but you won't tell me your problems?"

Her mouth spread into a thin smile. "Precisely."

"I see just what you value me for, then," he remarked. Did he sound wounded? Or just wry? She couldn't tell.

"The less you know about all of it the better." She didn't want Mr. Higgins threatening to break Gabriel's limbs—they were very attractive, after all, and she wouldn't allow him to shoulder her burden. "And it won't be a scandalous physical relationship if there is no scandal. We'll have to be discreet."

His brows drew together. "But open enough to encourage everyone to believe we are madly in love?"

She twisted her lips in thought. "Yes, that is a delicate balance, to be sure. So clever of you to figure that out."

He rolled his eyes in clear exasperation. "I wasn't being clever. I was pointing out how ludicrous your entire notion is."

She took a deep breath and stepped close to him. So close that her breasts brushed against his folded arms, and she could see the pulse beating at his neck. "Tell me you don't feel the pull, Gabriel. Tell me, and I will forget my ludicrous notion, as you call it. But I don't think you can. I think you feel it as strongly as I do, and trying to resist it will only make it harder."

He met her gaze, his jaw clenched, his nostrils flared. For a moment, she thought he was going to tell her all of what she demanded: that he didn't feel it, that all the attraction was entirely on her side, and she was a fool if she thought he struggled against his desire for her.

But then it looked as though something had broken, because he unfolded his arms and gathered her to him, claiming her mouth in a fiercely passionate kiss.

A warmth unfurled in her body as though she'd been set ablaze from the inside.

She moved closer to him, wrapping her arms around his neck and sliding her tongue into his mouth.

He groaned, and deepened the kiss, licking and sucking her tongue as his fingers clutched her waist.

Her nipples hardened, and her breasts felt tender pressed against his chest. Every part of her ached, but not in pain—as if she needed to be touched all over to assuage the feeling.

She opened her eyes, not realizing they'd fluttered closed, scanning his face as he continued to kiss her. His beautiful face, his eyes shut, strands of hair falling over his brow as he leaned toward her.

If the world were to end right now, she would be happy. This moment, out on a quiet village road, kissing him. It felt good and right, and she never wanted it to stop.

Chapter Eleven

Gabriel unleashed all his pent-up passion in kissing her. As she'd wanted.

He had tried to resist her, tried to pretend he hadn't felt the surge of attraction anytime they were in the same room together.

She was more observant than he, obviously. And also obviously far more audacious. He knew well enough the risks one took in giving into temptation—his father's entire life had been about luring people into temptation—and he'd prided himself on keeping his actions and emotions as reasonable as possible.

But it seemed that constant suppression had a price.

Her lips had parted for him, and her tongue was as eager as his, sliding in and out of his mouth with relish.

Her fingers were tangled in his hair, dragging him down to her, as though he was even thinking of pulling away.

Her breasts pressed against his chest, and it took every modicum of restraint not to slide his hand up and caress them. Instead, he kept his hand at her waist, his fingers gripping her tightly.

His cock was hard, and he forced himself not to press that part of himself against her as well. They were outdoors, for goodness' sake, on a road that anyone might come along and see them.

For an engaged couple to be caught kissing would be one thing—but for them to be seen with the length of their bodies pressed against one another, his hands on her breasts, would be entirely another.

Eventually, he broke the kiss, but only to place his mouth on her neck just below her ear, running his tongue down the slim column to her collarbone. She tilted her head back as she shifted her hands from his neck to his arms, her palms sliding up and down as he sucked gently on the soft skin of her throat.

He heard her moan, a low hum that made him long to hear more of her cries. Her fingers were now splayed against his upper body, frantically digging into the planes of his chest.

"Octavia," he growled, raising his head and taking her mouth once more. She clutched his shirt at the neckline, and he felt the fabric pull as her hands moved down.

He put his fingers on top of her hands to stay them, and she drew back, her gaze challenging. "You don't want me to do that?" she asked. Her voice was lower than usual, husky with passion.

"I don't want you to do that *now*," he corrected

her, his mouth curling into a smile. "You can tear my shirts to your heart's delight later, if you like. But it would be an awkward thing if I go into town looking like I've been ravished."

She snorted in laughter as she removed her hands, giving his chest a final pat before putting them behind her back. "It would certainly give Mrs. Hall plenty to talk about."

"I think," he replied, putting the pad of his thumb on her lip, "that we will be giving them plenty to talk about as it is. You look as though you've been thoroughly kissed."

Her eyes danced with amusement. "But not ravished." She mimicked his actions, placing her thumb on his mouth. "And you look the same. Only fitting for an affianced couple, after all." Her tone was wryly mocking.

He took a deep breath as he held his arm out. "The next nineteen days are going to be very interesting indeed," he said as she took his arm.

"More interesting now," she remarked, shooting him a sideways glance.

"Definitely."

They began to walk, her arm tucked into his. Her hip occasionally bumping his thigh.

"Do you need to buy anything in town?" he asked.

"No, but you'll need to buy a few new shirts," she replied slyly.

He barked out a laugh. "I have to say, I have never met a woman as forthright as you."

"Is that a problem?" There was a hint of vulnerability in her voice, something he hadn't heard from her before.

He shook his head. "No, it's just . . . unexpected."

She exhaled. "Good. I know I say things without thinking them through. It's been pointed out to me often enough," she said ruefully. "But I can't seem to stop. Or if I did, I would always be silent, and I don't think I could do that."

"I like hearing you speak."

Ironically, his words were met by a long silence.

But it was a companionable silence. Now that they'd cleared the air—not to mention kissed the lips—things felt suddenly more comfortable. Gabriel wasn't accustomed to feeling so comfortable with anybody else, to be honest. Except Nyx.

"What are you thinking about?" she asked suddenly, startling him.

He could prevaricate, or he could answer honestly. He chose the latter. After all, just because she wasn't willing to tell him everything didn't mean he had to follow her lead.

"I was thinking that you might be my first real friend."

He felt her head snap around to look up at him. "Pardon?"

He exhaled. "My first real friend. I had friends at school, boys whose parents my father fleeced. But I was always keenly aware that there was a not-insignificant chance my father would ruin everything, and so I always held back a part of myself."

Her hand squeezed his arm.

"What do you miss from a friendship, do you think?" she asked softly.

He glanced up at the sky. It was a mild day, a relief from the heat since he'd arrived at his house. It wouldn't last, but today was simply glorious: blue skies with an occasional cloud scudding by, a soft breeze lifting the hair just enough to cool any perspiration that might have occurred.

"I suppose I've missed sharing my ideas with someone else."

She hummed her agreement. "Probably why you were so skeptical of my curiosity about your work."

The idea took him by surprise.

"You might be right," he said slowly. "The only people who've ever asked before are—" He stopped, feeling odd about the revelation.

"Are ladies who are intrigued by your outside but not your inside?" she finished for him.

He made an inarticulate noise, and she laughed. "You are remarkably handsome, you know. I assume you know that?" she added, now making it into a question.

He shrugged. "I've never contemplated my appearance that much before."

"Fortunate you," she replied. "Ladies are taught to contemplate their appearance as soon as they realize their livelihood might depend on it." Her tone was derisive. "If you are pretty enough, you can marry well enough to be taken care of. If not—"

"You're certainly pretty enough," he remarked in a casual tone. "Why didn't you take that route? It might have been more secure than the literal gamble of running a gambling house."

He couldn't judge her so harshly for her decisions anymore. While it wasn't what he would have chosen, he couldn't know all of her circumstances. And not just because she wouldn't tell him.

She snorted. "My older sister, Ivy, made that choice for me, and I am grateful to her for it. If Ivy had done what she was supposed to, she would have married your father, and I would have—" She broke off.

"Married me."

There was a silence, and then the two of them turned to look at one another at the same time, bursting into laughter at the irony.

OCTAVIA WAS STILL smiling when they arrived in Greensett.

You're always acting before thinking, she heard her sister, Ivy, say in her head.

Yes, but look where that got me! she retorted.

He'd kissed her. He'd taken her at her word, wrapped her in his strong arms, and kissed her.

She shivered just thinking about it. He was kind and gentle in his everyday life, but when he kissed, it felt like something transformed inside him. As though there was an inner passionate beast who came alive at the touch of another's lips.

Feeling all that masterful energy made her want to sink into it, to explore every aspect of what it might mean.

Not that she could explore *every* aspect—she knew well enough the risks of all the exploration. She wasn't a sheltered woman who had no idea where children came from. But she could explore most of them, and that would have to be enough.

It would all have to be enough.

They went to Hall's Elaborate Emporium, where an effusive Mrs. Hall helped them purchase an enormous hunk of carbolic soap, a few tins of baking soda, and vinegar.

"Cleaning the house for after you two are married?" Mrs. Hall asked. "It has been a long time since that house has been— That is, I'm sorry, Miss Holton."

Octavia smiled to let the other woman know she was not offended—of course the entire village had known just how ramshackle her father was. And that his daughters had run off to face the dangers of London rather than stay under his care.

Soon she'd be running off again.

Leaving Gabriel. Leaving all of them—Mrs. Jennings, Mary, Mrs. Wycoff, Charlie, and Old Joe. People she'd begun to think of the same way she thought about her family.

"We want the house to become a beautiful home," Gabriel replied easily.

A home. A place she wouldn't belong, no matter who the house belonged to.

"Thank you, Mrs. Hall," Gabriel continued. He gestured toward the door. "Shall we?" he asked.

She nodded, waving goodbye to Mrs. Hall as she left the store. Her chest still tight.

"And now," he said, turning to her, "that is done. Where would you like to go next?"

She shook off her dark thoughts and looked up at him. The early afternoon sun picked up the gold in his hair and made his amber eyes look like gold as well. He was so beautiful he hurt her eyes. And he would be hers to play with until she went back home.

Home. She nearly snorted at the thought.

Her home was the apartment at the back of the gambling house she and her sister owned. It had been a home of sorts before her sister got married, but now it was just Octavia and Cerberus. Ivy visited, but the rooms weren't the same since her sister had left.

So much for shaking off the dark thoughts.

She took his arm and raised her face to the sun. "I want to sit outside and drink something refreshing." She swiveled her head to regard him again. "Is there a place like that here? I have so little recollection of the village from when I lived here before."

One corner of his mouth shot up as his eyes met hers. "There certainly is. Allow me to escort you there."

THE PLACE HE took her was a tea shop that he assured her also served other beverages. They walked through a small rustic room. The floor was polished to a blinding glow. The walls were covered in artwork of all sizes and talents, from a reasonable reproduction of the Mona Lisa to what appeared to be a child's interpretation of the Mona Lisa. The figure in the latter sported inexplicable cat ears and was a distinct shade of orange.

The shop had a few tables and chairs, and Octavia paused as they entered, waiting for the hostess to seat them. Instead, she walked them through the room and down a small flight of stairs to a backyard, enclosed on three sides with a white lattice fence.

Chairs and tables were set out here as well, and there were a few patrons who looked up as they came into the space.

"I will give you a few minutes to decide," the hostess said, dropping a well-worn menu on the table.

The table was covered with a piece of fabric that had faded in the sun, now only holding a hint of the floral print it must have begun life with.

She glanced around as they hitched their chairs forward, feeling an unexpected serenity at being here. With him.

She was so seldom calm it felt rather odd, she had to admit.

But this whole adventure felt odd—arriving by herself with no way of getting home, only to discover a gentleman in a pond. Suddenly living with a group of friendly strangers who believed certain things to be true about her that were most definitely not. Trying to unearth something of value in the decrepit house she vaguely remembered from her childhood.

"Do you know what you want?" he asked, pivoting the menu toward her.

She scanned it, making her decision quickly and decisively. That, at least, was the same.

"The Sloe Summer Day," she pronounced, sliding the menu back to him.

He read the description, a wry smile curling his mouth. "Sloe gin and lemonade?" He lifted his head to meet her gaze. "It sounds like an unusual combination, but one I imagine will be entirely refreshing."

The look in his eyes indicated he was speaking about far more than a beverage, and her breath hitched as she absorbed his words.

"Entirely," she promised. He raised an eyebrow—at how confident she sounded, perhaps—but didn't say anything more until the hostess came to take their order.

The drinks were indeed refreshing, and Octavia found she had finished her glass mere minutes after the server placed them on the table.

Mr. Fallon was taking more time with his drink, sipping from it while keeping his eyes locked on Octavia's face. Now that she had broached the subject, it seemed, he was allowing whatever feelings he'd smothered to surface.

His gaze felt like a brand. She felt uncomfortable, but it wasn't an unpleasant feeling. Instead, she felt warmed from the inside, certain parts of her aching for relief.

And that warmth wasn't just the intense attraction she felt for his outside; the warmth was because of his intelligence, his honor, his curiosity.

She chuckled to herself at the last. "In that story," she said, "Pandora unleashed all sorts of terrible things into the world merely because she opened a box—"

"A jar," he said.

"Whatever," she replied, waving her hand. "But I think the impetus for her opening the jar was her curiosity, and I cannot think curiosity to be a bad thing. Just think of all that has been discovered because someone wondered about something."

"I agree with you," he said, surprising her. "And I think that having evil and misery in the world, those terrible things you mention, help shape people for the better." He shrugged. "You can call it me being optimistic, but I think that humanity will triumph, even though the gods are tossing all sorts of things our way."

"How so?" she asked, intrigued.

"So much of who we are as adults is shaped by our experiences as children. Terrible things that happened to us, or might have happened to us, change us." He lifted an eyebrow. "You can't tell me that escaping the plans your father had for you—that my father had for you—didn't irrevocably alter you."

She inhaled sharply. She wished she could deny the truth of his words, wished she were who she was because of . . . who she was, but that wasn't it at all.

"I suppose," she began slowly, "that if I had not left with Ivy, I might not be me." Which would be a shame. She rather liked herself. And she thought he did, too. "I wouldn't own my establishment. I wouldn't live happily by myself." It wasn't entirely the truth. She wasn't completely happy by herself. She just hadn't given it much thought. "And I would probably be married with several children by now," she said, ending with an exaggerated shudder.

He crossed his arms over his chest and regarded her. "You don't want that? I thought—"

"You thought that every woman wants the same thing: a husband, a house, and children. Possibly a dog." She felt her cheeks heat as her anger surged. Not anger at him, but at every person who'd assumed that just because she wasn't doing what was expected of her, she was unhappy. "I have the dog, but the rest?" She shook her head. "Not until it makes sense for me."

He held his hands up in a gesture of surrender. "I didn't mean to malign you. I wasn't implying it was something you should want. I want those things, eventually." He regarded her coolly. "And I wonder at your vehemence about not wanting them."

She rolled her eyes. "I am not *vehement*. I am merely expressing my *opinion*." She spoke in a fiercely vehement tone, if she was being honest with herself.

Which she was. She wasn't always honest with others, but she was invariably honest with herself.

"I do want those things," she continued in a softer tone, gazing down at the table. "But I don't want anything forced on me," she said, raising her eyes to meet his.

"Choice is a luxury," he replied simply. "And we both have it, thank goodness."

She raised her glass, mouthing *two more* when she caught the server's eye. "And we have made our choice, at least in regard to one another, have we not?" She lifted an eyebrow as she spoke. She felt a profound urge to stop talking about the future, her future. Because it wouldn't have him in it, and she didn't want to think about any of that right now.

"We have," he replied. There was a wary look in his eyes that hadn't been there before. But she couldn't challenge him on that—on anything, really. They were working in opposition to one another in every way but one, and she assumed he knew his own mind well enough to raise any objections, if he had them.

Instead, she picked up her new glass of the Sloe Summer Day and lifted it toward him. "To choice," she said.

"To choice," he echoed as he tapped his glass against hers.

Chapter Twelve

They walked home, both flushed from the drinks, the heat of the day exacerbating the warmth they both felt.

But Gabriel couldn't blame a beverage or two or the swelter of a summer day for the fire burning within him.

It was her.

She walked beside him, offering a mischievous glance toward him every so often. As if they shared a secret. Which they did, of course.

He had some experience, naturally. He had urges, which he'd assuaged with the help of various equally urgent women in the past. They had been sufficiently pleasant that he understood why so many gods and goddesses spent their time chasing the feeling. But he had never felt the same fierce desire for anybody that he felt for her.

"What are you thinking about?" she asked suddenly.

Sex. "Uh—" he began.

She laughed, grasping his arm. "I know what you're thinking about. I can't stop thinking about it either. I'm startled I didn't suggest it before, given how generally overwhelming you are."

"Overwhelming?" he said, frowning in puzzlement.

The road back to the house was lined with wildflowers, a profusion of colors that were as riotously chaotic as she was. Lovely to view, but trying to gather them into a tidy bundle would be an impossible task.

"Overwhelming," she repeated firmly. She waved her hand in the air. "You're handsome, you are well-educated, you have money, you are interesting to talk to, and you have an adorable dog. As I said, overwhelming."

He shook his head in disbelief. "I have to say the same thing of you."

"Oh?" she said, sounding pleased. "Do tell me. I haven't had anyone compliment me since I arrived."

"I beg your pardon," he replied in mock outrage. "I believe I mentioned you were clever."

She shrugged. "Perhaps you did. But if we are to continue whatever this is," she said, flicking her hand in the air again, "then we should be confident of our mutual interest."

"You make it sound like a maths problem," he remarked. "I thought you found maths boring."

She burst out laughing, nudging him with her shoulder. He didn't think about it, but responded by wrapping his arm around her, his fingers resting on her opposite shoulder.

She gave a contented little wriggle, settling

herself more comfortably into the embrace. "What an excellent thought," she said, looking up at him. "And of course if anyone sees us, we have the perfect excuse, what with being engaged and all."

He gazed down at her, seeing the frank interest reflected in her brown eyes. How she met his gaze fearlessly without resorting to batting her eyelashes, as she'd done when they'd first met, or lowering her eyes to the ground in sudden shyness.

Octavia was likely the most confident, vibrant person he'd ever met. The flowers surrounding them seemed brighter when he was with her, the conversation more sparkling than with anybody he'd ever known. The feelings between them more intense than any he'd experienced before.

She was like a shooting star, lighting up the sky for a few precious moments only to burn out and disappear. She'd be returning to London in nineteen days, no matter what the ultimate resolution to their situation was. She'd made that absolutely clear.

But it was for the best. He didn't know how he'd resist falling in love with her if she was here for long. It was likely because he'd grown up in such isolation that he craved the kind of connection they seemed to have. If he grew accustomed to her presence, would he still feel the same way?

He didn't know. And likely wouldn't ever find out.

She'd be gone before she was a habit, thank God.

He'd retrieved the proof of ownership while she had been sorting out what to buy at Hall's. It was tucked safely in his pocket, feeling as though it was both a blessing and a curse.

Returning to normalcy—making his house a home, feeling settled and peaceful at last—should be something to which he was looking forward, but somehow his desperate desire for that boring, predictable life wasn't as fervent now that he'd met her.

It didn't matter. His feelings about her wouldn't matter because, like Persephone, she'd be returning to her world soon enough.

And he'd be alone with his dog again, the way it had always been. He slipped his arm away from her, making an exaggerated show of flexing his fingers as though he had a cramp or something.

When really it was that he was already anticipating the time when he wouldn't be able to touch her at all.

"THERE YOU LOVEBIRDS are," Mrs. Jennings chirped as Octavia and Gabriel walked up to the house.

Her smile widened as she glanced back and forth between them. "You've been gone a long time."

Octavia stepped inside the house, pausing as she took in all the changes. She hadn't noticed, since they had occurred with her there, but a few hours away made her look at everything with fresh eyes.

The foyer was substantially cleaner than it had been when Octavia had first arrived. She'd seen Gabriel cleaning nearly every day since then, and so she knew this was likely his handiwork. Where there had been a thin film of dust on everything, now the walls and furniture gleamed—at least as much as they could, given their age and general disrepair.

But more than that, the house was beginning to look like a home. Was that because of the increase in tidiness and the decrease in cobwebs? Or because there were people living here, interacting with one another as they lived their various lives?

A sudden pang struck Octavia's chest as though someone had shot an arrow at her heart. Even though she was here now, she was aware that she didn't truly belong.

She wasn't from Greensett, like everyone else was. She had ties to the place, of course, but she lived and worked in London, and while the other inhabitants, save Gabriel, thought she would be staying here, she would be returning in less than three weeks.

She missed her work. She already felt restless here, clattering around the house with a few memories sparking connections in her brain. Memories her mind shoved down into a place that wouldn't be examined. Memories of time spent with her sister, when all her future was supposed to be was marriage and children. In that order.

Her chest was tight just because she missed London, she told herself firmly.

What would happen when it was time for her to go?

Don't think of that now.

"I hope the two of you took time out to engage in some enjoyable pursuits?" Mrs. Jennings was saying.

"Oh yes. And we've made plans for more enjoyable pursuits," Octavia replied, arching an eyebrow. Right. At least she had that to think about rather than when it came time for her to leave.

Gabriel made a choking sound, quickly smothering it with his hand in front of his mouth.

"Will you be telling us another of your stories tonight?" Mrs. Jennings asked.

Gabriel met Octavia's gaze. "I will not. I believe I will be working on my own enjoyable pursuits."

Octavia felt an anticipatory shiver run through her, both at his words and at the look in his eyes. This was possibly the best idea she'd ever had.

Though given that her previous ideas included borrowing money from a vicious moneylender and arriving at a house with no possible exit plan, it might seem to indicate her ideas were not always the best.

But this one was. She just knew it was.

OCTAVIA SPRANG UP as she heard the soft knock. She leaped off her bed and hurried to the door, pulling it open just enough for her to see him on the other side. She grabbed his arm and yanked him inside, being careful to close the door as quietly as she could. Cerberus lifted his head, but lowered it again when he saw it was just Gabriel, and not Gabriel and Nyx.

"Are you cert—" he began, but stopped speaking as she put both palms on his chest and shoved him back against the door, getting on tiptoe to reach his mouth.

He made a noise of surprise, then followed her lead, pressing his lips against hers as he wrapped his arms around her body.

It felt delicious to be held by him, his strong hands at her waist, a few tendrils of hair spilling over his brow to tickle her nose. She nibbled on his mouth and heard him make a low growl deep in his throat as he allowed her tongue entrance.

Now that it was decided, now that they both knew what was happening, it was as though there were no constraints—his tongue tangled with hers, both of them kissing one another feverishly.

She relaxed against his body as she explored his mouth with her tongue, sliding her palms up so she could grip his shoulders to maintain her balance. His body was so deliciously muscled, so hard. Such a contrast to her own. She had the fanciful thought that she'd like to just melt her softness into him, her curves finding and surrounding every inch of his planed body.

He kept his hands at her waist, and she shifted, wishing he would slide one palm to cup her breast, ease the ache she felt there. Perhaps eventually slide his hand down to cup her there and ease her ache even further.

Octavia was familiar with what gave her body pleasure. She thought it was a waste of time to postpone one's sexual adventures until one found a suitable partner, so she'd searched out what made her respond. And she knew, she just *knew*, that if he touched her there, and she could guide him, she would experience the best climax of her life.

But she had to be patient.

His hands weren't moving, though his lips, tongue, and teeth were. She focused on the kiss, relishing all the sparks it sent shooting through her. He was an accomplished kisser, and she was pleased to find that he followed her lead as well as led her. The give and take, the clash of tongues, was a battle of the most enjoyable sort.

She felt his erection, and she shifted again to feel that hardness press against her in a fruitless attempt to satisfy her craving.

It only made her more eager to feel him everywhere.

Octavia knew a lot about what occurred between adults, but that didn't mean she'd experienced it firsthand, so to speak. She'd kissed gentlemen in her time, but she hadn't done anything more. With him, she was so tempted, even in this early stage of their sexual activity, but she knew she could not risk a child.

Though there were plenty of other things they could do, if he was willing.

His stiff cock told her he was most definitely willing.

She broke the kiss, leaning back to gaze at his face. His eyes were fierce with desire, with passion, and she felt as though she could almost glimpse fire glinting in his amber gaze. Fire, and hunger.

She spread her palms over the broad planes of his chest, her lips curling into a knowing smile.

His lips did the same, and then they were just staring into one another's eyes, exchanging grins.

As though they really were madly in love like the affianced couple they were pretending to be.

"Enough of that," she muttered, grasping his shoulders and tilting forward to kiss him again. "Touch me, Gabriel," she murmured, then put her hand on top of his and moved it to her breast so there would be no mistaking what she wanted.

He made that low throaty noise again, and there was an added intensity to his kiss, his hand squeezing her breast as his other hand gripped her hip.

She still wore her gown—even she wasn't bold enough to wait for him in her nightdress, or even less—but she'd loosened the ties at the neckline and removed her undergarments in expectation of what might happen tonight.

Of what she wanted to happen.

So it shouldn't have been a shock when the

fingers of the hand that had been on her breast were on her bare skin, just above the neckline.

But it was. She trembled, and ran her hand down his arm to his waist and then to the small of his back. Lower still, grasping the hard round-ness of his arse and pressing him to her.

His erection was still making its presence known between them, and she couldn't resist wriggling a little to increase the friction.

His response was to slide his fingers down more into her gown and find her nipple, squeezing it between his thumb and forefinger. The pain of the contact sent a sweet pleasure through her.

"More," she said against his lips, then put her other hand to the opening of his shirt and slid her palm underneath, his skin warm and firm against hers.

She broke the kiss, yanking the door open and whistling. Cerberus got up, snuffling, and went outside.

"Alone at last," Gabriel growled, his eyes ablaze. He leaned down and hoisted her up into his arms, then strode to her bed and tossed her onto it. She bounced, laughing, as he got onto his hands and knees and approached her, looking for all the world like a fearsome jungle creature. A lion, with that tawny gaze and sun-kissed hair, confident that he was the ruler here.

Though he would find she could rule as well as he.

She sat up and leaned forward, her hand going

to his shirt. "I want this off," she demanded, tugging at it.

He offered her a feral smile, then reached behind his head to remove the shirt, revealing that delicious chest she'd seen the first time they met.

She bit her lip as she drank him in, the impossibly broad shoulders, the light dusting of golden hair on his upper chest, the definition of his muscles.

The trail of hair that led down into his trousers, which were tented.

He jerked his chin. "And you. What are you going to take off?"

It was a challenge. As though he wondered if she was truly brave enough to match him in whatever they were doing. He clearly didn't know her well enough yet.

Or perhaps he did, and he knew that challenging her would be the best way to further her interest.

She shrugged in reply. "What do you want off?" She snorted. "Not that there's much to choose from. My gown, and then—that's it. I'm not wearing anything underneath," she told him, heat flooding her body as she heard his sharp intake of breath and saw his eyes narrow like the predator he was.

"The gown," he replied. "Only—" And then she was on her back, his weight on her, one hand yanking up the hem of her gown, the other hand cradling her head. "Perhaps I should take care of removing this. Unless you'll get cold?"

Not very likely, she thought. She was burning up. His hand was on her lower leg, then at her knee, and then paused on her thigh. She saw his throat work as his fingers spread out over her skin there, and she wanted to urge him to move up higher, to touch her there, but she also wanted to savor the delicious agony.

"Kiss me," she said in a low, husky voice.

He obliged, lowering his head to hers as his fingers flexed on her thigh. Tracing the shape of her ear with the fingers of his other hand.

She shivered, and she felt him smile against her mouth. "I can't have you getting cold," he murmured, and then his fingers went *there*, and she moaned, arching underneath him. "You like that?" he said, unnecessarily, because she was writhing beneath him, catching her lip with her teeth as he began to stroke and pet her.

He kissed her hard, again, as he continued what he was doing down there, finding a rhythm that seemed as though it would end in an inexorable orgasm.

"Who knew you were so skilled with your fingers, Mr. Fallon?" Her tone was breathy, and right as she stopped speaking he did something that made her shudder, the climax nearing.

"Come for me, Octavia," he urged, his gaze heated.

She couldn't speak now, she could just feel, and the combination of his naked chest on her body, the warm, heavy weight of him, and his fingers at her opening was enough to push her, the overwhelming rush of pleasure flooding her as she came.

The moment seemed to stretch for hours, the pulse of ecstasy a delicious drumbeat flowing through her body.

And then it was over, and she was gazing up at him through heavy-lidded eyes, a seductive languor coming over her.

"That was wonderful," she said at last.

One corner of his mouth curled up into a wicked smile. "It was," he agreed.

She raised one hand and pressed against his chest, pushing him onto his back. She straddled him, a knee on either side of his legs, her palm flat on his skin. She moved her fingers lower, slowly enough that he could stop her if he wanted.

He didn't stop her.

And then she reached the placket of his trousers and undid the buttons swiftly, reaching inside to grab hold of his throbbing cock.

He gasped, both hands fisting the coverlet, his eyes closed, the muscles of his jaw working.

"And now it is your turn, Gabriel," she said, sliding her palm over the long, hard length of him.

Chapter Thirteen

Gabriel opened his eyes, relishing the feel of her on top of him, the skirts of her gown hiked up over her thighs, her cheeks flushed from her climax.

He knew he'd wanted to see her come as soon as he had met her—that unflappable confidence set off-kilter in the throes of passion. And he had gotten his wish. He lifted his hand to his mouth, the hand that had worked her to climax, and slid his fingers inside, licking her sweetness off each digit.

Her eyes widened, and her grip on him tightened. She was stroking his cock, sliding her hand up and down, holding nearly as firmly as he liked.

"Harder," he said, his voice a ragged rasp. "Hold me harder. You won't hurt me."

She arched an eyebrow, but did as he instructed, now squeezing his aching cock in her hand as she kept up her movement.

"Let me see your beautiful breasts," he said, nodding toward the neckline of her gown. "But don't stop what you're doing," he commanded.

"So demanding," she chided, but put one hand up to her neckline and dragged the fabric down her chest, wriggling to shift the gown off her shoulders. The gown was tied at the neck, but it was much looser now, and so it took just a minute or two of her adjusting and pulling to reveal what he was dying to see. One breast popped out, a perfect handful of lush flesh, her pink-tipped nipple puckered and stiff.

"Well?" she asked, squeezing his shaft tighter as she kept up her rhythm.

He needed to taste her there. Everywhere, if he was being honest.

But right now, he needed to suck her nipple into his mouth and lick her, discover if she was as responsive as he anticipated she would be.

He tilted his head up and captured the sweet bud in his mouth, sliding his tongue around the hard nub.

"Oh!" she gasped, and her hand slowed.

"Don't stop," he murmured against her skin.

"Neither should you," she said, likely trying to sound commanding, but her words came out in a soft, pleading breath.

He shifted to nibble on the underside of her breast, feeling the warm, heavy weight of it. Nipping lightly, then licking and kissing. She squirmed and moaned, and her hand went faster on him.

And then he couldn't concentrate anymore. He had to let the feelings subsume him, overwhelm him, as he reached his climax, groaning as he spilled over her hand, shuddering as the delicious bliss seemed to flow through every part of him.

He forced out a ragged breath as he felt his heart racing, his limbs heavy. It was as though he was boneless, and he tugged her to lie down next to him, wrapping his arm around her and tucking her close.

"My hand—I've got—" she said, gesturing in the air.

Gabriel reached into his pocket, withdrew a handkerchief, and wiped her hand clean. Then he slid her hand up onto his chest and put his other hand on top.

"That was wonderful," she sighed, her body moving even closer to his.

He wondered what they looked like—her with her gown undone, one breast exposed, her skirts hiked up, him with his trousers open, his chest bared, his hair likely equally disheveled.

Both of them relaxing in post-orgasmic lethargy, a unique languor that made him forget everything that had come before and everything that might yet happen.

He only knew what was now.

And that he never wanted to leave.

"Have you done this before?" she asked suddenly, startling him.

"Done?" he replied.

She flicked her fingers in the air. "Not *that*," she snorted. "It's obvious you have. You are far too skilled for this to be your first time."

Gabriel felt smug.

She continued. "This—two people deciding to engage in enjoyable pursuits together. I mean, without any expectations." She shook her head. "Likely I'm not making myself clear. You've clouded my brain, Mr. Fallon."

He ran his hand down her arm, and then lower to her waist, and then, finally, cupped her arse.

It was full and round, and he wished he had spent some time touching it before. But her bosom was so alluring, he hadn't been able to resist.

Next time.

If there was a next time.

"This? The mutual exchange of enjoyable pursuits?"

She made a disparaging noise. "You make it sound like a transaction."

"Isn't that what you said?" he asked, trying to keep his tone light. The last thing she likely needed—the last thing she would want—would be for him to put any meaning on whatever this was beyond a mere exchange.

It would be so easy to fall in love with her, he mused. Her vivacity, her intelligence, her wicked sense of humor.

But then there was what she did for a living, and her being so different from anyone he'd ever met. He doubted if she would be happy living in Greensett, even if she was living in her old house. *Especially* if she was living in her old house.

She wasn't the type of person who would take well to domesticity, he thought wryly.

Nor would he want her to be. She wasn't someone to be tamed. She was someone you had to adjust to, rather than the other way around.

She was here, yes, for the moment. They were here for the moment.

But the moment would end.

"I suppose it is," she said at last. Sounding somewhat disappointed. What her disappointment was, he had no idea. He knew she didn't want anything more permanent. She'd made that absolutely clear. "It does seem rather mercenary. As though we are bargaining at a bazaar."

"If that is the kind of bargaining you do at a bazaar, I'd be very interested to go shopping with you," he said dryly.

She laughed, leaning up to kiss his jaw. "Perhaps we should employ that strategy next time—"

"There's to be a next time?" Damn, he hoped he didn't sound too eager.

She ran her hand down his chest to his abdomen, raking her nails over his skin. "Of course there is. Unless you don't want—"

"No, I do want." He raised his hand to give her arse a playful slap. "I most definitely want."

"Oh good," she replied. "Because I want, too."

And then her hand slipped lower, and found his already stiffening cock, wrapping her fingers around it as she pressed herself against him.

OCTAVIA STRETCHED, STARTLED to find Cerberus, and not Gabriel, pressed against her side. Gabriel must have let him back in when he left in the middle of the night. She had apparently been in a blissful post-wonderful-feeling sleep.

She patted her hound, then gazed up at the ceiling, a smile on her face.

Not that she was smiling at the ceiling; it was cracked in spots, and she suspected that if there was a hard rain, she might get wet.

But at the recollection of him, and what they'd done the night before.

He'd been far more . . . *adept* than she'd have thought he'd be, nothing like the scholars she'd always imagined—quiet, bookish people who knew more about their studies than anything in the real world.

But, she supposed, he was an expert in Greek myth, which was about nothing but what they'd spent the night doing.

"Perhaps I should start calling him Zeus," she mused. "Though I am definitely not Hera." Thus began and ended her knowledge of Greek gods.

And there would be more such encounters. She had asked because she wanted them to be absolutely clear in what they were doing. If he had assumed it was just the once, and that satisfied him—so to speak, she chuckled to herself—then she would accede. She would not force any situation on him that he didn't like.

Such as pretending to be affianced.

But that was, she could admit, a necessity, given how little thought she'd put into her insistence on staying.

Yet when she'd asked him, he'd responded so quickly she could be in no doubt about what—and who—he wanted.

Her.

And she him.

She rolled over onto her side toward Cerberus, who opened sleepy eyes at her. "This is turning out to be far more interesting than I thought it would be," she said, petting him.

He made a snuffling noise and closed his eyes again.

"So much for my fascinating conversation," she said, giving him one final pat before rolling back over to get out of bed.

It was early, and the sunlight felt new and fresh, as though it was as excited as she was about the day ahead.

Or perhaps that was just her interest in seeing him again.

Which was a lovely thought—until it wasn't. She was far more intrigued by him now than she had been before. Surprising, given her initial reaction to his looks and that powerfully strong body.

Drat. She couldn't allow herself to do anything close to falling in love with him. This was a temporary situation, something to pass the time until she was able to get enough money to pay Mr. Higgins.

And he definitely should not do anything close to falling in love with her either. That would be far too awkward, what with her leaving as soon as she could.

"You'll deal with it all later," she promised herself before getting dressed.

Though somewhere she thought she could hear her sister's voice: *That's what you always say. You don't anticipate anything, don't plan for anything.*

And look where it's gotten me, she wanted to reply to the imaginary voice in her head.

Where? Well, for one thing, you are in your childhood home, desperately trying to find something of value so you can pay off the ruthless moneylender you borrowed from.

That voice in her head was most definitely not her own.

And I am a successful business owner who's gotten to decide what it is I do with my life, she retorted.

Which is good if what you want to do with your life is risk losing a limb because you can't find something.

Oh, shut up.

And with that burst of optimism, she went down to the kitchen in search of breakfast. Cerberus trotted after, apparently deciding the possibility of food was better than the certainty of sleep.

AN HOUR OR so later, having consumed some muffins that were not absolutely terrible, Octavia found herself lingering outside the library door, negotiating whether or not to walk in, and if she did walk in, whether or not to appear surprised that he was there.

"Stop being an idiot," she muttered, before pushing the door open and walking inside, an expectant smile on her face.

Instead of seeing Mr. Fallon—Gabriel—as she'd expected, Mr. Higgins sat behind the ancient, scarred desk, an associate standing on either side of him.

"Oh!" she said, her throat starting to close over in panic.

Mr. Higgins rose slowly, keeping his gaze locked on her face. He was approximately fifty years old, with a thin, lined face, a hawkish nose, and piercing dark eyes that felt as though they were skewering her. "Yes, Miss Holton. *Oh.*" He slid a hand into his jacket, withdrawing a letter. Still staring at her, he shook it free of its envelope, which fluttered to the floor.

"Your sister writes you." He lowered his eyes to scan the words. "It seems you did not tell her where you were going. She is quite concerned." He cleared his throat. "'If you are in trouble, my dear, you need only come to me for help,'" he quoted. Again he looked at her, a nearly palpable anger emanating from his pores. "You and your sister have powerful, wealthy friends. The Duke of Hasford, for example? You are friends with his wife, are you not?"

Octavia raised her chin. "What are you doing here, Mr. Higgins?"

He clamped his teeth together and made a noise that was so full of menace, Octavia nearly stepped back. *Nearly.*

"I am here because you owe me monies, Miss Holton. And word is spreading that I have allowed a borrower to leave town without paying me." He walked to the front of the desk to face her, his walk casual, as though they were merely acquaintances and had run into one another unexpectedly as opposed to his traveling for at least six hours to find her.

She swallowed as she thought about that. He'd left London himself to come speak with her. She was in very deep trouble.

"I am here, sir, because my father has passed, leaving me this very valuable house. And its very valuable contents." She made an airy gesture.

He glanced around the room, skepticism written on his face. "This house?"

"Indeed." She nodded. "My father was a collector of sorts, and I am cataloging his treasures so I may reimburse you."

"Even though," he said through a clenched jaw, "you have missed a payment? I believe you promised I would have a portion of my money two weeks ago." He spread his hands out. "And yet here we are, and I have none of the money you owe me."

Her chest felt tight, and it was getting increasingly hard to breathe. "I will pay you back, Mr. Higgins. I signed my name to the chit, and I will honor my promise. It has just been a bit more difficult than I expected to go through my father's belongings." She put a tiny bit of sadness into her voice to imply it was more difficult because of her grief, when it was actually more difficult because she wasn't certain anything of value was here.

Hopefully he wouldn't figure that out.

"Octav—"

Octavia turned at the sound of Gabriel's voice, wishing she could just shoo him away so she could deal with this herself. But of course she could not. For one thing, he was already inside the room, swinging the door shut behind himself. For the next, his brow was furrowed, and he was glancing between her and Mr. Higgins, a clear question in his expression.

"My business is with this lady, sir, so if you do not mind?" Mr. Higgins said in an icy tone.

Octavia willed herself to breathe.

Instead of retreating, however, Gabriel walked closer, stopping to stand beside Octavia, catching her hand in his before speaking. "This lady is my fiancée, so anything you have to say to her can be said to me."

Mr. Higgins glanced between them, clearly amused. The scoundrel. "Are you certain you want your . . . *fiancé*," he said, emphasizing the word, "to know what you've been up to?"

Octavia lifted her chin. "I do not, but since you've gone ahead and said something, Mr. Higgins, we will have to explain ourselves."

"Please do." Gabriel spoke in a tone she hadn't heard before—authoritative. Commanding.

She wondered why that sent an entirely inappropriate shiver up her spine.

Mr. Higgins shrugged. "Who am I to sow discord between engaged couples?" he said silkily, making Octavia doubt his words. He sat on the edge of the desk, his hands folded on his knee.

"This lady happens to owe me a great sum of money."

"Not that great," Octavia expostulated.

Mr. Higgins gave her a menacing look. Which didn't menace her at all, especially since she had Gabriel's strong fingers entwined with hers.

"Great enough. You forget the penalties for late payments, my dear."

"You rapacious bast—"

"Ah, careful, Miss Holton," Mr. Higgins interrupted. "You wouldn't want your fiancé to get the wrong idea about you."

"Hardly," Gabriel murmured beside her, and she wondered if that was a compliment or not.

She rather doubted it was.

"The nature of my business requires that I charge interest," Mr. Higgins continued. "If you could have gotten the funds from another source, you would have." He shrugged again. "You did not. And those were my terms."

Octavia wanted to rail at him, but she knew he was right. He was a businessman, as was she. Businesspersons, they were, she supposed. She knew what she was doing when she'd borrowed that money.

It was just that she hadn't anticipated things making it difficult for her to repay him.

You never anticipate anything, her sister's voice echoed.

"How much does Miss Holton owe you?" Gabriel asked.

Octavia whirled to face him, dropping his

hand. "You can't," she said fiercely. "I won't let you."

"I don't care how I get my money, Miss Holton," Mr. Higgins said in a deceptively silky tone. Really, he could have been a model for the villain in any number of penny dreadfuls. "Just that I get it."

"You'll get it," Octavia asserted, aware that she had no basis on which to say this. Just that she did not want Gabriel to have to do even more for her than he already had. "In the meanwhile," she said, her eyes lighting on the book on the other edge of the desk, "I can offer you something as collateral." She strode forward and snatched the book from the desk, holding it out to Mr. Higgins.

"Octavia," she heard Gabriel say behind her, but she ignored him.

"What is this?" Mr. Higgins said, glaring at the book.

"It's a book," Octavia replied, in a tone that implied he was an idiot if he didn't know that. "It's a valuable book, isn't it, Mr. Fallon?" She turned to regard Gabriel, noting his barely repressed anger, the white lines bracketing his mouth.

Good. If he was angry with her, he would be less inclined to white knight his way to her rescue. She did not want to be rescued, thank you very much.

And it would be less likely he would do anything so foolish as to lose his heart to her. The easier for them to part at the end of this adventure if he was as irritated by her as he seemed to be now.

Though *irritated* was rather too mild a term for what he appeared to be experiencing.

"Isn't it, Mr. Fallon?" she repeated, her stomach clenching as she saw him visibly control his temper. This is what she wanted, though. In the long run, if not for right now. For him to be furious with her. For him to see their relationship as transactional.

The alternative was too frightening for her even to think about.

"It is," he replied shortly. "The entire set, if none of the volumes are missing, is priceless. But even that volume is worth a substantial sum to the right person."

Mr. Higgins took the book from her hand then, giving it a dubious glance before handing it to one of the two men still flanking the desk, their faces set in implacable expressions.

They must have seen this type of thing a lot, Octavia thought. Which one of them would be the one to break her limbs, or whatever it was that Mr. Higgins would do to her if she did not repay his money? Not that this kind of musing was doing anything to extricate her from the situation.

"I'll take this for now, seeing as how you do not yet have my money." Mr. Higgins spoke in a disapproving tone. "But if I do not have everything you owe me—plus interest—I will pay a visit to your sister, and perhaps she will be able to help me."

"Don't," Octavia shot out. "Please." She swallowed hard. Knowing the disappointment Ivy would feel if she found out about Octavia's current predicament. Knowing, too, that her sister would be hurt Octavia hadn't come to her first. But also knowing that Ivy and her husband, the former Duke of Hasford, were saving to buy a house for themselves and Sebastian's dogs.

She couldn't do that to her sister.

"I will not, unless you fail to repay me," Mr. Higgins said. Now he did sound menacing. At least, Octavia now felt menaced, whereas she hadn't before. "I want it within the month." He jerked his chin toward Gabriel. "Perhaps you can persuade her to honor her word. Since it seems you will be expecting the same of her when she speaks her wedding vows."

Octavia was launching herself forward before she realized it, only to be grasped in strong arms and hauled backward, pulled up close to Gabriel's chest.

"Octavia," he warned, and she ground her teeth but didn't fight against his hold.

"Your fiancée has quite a temper," Mr. Higgins said with a cold smile. "Fortunate for you that I don't care about anything but my money. I'll take this and have it valued," he continued, holding the book aloft, "and I will see you within the month."

He gave them both a curt nod, summoning his henchmen and walking out of the library.

Only then did Octavia struggle in Gabriel's arms, breaking his hold to spin and face him. "You should have let me—"

"Let you what? Attack him? How would that possibly help?" He spoke in a derisive tone, and Octavia felt a rising surge of anger, even though she knew it wasn't justified. She was just taking out her frustration on him, which wasn't fair.

Though none of this was fair. Starting from when her father had decided that gambling his family away—literally—was worth more than love. Than safety, and comfort, and stability.

She slumped, and he stepped forward, wrapping her in his arms. "It will be fine, Octavia," he murmured, his lips brushing her hair. "You will take care of this."

"Alone," she replied, her word muffled by his chest.

She felt him chuckle. "Alone. Of course. You would not have it any other way."

She nodded, relieved he wasn't insisting on helping her. Relieved and more comfortable now—after all, she wasn't accustomed to depending on anyone but herself and her sister. And even then she preferred to depend entirely on herself. Ivy lectured too much to make it worthwhile. That was only one of the many reasons she hadn't gone to Ivy in the first place.

She wouldn't lecture. But she would give her one of those hard stares that made her want to squirm, knowing she had done wrong, and was going to continue doing wrong.

She could handle this all herself.

But in the meantime, it was nice, she could admit, to be held in Gabriel's arms, even though it was just temporary.

This was all just temporary.

Chapter Fourteen

Gabriel didn't know what to do with his emotions. He'd never felt flooded by so many different feelings all at one time, feelings that were contradictory to one another. Rage, concern, sympathy, protectiveness, irritation—and those were only the ones he could name at the moment. He knew there were more.

He held her in his embrace, gazing over her head to the outside. The pond where they'd first met. She was settling in his arms now, rather like a small bird tucking its wings in after flying.

And they had flown, hadn't they?

He'd woken up with an unfamiliar sense of satisfaction, tinged with an eagerness to be satisfied as much as possible until she left.

That remained true, he supposed. This encounter merely reinforced that they came from two different worlds. That this was all temporary.

And she'd leave, and he'd be here alone in his house. Well, except for all the people who seemed to also live here now.

"You didn't have to stay," she said, drawing

away from him. She looked up, and he was surprised to see she hadn't cried. Most people would have cried after such an encounter.

But not Octavia.

He forced himself to give her a smile, as warm as he could make it. Which honestly wasn't very warm, he supposed. "What kind of fake fiancé would I be if I let you deal with that alone?"

"I gave him the book," she said dully, glancing away.

"I know. It's yours to give."

"Though I gave it to you." Again she met his eyes, and he felt the impact of that unflinching gaze. "And then I took it away. Like your father, perhaps."

The similarity made him inhale sharply, and he felt his chest grow tight. She was correct— it was like his life with his father. Except for Nyx, who the older Mr. Fallon had known would be a bridge—or a dog—too far. Even if Nyx hadn't already been popular with Gabriel's classmates.

But anything else that Gabriel had found pleasurable to be around him, whether it was a particularly comfortable sofa, or a pair of carriage horses that inspired his imagination, could be gone at any moment. Not because his father had lost them gambling, as he presumed Octavia's father would have, but because his father had found a way to leverage the sofa or the horses into something better. But not better for Gabriel. Just better for him.

"I suppose," he replied, realizing she was waiting for his response.

She nodded, as though he'd confirmed what she already knew, her expression growing guarded as she moved to the desk, running her hand along its gnarled surface. "I would not blame you if you wished to keep distance between us," she said in a low voice. "Because that was a rather forceful reminder of who I am and what I do."

He jerked forward, stopping himself before he touched her again. "Is that what you want?" he asked.

She turned to face him, and now he could see the glimmer of tears in her eyes. "No." She lifted her chin. "But I would not blame you," she said again, "if you—" She made a vague gesture that he took to mean their current relationship.

"No," Gabriel said again, shaking his head to emphasize his word. "I know who you are, Octavia. This hasn't changed anything, it isn't as though I wasn't fully aware of all that before." He shrugged, trying to appear indifferent. Though that was the last thing he was when thinking about her. "Our interlude is just that, and nothing about today is going to change it. Besides," he said, making a conscious effort to lighten the atmosphere, "you're going to have to find something of value to pay off that modern-day Ploutos."

She raised an eyebrow, and he continued speaking, knowing what she was going to ask. "He was the god of wealth."

"Ah," she said, and he was relieved to see a

genuine smile curling her lips. "Of course he was." She paused, and her smile ebbed. "Thank you," she said at last. "For not leaving me to it. For continuing this—" Again, she made that hand wave that indicated everything between them. "For being my friend." She exhaled, then her tone shifted to something brighter. "And for being my fake fiancé, even though you were the one who imposed that on us."

"Yes, I didn't think it through when I said it," he admitted ruefully.

Her eyebrows arched. "My sister says I never think anything through. I am pleased to find we have common ground."

"I don't think it's an admirable trait," he replied.

She made a gesture of indifference. "It has caused some . . . difficulty in my life, that is true, but I like spontaneous action. Not knowing what might happen from one day to the next. Trusting your instincts rather than your plan."

He folded his arms over his chest. "Is spontaneity what led you to suggest—" He made that same vague movement she'd done earlier.

Her cheeks turned pink, and he found himself surprised that she was capable of embarrassment—this bold woman who strode around taking what she wanted, damn the consequences.

Because, he presumed, she never considered the consequences.

"How are you going to get the money you owe him?" he asked.

Her expression shuttered. "I wish you didn't

know about that." She struck a defiant pose. "I had no choice."

"You always have a choice, Octavia," he replied.

He met her gaze as he spoke, and he saw the immediate anger flicker in those dark brown depths. Then she looked away, biting her lip as though in regret.

"I suppose I do," she said, after a very long silence. "And I suppose I should have thought more about borrowing money from Mr. Higgins. But I didn't have a choi—I mean, I couldn't get the money from anywhere else. And I thought it was a certainty that if I could improve the club, business would also improve. But then it rained for nearly two weeks, and there was some sort of political crisis that made all my wealthy patrons stay home so they could pretend they weren't wealthy." She rolled her eyes in disdain.

"How are you going to get the money?" he repeated, more strongly now.

"I don't know!" Her frustration was palpable. "If I can't find proof—"

He heard a note of defeat in her tone, something he hadn't heard from her before.

"I've got something I need to discuss with Mrs. Jennings," he said, knowing she would hate what he was about to do, but it wouldn't matter in the long run.

They had agreed. Eighteen more days of this, and then everything would be over.

She'd be furious with him if she found out, but it wouldn't matter.

"THERE YOU ARE!" she exclaimed as he walked in.

She'd asked Mrs. Jennings, who said she hadn't seen him, and then she had popped into nearly every room of the house, unable to locate him.

And here he was, coming in from outside. If she weren't bursting to tell him what she'd thought of, she'd wonder where he had been.

"I've had an idea," she said, taking his arm and dragging him to the library.

He came without question, shutting the door behind them as she strode to the desk—the same desk Mr. Higgins had been leaning against only an hour or two earlier.

"What is it, Octavia?" he said.

She bit her lip. "Could you sit down? You're far too overwhelming standing over there."

He shrugged, going to sit in the chair opposite. He leaned forward and gazed at her expectantly.

"I was thinking," she began. "We both believe we own this house."

"We do," he said.

"And if we both believe it, then we could both have things happen here before the time for proving it one way or the other is up."

Now he looked wary. "What is your idea, Octavia?"

"A gambling event," she exclaimed.

"A gambling event?" he replied in disbelief, his mouth tautening. "Why would I possibly agree to that? And how could you possibly do it here?"

"Even if you don't agree that it is my right to do so because this is my house"—she took a deep breath—"it is the right thing to do. And it would be remarkably easy to implement, at least what I've envisioned."

"Explain."

Another deep breath. "Which? What I want to do here, or why it is the right thing to do?"

He leaned back in his chair and folded his arms over his chest, jerking his chin toward her. "Either one. Your choice," he added.

Her cheeks flushed again. "Fine." She mirrored his posture as she thought.

"The event would be for one night only. I would invite my usual customers to come, promising them a different type of experience than they usually get in London. They're all in the country anyway, and they're likely dying of boredom, so this would be the perfect entertainment."

"You want them to come here and lose enough money so that no matter what happens, you can pay off that Higgins?" His tone was harsh, and she flinched.

"Well, yes. I know you would loan me the money, but then I'd owe *you*." She shook her head. "I can't have that."

"I would not threaten your person, Octavia."

"But this is the perfect solution!" Why couldn't he see it?

"This would be the most efficient way to solve your problems," he said slowly, leaning back in his chair. "So you can return to London." He nodded. "In which case, I agree."

His words were like a splash of cold water

in her face. He was doing this just because he wanted her to go?

Some of what she was feeling must have shown in her expression, since he held his hand up. "It is not that I wish to get rid of you," he said. "It is just that I do not trust that blackguard not to do you damage if you don't repay him." He raised a brow. "I happen to prefer my fiancées—fake or otherwise—not to be threatened with imminent danger."

"Very kind of you, sir," she replied. "I happen to value my person as well."

His eyes flashed with a knowing heat, and she felt her body respond. "As do I, Octavia."

"Wait," she said, suddenly horrified, "you're not agreeing to this because of—" She waved her hands in the air.

"Because of our transactional relationship?" he said. "Of course not. And if it was that kind of situation, don't you think *you* would be the one owing *me*?"

His lips quirked as he spoke, and she sighed in relief. "You believe yourself to be quite capable in that regard, then?"

"I know I am." He gave her a look of superiority. "If your moans and cries from last night were any indication."

She felt her face flush. How was it possible this scholar, this man who had a sweet, tiny dog, who spent his evenings telling myths to mothers and children, could be so thoroughly wicked in certain ways?

And thank goodness he was. It was going to make the rest of her time here thoroughly diverting. And provide excellent memories for when she was back in London.

"Well," she said, speaking in a rush, "if I'm to do this, I need to get to work." *And not get to work undoing you, as I wish I could do.*

OCTAVIA HAD A plan. For the first time in her life, she had a plan.

Granted, it wasn't much of a plan. She stared down at what she'd written thus far.

> *Host event.*
> *Make enough money to pay Mr. Higgins and get back to London.*

But it was a start. Ivy would be so—

"Ivy!" she exclaimed, grabbing another piece of paper. She needed to write her sister a letter so she wouldn't worry about her. Or worry as much about her—she knew Ivy worried about her no matter what.

She was halfway through the letter when she heard the footsteps pounding up the stairs. Was Mr. Higgins back? Was he threatening the rest of the household?

She bolted out of her chair and ran to the door, flinging it open as Cerberus roused himself from where he'd been sleeping to stand beside her.

Mrs. Jennings stood there, a grin on her face, her daughter on one side and Mary on the other.

"Mrs. Jennings! And Mrs. Wycoff, and Mary. How may I help you?"

Mrs. Jennings clasped her hands together, her excitement palpable. "We heard you are going to be hosting a party, Miss Holton."

News certainly traveled fast—she and Gabriel had spoken only a few hours ago.

"And we're wanting to help."

"Uh . . ." Octavia began. She hadn't thought, when she'd made the proposal, that she would have to explain the idea of a gambling event. They would likely be scandalized.

She hadn't thought.

Of course you didn't.

Her inability to forecast anything was becoming a bit of a problem.

She'd have to write that on her plan: *Figure out how to explain my business to everyone in Greensett so they won't be too entirely shocked by it.*

Though if they *were* entirely shocked by it, they wouldn't ask too many questions when they discovered she and Gabriel had called off their engagement. They'd probably think he was shocked to discover his bride-to-be was a businesswoman.

"When were you thinking of having this party?" Mrs. Jennings continued. "We want to help. You'll need food, of course."

"I've been working on some new recipes," Mary said. "Something nobody has tasted before."

Something nobody has tasted before. "Lovely," Octavia replied, hoping her opinion of Mary's cooking did not show on her face or in her voice.

"I'm working with Mary on it, too," Mrs. Wycoff said, sharing a conspiratorial glance with Octavia. "I've been helping her in the kitchen a bit. It seems I have somewhat of a knack for cookery."

"Oh, I was wondering why it was—" Octavia began, then snapped her mouth shut as she realized what she was about to say: *why it was better than before.* "Anyway, I will gladly accept any help you can offer," she said quickly.

She'd need tables, and beverages, and food— she'd think about food later, she hastily corrected herself, wincing as she thought about Mary's cooking—and candles, and for the house to be presentable enough to make it seem as though the event was an exotic experience, not just a few people out losing money in the country.

Hopefully *losing* money. For her plan to work, they had to lose money, or she would be in worse shape after the weekend than before.

"When will it take place?" Mrs. Wycoff asked.

"Uh—" She'd need time to prepare, but it had to be within the time she and Gabriel had agreed upon. "Let's say in two weeks and three days?"

That would take her to the night before they each had to produce evidence of house ownership. She hoped she'd found something by then.

But if she didn't, she had devised another way to get some money so her limbs, not to mention her sister's love for her, wouldn't be in jeopardy.

She couldn't think about that. About any of it. She had to concentrate on what had to be done now.

"I'll train people to be the—the hosts," she said

brightly. She would explain the whole gambling concept later on, when they had grown more accustomed to the idea. Right now she just needed them to be excited about the event, regardless of the details. She wouldn't be able to run the whole thing entirely on her own, and she didn't think she could count on Gabriel to help—it was enough he was allowing her to do it in the first place. She didn't think he would want to be an active participant.

"I can do that," Mrs. Jennings said brightly.

Octavia couldn't help but smile at the older woman's enthusiasm. Had anyone ever been as willing to do or try anything as Mrs. Jennings? It seemed that she relished new challenges, whether it was moving herself and her small family to live with a former pupil, picking up housekeeping skills, or cheering on everyone else's successes.

Octavia had a bit of that enthusiasm herself, but too often her enthusiasm lacked specifics—instead, she thought of things like *engage in physical relations with Mr. Fallon* without thinking of the consequences to her heart, or *get a carriage ride to a remote village several hours from London* without thinking of how she'd be able to get back.

Borrow money from Mr. Higgins was another such venture.

Perhaps she should embrace the whole notion of planning for things, even if it was contrary to who she was.

Chapter Fifteen

I heard Mrs. Jennings and the others discussing your gambling event," Gabriel said, as they met in the foyer. His heart should not have started beating faster when he saw her, and yet it had.

They'd agreed to continue searching together— her for her father's papers, and him for more books of the *Mythologiae*, though he'd keep his eye out for the former—even though she now had another goal, perhaps meaning she wouldn't need to find the thus-far-elusive proof that she owned this house.

"I was astonished at how quickly they agreed to everything," she replied. "Usually when I have an idea, it takes a bit of time to convince others. Not everyone is as spontaneous as I am—though I am now able to acknowledge that planning has its place."

"When planned for," he said dryly.

"But spontaneity is an excellent characteristic," Octavia said firmly. Either missing or ignoring his barb. "It shows that your mind is agile, that you are able to juggle multiple ideas in your head, and that you are seldom surprised for long."

"It also," Gabriel pointed out, "means that sometimes you are left without a solution to a problem because you have launched into something without thinking it entirely through."

He was so acutely conscious of her, so close to him, but not touching. Their minds sparring with one another, exchanging ideas and opinions as though they were paired in a complicated dance.

He had never felt so inspired, as though his brain was on fire with a surfeit of ideas. It wasn't just the reconfiguring of Greek mythology he'd done to share with the people he was unexpectedly living with; it was the combination of mind and body she brought. The passion and appreciation for physical things as well as the mental flirtation they were engaged in since the moment they first met.

He also had to admit spontaneity could be useful. After all, he knew she hadn't thought before she suggested they take their attraction to a physical relationship, and that had worked out well beyond his imaginings, which had been robust.

They walked down the hall to the library together, him trying to keep his mind on looking for books and papers—not looking to see if he could slide his hands up her skirts to find the warm, wet place between her thighs, or if he could hoist her legs up around his waist and put her back to the door so he could feast on her mouth and neck.

She followed him into the room, giving a gusty sigh as she glanced around at all the books they hadn't looked through yet. "For a person who didn't read, my father certainly collected a fair number of books," she muttered. And then sneezed.

Gabriel withdrew a handkerchief from his pocket and offered it to her.

"Of course you'd carry a handkerchief," she said, glaring at him. And then wiping her nose.

"Your father seems to have accepted a wide variety of items for stakes. Books, houses. People," he added, after a pause.

"Yes, true," she replied, her voice more strained than usual. She picked up the top book on a pile, flipping it open and scrutinizing it. Then made a noise of disgust and looked up at him. *"Lives of the Most Eminent English Poets,"* she read aloud, her tone disdainful. She closed the book and put it to the side. "Not even as useful as that fox book we found earlier."

"But interesting," Gabriel said, advancing to the desk.

"Let me guess," she said, holding her hand up. "All of them are men. Because the women had to do practical things, like running a household or raising the children while their husbands, fathers, and sons spent time writing poetry."

Gabriel's brows rose at her scathing tone. "You

want to write poetry?" he asked, deliberately being obtuse just to get her strongest reaction.

"Of course not!" She glowered as she folded her arms over her chest. "You're just saying that to irk me."

He made a bow. "At your service, my lady."

"Hmph. The thing is," she continued, "I want to be able to write poetry if I choose. But I cannot, because I have to spend my time—"

"Creating a space for people to lose their life savings?" he replied in a deceptively mild tone.

She threw her hands up in exasperation. "Yes, Gabriel, that is what I do. I don't care at all about how these people are going to feed their families. I don't take pains to listen to rumors about their potential insolvency. I don't insist that they pay their debts the very night they incur them." She shook her head as she met his gaze. "I understand your antipathy to the pastime, given your history. But do me some credit and understand that I am responsible for what I do."

He stared at her for a long moment, then gave a slow nod. "I apologized for my preconceptions when we first met, and now I have to do it again. I am sorry, Octavia."

She blinked as if surprised. "Oh. Well. Thank you."

"Did you know," he said, drawing closer to her, "that you are beautiful when you are angry?" He nearly laughed aloud at how quickly her expression changed. She scowled, and opened her mouth as though to say something—no doubt something cutting and dismissive, something that would make their spark burn more intensely—when he held his hand up and kept speaking.

"AND YOU ARE beautiful when you are calm, not that I have seen that too much in the time I've known you." The last part was said in a pointed tone Octavia did not care for, even though she did like compliments. "And beautiful when you are being spontaneous, and when you are disheveled in your bed." By now he was standing very close to her, so close she could see the faint stubble along his jaw.

"You are beautiful as well," she said in a disgruntled tone. She couldn't resist lifting her hand to slide her fingers along that strong jaw, feel the stubble prickling her fingertips. "If only we were—" she said, breaking off as she shook her head.

"If only we were?" he echoed, making the repetition into a question.

She sighed. "Different people. Though if we were, we likely wouldn't be here together at all." She raised her gaze to his, removing her hand from his face. "But you are a scholar, a man brought up in the country, someone who wants to make this house into a home. Not to mention treating everyone who lives here now like your family."

"And you?" he said.

She glanced away, out the window. To the

pond where they'd first met. The image of him and his glorious chest came to her mind, and she bit her lip. "I belong in London. My business is there, my sister is there, and London is where we went when there was no place else to go." She looked back at him. "Not that you are saying you would—if I were different—but you have to see it's impossible."

"Nothing is impossible, Octavia," he said gently. He cupped her neck and rubbed his fingers against her skin. "Not even the likelihood that two people who are on opposite sides of a dispute will realize they have an undeniable connection."

And then he lowered his mouth to hers and kissed her.

Glorious. That was her first thought as she opened her lips to allow his tongue entrance. She gripped his arms, relishing the strength she felt there, and then slid her hands up to his shoulders. Their breadth would have made her gasp, but her breathing was already faster thanks to him, his wicked mouth and that even more wicked tongue.

She wished it were nighttime already, and he could creep into her bedroom again so they could thoroughly explore one another.

She hadn't gotten to touch his chest much, for example. He'd distracted her with what he'd done with those capable fingers and then his mouth on her breast. She wanted to strip him naked, run her fingers along every hard plane of him. Mark the places where he was more sensitive to her touch, see what would make him shudder the way she had.

And since she was the other half to this bargain, she wanted him to do the same to her. Put those big, strong hands all over her. Pinch and caress her nipples, hold her still as he brought her to another one of those shuddering moments of ecstasy.

He pulled her closer now, and she felt the hard length of him against her lower belly. She shifted onto her tiptoes so she could angle that hardness against her cunny. Wanting to rub up against him and create a delicious friction that would leave her aching and eager.

So that he could slide his fingers under her skirts and work that magic again.

His hand was on her arse, squeezing it, and she couldn't help but moan. Now his mouth was at her neck, sucking softly on the sensitive skin there as his fingers caressed her curves. Her breasts ached, and she moved side to side so she could rub them against his chest.

"Should we clear off that desk, Octavia?" he murmured. She twisted to look at it, then glanced back at him. His whisky eyes were dark with passion, and his lips were curled up into a wicked smile that sent shivers all over.

"We should," she said, immediately going to the desk and hoisting a stack of books off it and onto the floor.

"Get up on it," he ordered, and she shivered again at the clear command she heard in his voice.

"And if I don't?" She couldn't help but challenge him. Because that was who she was.

"If you don't," he said in a growl, "I'll slap your pretty arse until you do what I say."

"Oh," she sighed, placing her hands on the desk and twisting her neck to look back at him. "I would like that, please."

His gaze darkened even more, and he advanced toward her, a clear intention in his stance. He held his hand up, one eyebrow raised, and kept his eyes locked with hers. "You'll tell me if you don't—" he began, and she nodded.

Still keeping his eyes on her face, he lowered himself to the floor and grabbed hold of the bottom of her gown, beginning to raise it up slowly. He clamped his hand on her ankle, then her calf, sliding up as he drew the gown up. She felt the cool air on her bare skin, and she bit her lip again in anticipation.

"Are you certain you won't do what I say, Octavia?" he asked.

She shook her head. "I won't." Her voice sounded shaky. He had barely touched her, and already she felt as though she was burning up inside.

What would it be like when he delivered on his promise?

"Then you leave me with no choice." By now her gown was up at her waist, her buttocks bare to his gaze.

"You always have a choice, Gabriel," she said in a sly tone of voice.

He barked out a laugh as his palm slid along her bare skin. And then he lifted it to slap the cheek of her buttock, and she gasped, the shock of it making her body tingle.

"Now will you get up on the desk?" he demanded. His palm soothed the skin where he'd slapped her.

"No," she replied, shaking her head in emphasis.

"You don't even know why I want you there," he said.

"Why—why do you want me there?" she asked, before his hand slapped her again. "Oh!" she blurted, and his brows drew together in concern.

"Are you all right?" he asked.

"Very all right," she said, wiggling her lower body in provocation.

"You are," he agreed, and she knew he was speaking about her, not just how she felt right at this moment. If only—

But now wasn't the time to regret their respective situations.

"So, are you going to tell me?" she asked impatiently.

He curled into her, his front pressed against her back, the rough fabric of his clothing against her newly sensitive skin.

It felt amazing.

"I want to have you on your back on this desk here," he said, murmuring low into her neck, "with your gown up around your ears so I can see all of you. Have your legs dangling over the edge, spread wide so I can see you there, too."

She uttered a garbled noise in response, and he chuckled against her skin.

"I'll kneel down on the floor, one hand on each of your knees, holding you open for me. And then . . ." He paused, his tongue darting out to lick her skin. "I'll kiss you there."

She shuddered in response, her hair falling around her face, her whole body quivering in anticipation.

"But only if you get on the desk for me, Octavia." He drew back as he spoke, and then he slapped her arse again, this time on the other side, making her jump. "Are you going to?" he demanded, and then his hand was on her again, the impact of palm on tender flesh making a resounding noise.

Her breasts were aching so much they were nearly painful, and her arse throbbed from the sensation of his slapping her there.

It was remarkable not to be in control, and she realized she craved that, since it happened so seldom—she was always the one guiding things, especially now that her sister, Ivy, had ceded the running of the club to Octavia. It was blissful not to have to make a decision beyond whether or not she would splay herself out for his—and her—enjoyment on the desk.

Which, put that way, made it ridiculous she wasn't already up on it, but the way he demanded she obey and his subsequent actions made her squirm with an even greater passion.

"You haven't answered me, Octavia." His palm

rubbed her buttock, and then his hand slipped between her legs, cupping her. "You're so wet," he said, his voice ragged. "You're wet for me."

She reached back, her fingers spread wide as she laid her palm on his hardness. "And this is for me," she said, curling her fingers as much around him as she could, given their awkward position and that he still wore clothes.

Why was that, anyway? With her gown hiked up and her lower body exposed, why wasn't he keeping up his end of the mutually pleasurable bargain?

She raised herself up off the surface of the desk, turning to him. Dropping her hand away from him as she straightened, then putting it back as soon as they were face-to-face.

She gripped his hardness and stepped closer to him, her gown falling back down to her ankles. The fabric brushed against her tender flesh, making her shiver all over again.

He groaned, catching her wrist.

"Mr. Fallon!"

They both looked toward the door, which remained mercifully shut. Though they heard someone grasping the knob. "Mr. Fallon!" the voice called again. It sounded like Mrs. Jennings.

Octavia leaped away from him, scurrying to the other side of the desk as she batted at the skirts of her gown in a vain attempt to tidy herself.

Thank goodness they weren't still rucked up about her waist.

She glanced at him, and immediately began to laugh—he'd grabbed a book from the floor and was holding it awkwardly in front of himself.

"Come in, Mrs. Jennings," he said in a calm tone. He glared at Octavia as she smothered her laughter. "This isn't over," he said in a low growl.

She arched an eyebrow and looked pointedly toward where he held the book. "No, it most certainly is not," she said, feeling herself start to laugh even harder at his expression.

Mrs. Jennings stepped into the room, her eyes wide.

"Excellent, you are both here!" she exclaimed. She didn't seem to notice anything untoward.

"What is it, Mrs. Jennings?" Octavia asked after a moment.

"There is a *spider* in the corner of the room I am mopping, and I am not certain how to handle it. I didn't want to let it go onto the floor, because the water might cause some damage to it," she said, speaking so earnestly Octavia wondered if the spider was another one of her relations.

"How to handle it?" Gabriel said. "If you could—"

"And I was thinking that if you could come take care of it, that would be best," Mrs. Jennings interrupted, giving him an encouraging look.

"Yes, do go take care of the spider," Octavia said, making a shooing gesture. "You don't want it to get wet, do you?" she continued, biting her lip to suppress her grin.

"Of course he doesn't!" Mrs. Jennings exclaimed. She walked back out, clearly expecting him to follow.

He stalked out of the room, giving her one last glance that was both enticing and threatening, still holding the book in front of himself, and she succumbed to her laughter when they were out of earshot.

Chapter Sixteen

Gabriel had considered adjusting his story that evening to speak about Arachne in light of the whole spider incident, but he didn't want to remind Mrs. Jennings of how he'd had to ultimately dispose of the creature.

So he stuck with Heracles, as he'd planned.

All the house's inhabitants were in the living room again, this time having had a surprisingly palatable meal. They'd discussed the Big Event, as Charlie had dubbed it, and even Gabriel had felt enthusiastic about some of the plans. If she could get enough money, she wouldn't have to worry so much about owning the house.

"Heracles was a very strong and powerful man," he began. "He had the powers of a god, but wasn't actually a god."

"How many gods are there? I thought there was only one," Charlie said.

He blinked in surprise as he realized he'd have to take a step back and explain polytheism. Not quite how he'd anticipated the night going.

He was being spontaneous, though. Which

was, he had to admit, sometimes a good thing. What had Octavia said? *Spontaneity shows that your mind is agile, that you are able to juggle multiple ideas in your head, and that you are seldom surprised for long.* This would be a lesson in self-improvement for him, and learning about other beliefs for them.

He'd just need to tamp down the various and voracious appetites of the gods in his explanation, which was getting more difficult now that his own various and voracious appetites had been awoken.

Once that was taken care of, he could continue with Heracles's story. "Heracles had a lot of strength and skill, and was rightfully proud of that." He met her gaze. "He did things he had to for survival—when he was just a baby, the jealous goddess Hera sent snakes to kill him, but he killed them instead."

Her eyebrows rose in surprise. "A child? Who would do that to a child?" she asked, her tone outraged.

He gave her a wry glance. "People seldom realize the hurt they do to others, even children, because of their own passions. And Hera was very passionate. She couldn't keep Zeus from doing what he wanted, though." He saw the blank looks on their faces and gave a quick explanation. "Zeus was Heracles's father, but Hera was not Heracles's mother."

"Ah," Mrs. Jennings said, nodding her head in understanding. "Zeus was a scamp."

Gabriel suppressed a snort at hearing the strongest god described as *a scamp*.

"And Hera made it so Heracles did some things he didn't intend to. Things that hurt people, even though he wasn't himself to blame."

"What did he think about those things?" Octavia asked. "Or the people who loved him. What did they think?"

"The people who loved him understood, but he blamed himself. So he went to Apollo, who assigned him twelve labors. If he could do all twelve, not only would he be forgiven, but he would ascend to Mount Olympus as a god."

"My goodness," Mrs. Wycoff said. "If only it was that easy."

He saw Octavia give the other woman an understanding look, and wondered what was going on there, then realized it wasn't his business. But apparently Mrs. Wycoff and Octavia had spoken about things beyond the everyday—she wasn't nearly as selfish as she thought if she could offer comfort to someone else. Something he knew about her as well, though her comfort to him was repaid in kind.

"And for the last labor," Gabriel said with a smile, "Heracles was tasked with kidnapping Cerberus."

"Don't you mean dognapping?" she asked, resulting in laughter.

"Heracles was so strong he was able to wrestle Cerberus and capture him," Gabriel said when the laughter had eased.

"He should have just waved a bit of beef in front of him," Octavia observed, giving a fond glance to her own Cerberus, who lay snoozing on the floor. "Or sent an alluring lady dog, like Nyx," she added.

"Yes, alluring ladies can accomplish the most incredible things," Gabriel said in as neutral a tone as he could manage.

"Our lovebirds!" Mrs. Jennings exclaimed, clasping her hands to her chest. "To think of having such a past together and to be reunited in true love. That deserves its own story," she said, nodding.

A story where the couple parts after a few weeks of bliss, Gabriel thought. Wishing it wasn't true, but knowing it had to be. There was no possibility of her staying here, and he did not belong in London. Besides, it was clear he was needed here. Who else would give Mary a job as a cook, and allow Old Joe to live in the stables?

Besides her, of course.

If he could go back in time and cede the house to her, he might have. But she would have immediately set about her plans to sell it, and would have never gotten the chance to meet and know these people. To meet and know him, and vice versa.

He was better off having known her, even if it meant eventual heartache and pain. He would rather suffer the torture of her departure than of never having known the pleasure of her.

That made him understand some of the gods' actions a bit better, he had to admit.

"What did Heracles learn after his labors?" Mrs. Jennings asked, clearly still abiding by her teacher-like ways.

"He had to accept help from others," Gabriel replied, unable to resist giving Octavia a pointed look. "To acknowledge that he couldn't do it all alone."

OCTAVIA LISTENED IN rapt appreciation as Gabriel spun his story; an appropriate description, given their interlude had been interrupted by a spider.

He was wasted as a scholar, she thought. Or at least wasted sitting in libraries by himself reading dusty tomes, which is what she assumed a scholar was.

He was a born teacher, able to spark the imagination with a few clever phrases, putting things in terms his listeners would understand.

She wasn't one for admiring others. Life was too busy, and she was too pragmatic to indulge in wonder at another's abilities. But he was remarkable, keeping everyone's attention as he told them the story of Heracles and his labors, making the lesson of perseverance and belief in oneself clear without pedantry.

"He had to accept help from others," Gabriel said. "To acknowledge that he couldn't do it all alone."

She had people she could ask for help if she wanted to, but she never wanted to.

That was why she was in her current predicament. If she had come clean to Ivy and asked for her help in making what Octavia believed were necessary repairs, she might not have had to borrow money from Mr. Higgins, and would not be currently hoping for some sort of bibliographic miracle in the form of locating the rest of the books in that series Gabriel seemed to think were so valuable.

Of course she wouldn't have met Gabriel at all.

But still.

It stung, to think she might have been wrong all this time. That perhaps she should have swallowed her pride and asked for assistance.

Ivy must be frantic with worry about her. And she had decided not to think about it, because she didn't want Ivy to be able to tell her she'd done something without thinking. Again.

Even though she absolutely had.

She had started to make a plan for her event, hadn't she? If she could just learn how to strategize, perhaps she wouldn't be under threat of losing a limb or two from a ruthless moneylender.

Though he was just conducting his business, she knew. It was her choice to enter into a business arrangement with him. She couldn't blame anybody but herself for the consequences. Mostly because she hadn't thought of the consequences.

"Are you all right?"

Gabriel's voice interrupted her fog of self-recrimination. They were in the living room still, but the others had drifted out in search of their beds after Gabriel had finished. She hadn't realized she'd just been sitting there thinking.

"You were wonderful," she said, sounding as enthusiastic as she ever had. Even when he had brought her to—no. Now was not the time to be thinking about *that*.

She felt her cheeks heat.

"I was, was I?" His tone made it clear he was no longer talking about the story he'd told that evening.

She arched a brow. "Tolerable, I suppose," she said.

"Until we were interrupted."

"Yes, we'll have to—that is, we need to be more cautious."

He blinked in surprise. "You? Cautious?"

She rolled her eyes. "I can be cautious. I can plan." Even though she had no idea how to go about either one of those things. But she was intelligent and capable. Surely she could figure it out. With some help.

"Actually," she continued, "would you be able to help me?"

His eyebrows rose. "Miss Octavia Holton, asking for help?"

She exhaled. "I can do it. I just haven't had to very often." There. That sounded more like her.

"Of course you haven't had to," he replied in a sarcastic voice.

She resorted to what she'd usually done when Ivy had used such a tone on her—she stuck out her tongue at him, making him double over in laughter. Which she hadn't seen him do yet. There was so much to learn about him, and only a bit more than two more weeks to do it in.

She'd just have to be extra-efficient.

"THESE," GABRIEL SAID, flourishing a notebook and a pen, "are your implements of destruction."

He and Octavia were in the library again the following day, it being the only place that wasn't currently the focus of intense cleaning.

Mrs. Jennings had marshaled the various forces currently residing in the house—of which there were many, Gabriel thought ruefully—to get the house absolutely clean by the time of Octavia's Big Event. Mary and Mrs. Wycoff were testing some new dishes, including a rather daring combination of turnip and carrot in the evening's pasties rather than the traditional meat.

The pasties were surprisingly good, and the conversation moved to what else they would serve when the gamblers were in residence. And then Mrs. Jennings had looked around the dining room and pointed out that it didn't matter what they served if the house was too disheveled for company.

Octavia seemed to bristle at the implication that her cleaning efforts hadn't been enough, but was soothed when Mrs. Jennings pointed out that Octavia's clientele was accustomed to a higher standard and were likely ready to find fault with everything, particularly if they were losing.

And since Octavia needed everyone to lose in order to get enough money to pay her loan back, she agreed that they'd have to redouble their efforts to prepare the house.

So now it was the next day, and they were in the library to embark on planning efforts.

"I should be helping Mrs. Jennings," Octavia said plaintively. "She's out there laboring for something I need done, and—"

"And if you don't have a plan for what you are going to do, it won't matter," Gabriel said flatly. "Look, I understand this is anathema to you—"

"I don't know what that means," she muttered.

"But it's important to ensure this event goes as smoothly as possible. That's why you asked for my help, is it not?"

She made a grumbling noise as she crossed her arms over her chest. "It is," she said, "but it is not fun."

Gabriel smothered a laugh.

"How about this," he said, putting the implements of destruction on the desk and walking to where she sat. He knelt down in front of her and placed his hands over hers, which were resting in her lap. "I'll do something nice for you if you complete your plan."

"Nice?" she said, raising her brows.

"Nice," he replied, giving her a wicked smile.

She rolled her eyes. "That would be nice for you as well."

He shrugged. "True. Every bargain has some sort of reciprocity, does it not? And we do have a bargain."

She gave him an amused glance. "We do. Fine. I'll work on my plan." She paused, then twisted her lips in thought.

It struck him then that he was in a bargain with a woman who not only owned and managed a gambling house, but one who had risked her actual life by borrowing money from an unscrupulous source. Not the sort of person one would expect would be content to live a quiet life in the country as the wife of a scholar.

Unfortunately, that realization came at the same time he realized he'd done the impossible and fallen in love with her.

He'd. Fallen. In. Love. With. Her.

"Are you all right?" she asked, her tone concerned. She reached forward and slapped his cheek gently. "Gabriel?"

I've fallen in love with her. And he couldn't tell her. He couldn't do anything more than fulfill his end of the bargain: the mutual exchange of enjoyable pursuits. Help her plan the event that would allow her to leave him permanently. If needed, give up this house to pay her debt, one that would allow her to live in London in safety.

Taking his heart with her.

And now he was being maudlin, like Apollo chasing Daphne when she wanted nothing to do with him.

But Gabriel was not a Greek god, and Octavia

liked him well enough. Just not enough, he knew, to open herself up to the possibility of their fake engagement being real. To compromise.

She'd spoken of London—*my business is there, my sister is there*—and he knew she loved it as much as he loved Greensett. He could never ask her to give it up just for him.

Nor would he ask her.

"I'm fine," he said at last, shaking his head to clear it. He rose and walked back to the desk, gesturing to the notepad. "Let us work on this because the sooner it is done, the sooner you can have your reward."

She stood and walked to him, an impudent gleam in her eye. "We will have to search your bedroom for the books, you know."

"I am counting on that," he said, unable to resist pulling her into him for a quick, fierce kiss.

Chapter Seventeen

"You can't just write *food* on your list and think that's enough," Gabriel pointed out.

Octavia sat at the desk as Gabriel leaned over her, her face scrunched up into an adorable expression as she concentrated on what she was doing.

Not that he would tell her she was adorable; he wasn't that foolhardy.

Even though he'd foolishly fallen in love with her.

"But if I write it down, then I will remember I have to accommodate for it," she replied in a reasonable tone. Accompanied by a gesture indicating reasonableness.

Which meant that she was prevaricating. Octavia wasn't reasonable; she was impetuous, and brave, and stubborn, and fierce, but she was not reasonable.

His eyes narrowed. Not that she could see him; he was bent over her, not vice versa.

Though that might be interesting to try.

"How are you going to accommodate for it?" he asked. "You cannot expect Mary will be able to provide food—*edible* food—for everyone you hope to have here. Even if the pasties were remarkably edible." He shook his head in exasperation. "Never mind you haven't even told anyone about it in the first place, so perhaps the food shouldn't be on your list at all, at least not until you know anyone is going to come."

She gave a satisfied nod. "That is precisely why I just wrote *food*. Why would I bother figuring it all out until I have dealt with the invitations?"

"So, where are invitations on your list?" Gabriel said.

She covered the paper with her hand and scribbled hastily, drawing back in triumph. "There!" she exclaimed, pointing to the word she'd just written.

Which looked like *initiations*, but Gabriel presumed that wasn't what it said.

"How do you alert your customers to events at your own gambling establishment? Surely you must do something more than hope they will appear."

Gabriel straightened, walking to the other side of the desk and taking a seat.

She shrugged, not meeting his gaze. "My sister, Ivy, and her husband, Sebastian, used to manage that. I am more of the day-to-day person."

"Which means you don't know what it entails," Gabriel remarked.

She scowled again. Still adorable, despite how irritated he was at her.

She flicked a piece of hair away from her face,

put the pen down, and folded her arms over her chest. Then glared at him. "You are right," she said, surprising him. Or not; he knew she was able to admit when she was wrong, even if she was also incredibly stubborn. "And this is why I need help." She made a helpless gesture toward the paper. "I know what has to be done. It is just a matter of sorting out all the pieces."

This he could do. He slid the paper toward himself, picking up the pen. "Whenever I am faced with a daunting amount of work, I break it down into sections. Like this," he said, writing quickly. He felt her eyes on him, that Octavia enthusiasm focused intently on the task.

Similar to how she focused on—but he shouldn't let his mind go there, or he'd say forget the Big Event if he could sweep her away and give her her own Big Event. Or several of them.

He was besotted.

That was the only explanation for why his mind kept wandering there so often.

He was in love with her, he wanted to spend all of his time loving her, and he wanted to know she would be in this house forever. With him.

Unfortunately, the reality was that she would be leaving in less than two weeks, after her own Big Event—and not the enjoyable kind—and he would likely never see her again.

His heart hurt already.

"Gabriel?" she said, sounding impatient.

Of course. Just because she was humble enough

to admit she needed help didn't mean she was going to allow him to take his time showing her.

Though he did take his time when—

Goddamn it, Gabriel, he thought.

Not every road led to sex. Though he could say he understood the motivation of the gods and goddesses he studied better; they were all obsessed with their own pleasure, and they wouldn't stop at anything to get it.

But if he didn't stop at anything to get it, and he got it, she would be miserable. Even if she— miracle of miracles—believed she loved him as well, she would never tolerate being stuck in this house, in this tiny village, so far away from London. He knew, from how she'd spoken of it, that while her gambling house provided her means of support, owning it and running it provided so much more than mere food and lodging. She was able to utilize her excellently sharp mind to forward its success. She would be stifled in Greensett, even if she loved him.

Even if she initially persuaded herself that it would be fine, that love would carry them through difficulties.

"Gabriel!" she said again, her tone sharper. "Are you going to help me, or are you going to sit there and think about Zeus all day?"

He raised a brow. "You have been listening to my stories, then."

"Of course I have!" she shot back. "You're brilliant!" She accompanied her words with an exasperated flinging up of her hands, and he shook his head, keenly aware of how very Octavia the moment was—her paying a compliment to someone else while also being incredibly annoyed.

"Fine," he replied in a mild tone. "What are the elements of the invitations?"

The rest of the time was spent relatively peacefully, as Octavia went over the various parts that would go into a Big Event. Gabriel wasn't surprised to discover that she actually knew precisely what she was supposed to do— she just hadn't been prepared to assemble it all together in her mind.

She leaned back in her chair, wiping a pen-streaked hand over her forehead and leaving a trail of ink. "I think that is it. I will go to Greensett tomorrow and order the cards." She frowned, looking down at the list, which was actually robust now, and not just random words written on a piece of paper. "Do you think they'll be able to produce the cards in enough time?"

Gabriel nodded. "More than most, Mrs. Hall understands how crucial it is to maintain a good reputation, because people will talk."

She snorted. "You mean Mrs. Hall talks."

Gabriel shrugged. "She is a terrible gossip, but she is not terrible herself. I believe she truly wants the best for everyone. She just wants to know about everyone's lives."

"Which is why we have this whole fake engagement thing," she replied, with a wave of her fingers.

"And because it would have been beyond scandalous for the two of us to live together without the benefit of some kind of relationship," Gabriel reminded her. "And even then, we would have been barely skating by on people's good graces, since you didn't even bother to bring a maid or anybody with you."

"Didn't bother?" she replied, her eyebrows shooting up. "I didn't know I would find a naked gentleman in my pond."

Gabriel leaned back, folding his arms over his chest, feeling a wry smile curl his lips. "And I didn't know I would be facing off against the woman I was supposed to marry years ago." He paused, his newly realized feelings threatening to overwhelm him. "It hasn't been that terrible, has it?"

"You look good naked" was her quick retort.

He waited, knowing that she would have more to add.

"It's been . . . interesting," she said, this time more slowly. "I never realized I was lacking family until I came here." Her expression was stoic, though her voice trembled. "Mrs. Jennings, and Mrs. Wycoff, and Mary, and Charlie, and even Old Joe. They're people I care about, and when I am around them, like when we are listening to your stories in the evenings, it feels so settled." Her eyes got a faraway look in them.

"And I don't know if I like it, feeling this comfortable, if that makes sense."

Of course it did, since it was her. Octavia the Bold would never seek comfort. And it would make her uncomfortable, ironically enough.

Which just returned him to his earlier thoughts, that she would never fit into this life, even if she wanted to. It just wasn't in her nature. And he would never ask her to, to compromise a part of herself because he selfishly wanted to be with her for the rest of their lives.

But he would enjoy the hell out of her while she was here.

OCTAVIA WASN'T SURE why his expression changed, but it had. And she already felt vulnerable. She wasn't going to ask him what he was thinking about. They were veering so close to territory where she might say something she would regret—not that she had ever truly regretted anything. Even the loan from Mr. Higgins was an error of judgment on her part, but not how she had come to her decision. Perhaps she was splitting hairs because she was so stubborn she refused to ever admit a mistake.

Wait. Did that mean she had made a mistake?

She shook her head, as though she could dislodge the idea from her brain with a physical action.

"What are you saying no about?" he asked. He gazed intently at her, as though he was peering into her soul.

Which was a far more fanciful idea than she'd ever had. What was happening to her? First she admitted to feeling as though these strangers were family, and then she'd considered the ridiculous notion that she might regret something.

And now she was thinking about her soul. When she usually barely thought about her knees, or the small of her back, both of which were much closer to her.

"Nothing," she said, pasting a bright smile on her face. A thought crossed her mind, and she snatched it up, relieved not to be thinking about feelings, and souls, and anything close to an emotion. "I have a splendid idea! Instead of you sharing a story this evening, how about we conduct a general meeting about the Big Event? I could explain what is to happen and who is to do it, and then we could go over the particulars. I was thinking"—even though she hadn't been thinking of it at all, at least not until this very minute—"that you could run one of the tables. I am certain many of my patrons will appreciate having such a . . . scholar as their dealer."

"You want me to run one of your gambling tables?" He didn't precisely spit out the words, but his tone was sharp.

She decided to ignore it. "I do," she replied firmly. "It will be like your own Labor of Heracles," she said, with a cheeky grin. "I believe you will handle the table well, and resolve any issues that might come up during the course of the game. I also know that players like to have a sympathetic ear when they lose, and you are so softhearted, I believe you will listen to every tale of woe."

"I'm softhearted?" he replied, sounding skeptical.

She rolled her eyes. "No, not at all. Because only the hardest of hearts would allow an actual stranger who challenged the ownership of a house to stay in the house with her enormous dog. Never mind encouraging the entire village to live here—"

"I didn't do that. You did," he retorted.

"—and praise the food prepared by someone who might have a second career as a brick maker. If the bricks were made of—"

"You've made your point." He shoved back from the desk and rose, holding his hand out to her. "I think a meeting is an excellent idea. And you'll be able to identify any flaws or omissions in your plan by talking it out with the others."

She felt herself flush at his words. Not necessarily because it was the first time she'd been complimented on anything close to a plan, though that was certainly part of it. It was because he was so genuinely admiring; he didn't judge her for being as she was. He just . . . wanted her to get better.

And she discovered she did, too.

She took his hand, picking up the piece of paper they'd worked on together in the other. "Let us review the troops," she said, adopting a haughty tone.

He inclined his head, a lock of hair falling over his forehead. She smoothed it away, taking a moment to run her palm over his cheek. Meeting his eyes, which were still focused intently—so intently—on her.

She shivered, not only because of the connection they were sharing, but because she felt seen by him. Truly seen, as someone who had flaws and good qualities, who was someone of value. She didn't think he would be nearly as enthusiastic about all of that if he didn't also treasure her brain as much as her body.

And he seemed to treasure her body a lot.

OCTAVIA BOUNDED AHEAD of him, calling everyone's name as she walked swiftly down the hall.

Mrs. Jennings popped up first, emerging from the enormous parlor, brandishing a broom in one hand and a filthy rag in the other. "What is it, Miss Octavia? Not another spider, I hope?"

Octavia laughed in response. "No, nothing like that. I was hoping you and the rest of the cleaning crew could join me in the dining room? I'd like to share some ideas on the Big Event."

Mrs. Jennings's eyes got bright, and she clapped her hands together, apparently forgetting she was holding cleaning tools in both, which made the broom handle hit her on the side of the head. Mrs. Jennings wobbled, but righted herself, offering a vaguely embarrassed smile.

"Mrs. Jennings!" Octavia exclaimed, rushing toward her. She plucked the broom from the other woman's hands, thrusting it behind her to give to Gabriel, then turned to him with her hand held out.

He didn't ask her what she wanted. He just handed his handkerchief over, and she whirled back around to offer it to Mrs. Jennings, who took it with a relieved exhale.

"I think you are done cleaning for now, Mrs. Jennings," Octavia said in a soft voice. "Are you up to coming to the dining room for a strategy discussion?"

Mrs. Jennings gave a vigorous nod. "Yes, I will just go round up the others. I left Charlie in the stables with Old Joe. They are cleaning the unused stalls for the guests to put their horse companions in."

Octavia bit her lip and averted her gaze so she wouldn't laugh.

"Very thoughtful of them to think of the horse companions," Gabriel said in a grave voice behind her.

She twisted to meet his gaze, glaring at him. He widened his eyes as though protesting his innocence, and she shook her head before turning back around.

"Mary and Mrs. Wycoff are already in the dining room, I believe," Mrs. Jennings said. "They were going to see how many platters the tables could hold without crowding the people who might be seated for food."

"Excellent," Octavia said, taking Mrs. Jennings's

arm. "Gabriel, could you let Old Joe and Charlie know? We will meet you there."

She didn't wait for his reply, but began to walk, more slowly now that she had Mrs. Jennings with her. The other woman explained everything she'd done thus far, which apparently included a lot of sweeping and corner cleaning. Explaining both the broom and the rag.

WHEN THEY WERE all assembled, Octavia rose, holding her paper in front of her, and began to speak. Gabriel stood on the other side of the table, the rest of the household between them, seated. From this vantage point, he could see all of the members of the household, ranging from Old Joe through to Nyx, who lay in front of Octavia, gazing up at her adoringly.

Like master, like dog, he thought ruefully.

Cerberus was in front of the fireplace, gazing adoringly at Nyx.

"Thank you for joining me here, everyone," she began. The paper she held trembled. Was she nervous? Octavia the Fearless?

"Mr. Fallon and I worked on a schedule for the Big Event," she continued. Her eyes flicked up at him for a brief moment, and he saw the anxiety in her expression. She was nervous. Which was entirely odd, given who she was.

"Mary and Mrs. Wycoff will be in charge of the food. Have the two of you discussed anything beyond the pasties you served the other night?"

Both ladies shook their heads.

Octavia nodded, as though she'd expected that. "I would encourage you to think of something simple yet delicious—something that could be eaten without having to leave the play."

"Like a pasty," Mary confirmed. "People can eat those with one hand, if there's not too much sauce."

"Yes, but we will need more than that. We want them to be intrigued by everything we are providing here, from the food and drink to the various games of chance we will be offering."

"And horse rides?" Charlie piped up.

"I am not certain these people will want horse rides," Octavia replied gently. "But that already leads me to your assignment, which will be to take care of the horses. Do you think you can do that?"

"Oh yes, that would be wonderful!" Charlie enthused, and Gabriel's heart warmed that she knew just how to deal with Charlie's potential disappointment, and was going to trust him with the task.

"Back to the food," Octavia said, squinting her eyes in concentration.

Once again, Gabriel couldn't help but think she looked adorable. Even though she would be mortally offended if he dared suggest she was anything less than an Amazon—even if she didn't know precisely what one was.

"Mary and I could make savory scones," Mrs.

Wycoff suggested. "And we could serve soup, but not in a soup bowl—I think there are some boxes of teacups in the corner over there," she said, inclining her head to one of the few areas they hadn't cleaned yet.

Octavia gave an encouraging nod. "Yes, splendid! That adds a unique element to the event. How many different kinds of soups should we have?"

"I have a pea soup that some have said is quite good," Mrs. Wycoff ventured. "And I was thinking we could have oyster soup, and perhaps an almond soup. That would be a good variety. And for the scones—"

"Cheddar cheese and plain, I think," Mary said in a firm tone.

"Excellent," Octavia replied, sounding relieved. "The food is settled. I am so grateful to the two of you for working on it."

"It's the least we can do, since the two of you have opened this home to us," Mrs. Wycoff said.

Octavia gave him a triumphant *you are a kind person, see?* look before glancing back down at her paper. "On to the games themselves. We will offer card games, several varieties, though we will need dealers." She looked up. "Besides Mr. Fallon, who has already volunteered, do any of you feel comfortable being dealers? I can do it, certainly. But we will need—"

"I can," Old Joe said, surprising everyone in the room. They all turned to look at him, at which he promptly lowered his head. "I useta be the batman to a colonel in Her Majesty's Army. He had me organizing the supplies when he realized I was good with numbers."

"Wonderful!" Octavia exclaimed, meeting Gabriel's eyes, her own shining with pleasure.

"And I can do it, too, I am sure," Mrs. Jennings said. She turned to wink at Gabriel. "Do you recall when you were in my class, how we used to play old maid to see who would sweep the classroom floor at the end of the day?"

"And you were never the old maid," Gabriel replied, a grin on his face.

"Precisely," Mrs. Jennings said smugly. "I can always tell where the old maid is."

Octavia made a noise as though she was smothering a cough. "I don't know that we will be playing old maid at the Big Event, but I think your expertise with cards will come in handy."

"And," Mrs. Jennings said in a sly tone, "I can talk to the players as they play, which will keep them from telling where their old maids are. They'll be too distracted."

Octavia burst out laughing. "Oh, you are very clever, Mrs. Jennings. I will mark you down as a dealer, and I will fill in when necessary."

"Where are the guests going to stay?" Gabriel asked.

Octavia's face fell, and he immediately regretted asking the question. But in a few more seconds, her face lit up again. "Lady Montague lives close-ish to here, I believe. She is how I—"

she began, but stopped speaking when she saw Gabriel shaking his head no.

They couldn't know that she had just . . . arrived. Nobody except for Mrs. Jennings even truly knew that they'd said Octavia's lady's maid had gotten ill. And thankfully, Mrs. Jennings hadn't thought to ask where Octavia's carriage might be, if she had arrived on her own. Or where the coachman was.

Thank goodness Mrs. Jennings was just too excited for the news of their engagement to question anything about how Octavia had ended up in Greensett.

"Anyway," she continued hastily, "Lady Montague has a vast estate, and she would likely love to have some of our guests stay with her. The rest can stay with us—there are plenty of unused rooms."

"And there's the Packhams' inn," Mrs. Wycoff added. "They have some rooms, I believe."

Octavia made a note on her paper. "I'll write to Lady Montague directly. And perhaps one of you could speak to the Packhams?"

Mrs. Jennings raised her hand, and Octavia made another note. "And then we will have to clean the rest of the rooms."

Everyone groaned.

"I know," Octavia said, her voice sympathetic. "But the house will need to be clean when—"

"When we are married," Gabriel cut in.

Mrs. Jennings clapped her hands together. "It will be our wedding gift! Making certain

the house is ready for a young couple in love."
She turned to look at Gabriel, then at Octavia, a
pleased smile on her friendly face.

"Thank you," Octavia said hastily. She folded
the paper and slid it into her pocket. "We all
have our duties, then? And we have less than
two weeks to prepare." Then her expression fell
again. "Drat. I didn't think about what we'd wear.
We'll need to look our best, only—" Her words
faltered as she looked down at her worn gown.

Except for when she'd first arrived, she'd been
wearing a variety of increasingly old gowns, presumably so she could properly work in the house.

"I am handy with a needle and thread, miss,"
Mary replied.

Everyone looked warily at her, likely all of
them wondering if she was as handy with a
needle and thread as she was in the kitchen. At
least, all of them except Charlie, who appeared
to be enthusiastic about Mary's cooking.

"She is excellent," Mrs. Wycoff confirmed. "She
helps me with mending Charlie's clothing."

"Octavia, you have that ensemble you wore
when you—" Gabriel said, stopping short as he
realized he was about to give away the game, too.
Was there something in the air that was making
them so indiscreet?

Well, yes. Because they were far more indiscreet
together than they were being now about how
Octavia came to be in the household.

"Yes, you are correct," she replied quickly. "I

will try it on tomorrow, Mary, and you can see what you might do with it."

Mrs. Jennings and Mrs. Wycoff, it turned out, also had gowns they wanted altered, and then the conversation ebbed until Octavia clapped her hands together.

"I think we are finished," she said, looking relieved.

They all bade each other good night, with Gabriel the last to leave. He snapped his fingers for Nyx to join him, and the two of them walked up the stairs, Gabriel shooting a last, longing look at her bedroom, the door of which was closed. Mrs. Wycoff was at the other end of the hall, trying to get Charlie to bed. She met Gabriel's gaze over Charlie's head, an exasperated expression on her face.

It was a good thing, he told himself, that he had decided to be discreet. Because otherwise he would go to Octavia and demand entrance— to her room, to her body, and to her heart.

It was the last item that made him hurt the most, to think of how soon she'd be leaving.

Leaving him alone. Leaving him in this house they were gradually turning into a home.

Leaving.

Chapter Eighteen

Octavia smoothed the paper out when she'd returned to her bedroom. *My plan.* Which would not be possible to implement without the help and encouragement of all the people in the house. "And," she said, looking down at Cerberus, who lay at her feet, "not to mention a few dogs."

Cerberus raised his head and made a snuffling noise.

It didn't *have* to be just her out here on her own. In fact, with as many people currently residing here, it wasn't possible to be just her.

She hadn't meant to share her financial concerns with him, for example, but then Mr. Higgins and his threats had appeared, and she'd been forced to. And he hadn't judged her; instead, he'd agreed to help.

Even though she knew full well how he felt about her way of life.

That was true kindness, what he was going to do for her. What he *had* done for her, she thought with a smirk. Though of course, as she'd pointed out, the kindness had been reciprocal. He'd certainly seemed to enjoy it, at least.

For the first time, she wasn't in a complete rush to finish everything. To get her money and get out, as she'd planned when she'd first heard about her father's death. She'd miss these people when she left. Not just him, though he was the one she found herself caring the most about. And not just because of his kisses and the rest of it.

Would Mary ever make an edible pie? Would Mrs. Wycoff's face lose that haunted look? Would Old Joe find more of a purpose?

Would Gabriel eventually find a woman who suited his quiet lifestyle? Who would encourage his scholarly pursuits, not give him a puzzled look when he used a word she didn't know?

She already envied the unknown woman. Having that man in her care, and in her bed, would be wondrous. She knew that herself. He was a marvel: intelligent, passionate, considerate, and curious. He was willing to change his mind if given sufficient reason. He was tall, so he could reach high places. He was handsome, so he was pleasant to look at for long periods of time. He was gentle when he needed to be, fierce and powerful when he wanted to be.

She liked it when he was the latter, particularly when he was telling her what he was going to do to her. When he was slapping her arse in sexual play.

If only she could have that always. They had just begun their mutual benefits relationship; imagine how much more they could discover and explore if they had more time.

But she had less than two weeks. Hopefully she would make enough from the Big Event to pay Mr. Higgins, and perhaps she'd find proof she owned the house, which would add to her solvency. Her short-term problems would then be solved, leaving her with a lifelong problem: What was she to do for the rest of her life?

She had nothing against marriage, but she didn't long for it. She knew she would be too restless to be content being someone's wife, someone's mother, if that was all she was. She wanted to be a wife and mother eventually, but there had to be something more. Her sister, Ivy, was still involved with the club, albeit not in the day-to-day business. Her friends Lavinia and Ana Maria had both married dukes, but that didn't stop them from taking on projects that spoke to their souls.

She wanted the club to be successful. She wanted something she could point to with pride, knowing that she had done something of note.

But she would not get that opportunity if she didn't earn enough money to avoid getting her limbs broken, if she wasn't able to return to London soon to work on plans—now that she had more of an idea of how to plan—for when all the titled, wealthy people would return to London after their summer in the country.

THAT NIGHT, SHE settled into her usual place on the sofa in the living room, prepared to hear that evening's story.

Gabriel had a dangerous look in his eye, the one that brought her enormous amounts of pleasure. Mischievous, and charming, and almost— though he'd deny it—reckless. He had firmly told her she had no claim to the house—but was willing to help her search for items of value. He had agreed to her bargain, and had defended her when Mr. Higgins was a threat. He had turned over a valuable book to that gentleman as an inducement to leave.

And he was teaching her about the family you find, and how to help yourself improve through helping people.

"THIS IS ONE of the first stories I told," he began. "But I wanted to return to it. The story of Hades and Persephone."

"Huzzah!" Charlie cheered. Octavia smiled at him.

"Tonight, I will tell you a bit of the story, and then Miss Holton will assist." She gave him a surprised look.

His eyes crinkled in amusement as her expression changed, shifting from surprise to determination. *Spontaneity shows that your mind is agile, that you are able to juggle multiple ideas in your head, and that you are seldom surprised for long.*

"Hades fell in love with Persephone," he began, "as I told you before. But what about Persephone?"

He inclined his head. "That is where I want Miss Holton's assistance.

"Perhaps you could speak about how Persephone might have felt during all this?"

Octavia thought for a moment, then lifted her chin. "I have a better idea. Why don't I speak about how *Hades* might have felt about all of this?"

He gestured for her to rise, and she did, coming to stand beside him, then waiting as he sat where she had been.

Her eyes sparkled, and he found himself holding his breath as he waited for her to speak.

"Hades was the god of the Underworld, as Mr. Fallon has explained. But what does that mean exactly?" she said, looking at Charlie.

"He is in charge of the devils," the boy answered.

"Yes, true. But as Mr. Fallon has said, this is Greek mythology, which is very different from what we know of God here. Is that right, Mr. Fallon?" she asked.

Gabriel nodded. "Yes. Hades was the god of the Underworld, but everybody went to the Underworld, no matter how well-behaved or not you were when you were alive."

"So it is possible that Hades got to visit some of the nicer parts of the Underworld?" she asked, sounding like she was arguing a point of law in the Court of Chancery.

"It is," he admitted.

"And he could have taken Persephone there, especially if he wished to please her?"

"He could have."

She paced as she spoke. "Hades had a position among the gods. It was his job to see to all the people who came to the Underworld, and that was a great responsibility. He presumably liked where he lived, and he wanted someone to share it with him. But he knew that not many people would willingly go to the Underworld, especially if they weren't, er, headed there because of natural causes."

He smothered a chuckle, and she glared at him.

"And when he saw Persephone," she continued, waving her hand in the air, "she was doing something in one of her mother's fields, growing wheat or whatever."

He bit his lip to keep from laughing. *Doing something in one of her mother's fields.*

"She was so beautiful." Her voice was wistful. "And she stood there in the field and was part of nature, and growing things, and perhaps Hades longed to be a part of that growth."

His brows drew together in puzzlement. Why did she sound sad?

"Most importantly, he wanted to have someone with him no matter where he went. His job could take him to some dark places," she said. "Places with—with—"

"Places with more devils!" Charlie said with enthusiasm.

"Yes, and places for people who eat all the best sandwiches at tea and leave you the ones with the smelly fish," she replied, wrinkling her nose in an exaggerated expression of distaste. "It was Hades's job to do all of this, so he couldn't just stop. But he got lonely." She took a breath. "And isn't it nicer when you have someone with you?" she asked. She flicked a glance toward him, and he could have sworn he saw her smile for a moment. "And Hades didn't *want* to steal Persephone from her mother, but maybe he didn't know how to talk to a living person, what with dealing with his Underworlders so much."

"So you're saying the myth is really about miscommunication?" Gabriel said, his eyebrows raised. Mrs. Jennings chuckled as Mrs. Wycoff nodded in agreement.

She shrugged. "I don't know what I'm saying." She gave a rueful shake of her head. "Obviously."

"You're doing wonderfully, dear," Mrs. Jennings said in an encouraging tone of voice.

"Yes," Old Joe confirmed, making everyone turn to look at him. He seldom spoke.

She made a visible effort to rally, speaking brightly. "But I do know that things are not always what they seem, and it is important to find out why someone does what they do before deciding where in the Underworld they should go."

She accompanied her words with a firm nod, as though punctuating the thought. Not that he knew at all what she was saying—which he suspected was the case with her as well.

"Hades knew it was better to have company, even when he went to the very worst places. Being with someone else, someone he could trust and love, that made it all tolerable."

For a moment, Gabriel thought Octavia was going to cry. Her eyes got moist, and her chin trembled. He had never seen her so vulnerable before.

"So while it might be easy to blame Hades for stealing Persephone away from her mother, you have to wonder if she understood what he was going through. After all, she might have been in the best place in the world, but she only had her mother for company. Perhaps she was lonely, too." Her gaze met his. "The best place in the world, the worst place in the world, are all changed if there are people you care about there."

His breath caught.

What was she saying?

Was there a chance?

But no. She'd just talked about the best places and the worst places in the world, and he knew her best place was London. What's more, if she discovered what he'd done, how he'd chased after Mr. Higgins and promised to pay her debt if she couldn't—well, she would never forgive him. He knew that.

Better to have her in the best place in the world for now, and leave the rest of his life up to whatever spontaneity he might conjure up.

Chapter Nineteen

*S*even days now. Seven more days of all of this, and then—and then she'd be back in London.

Octavia shook the thoughts away, pushing her focus back onto her task. Unfortunately, she was polishing silver, which meant there was a lot of time for her mind to wander. And it kept wandering toward *him*.

The other night she'd talked about Hades and Persephone, and how lonely the god of the Underworld might have been, even though he had a whole kingdom to rule. Not to mention a dog, she thought, glancing down at Cerberus, who was resting at her feet.

"You'll be with me always, won't you?" she said in a low voice.

Cerberus did not respond.

Suddenly, she felt herself being pulled up out of her chair and hoisted over Gabriel's shoulder, his backside the only thing she could see.

"Gabriel!" Octavia exclaimed, whacking his arse as he walked up the stairs.

She hadn't even known he was there; of course, she'd been musing about Greek myths and their meanings while polishing silver. Perhaps she'd somehow learned how to conjure him.

He carried her easily, and she couldn't help but revel for a moment in his pure strength. Even though she was upside down, his arm banded around her legs, his other arm holding her still on his shoulder.

"What is it?" he said, sounding as though he was asking her to pass the salt at dinner.

"What are you doing with me?" she asked. She didn't want to insist he put her down, because she knew he would do as she said, and she was curious what he had in mind.

She hoped it was the nice thing he'd promised when he'd offered to help her with her planning. That promise hadn't been absent from her thoughts for too long, even as she spoke about Hades and Persephone, and love, and connection.

Perhaps more so, because of that.

And the promise would be nice for him as well.

A reciprocal bargain. An exchange of pleasure that would pass the time while she was here, and ensure that others believed their fake engagement was real. Not to mention teaching her things about her own body, as well as his.

"I am taking you to my bedroom," he replied.

"Gabriel!" she heard Mrs. Jennings exclaim. Octavia twisted her head to see the older woman on the upper landing, a shocked expression on her face.

"It's fine, Mrs. Jennings," she called.

"We're practicing for when I bring her over the threshold," Gabriel said.

Octavia glared at his arse.

Which did not deserve it. It was truly a remarkable specimen. Firm, and round, and delightfully and surprisingly muscled. She slapped it lightly, not enough to make a noise, but enough to make him notice.

He yelped, and his grip on her legs tightened.

"That is not how you are supposed to bring your bride inside," Mrs. Jennings said, her tone earnest. "You are supposed to carry her in your arms, not hoist her over your shoulder as though she is a bag of potatoes."

"Oh, of course," Gabriel said, easily swinging Octavia back down to the ground, then swooping her up so she was cradled against his chest. "Like this?"

Mrs. Jennings beamed. "Precisely."

"And here I thought you had nothing left to teach me," Gabriel said in a teasing voice. "But you continue to surprise me, Mrs. Jennings."

Mrs. Jennings leaned forward to pat Gabriel's arm. "I am glad you are open to learning new things."

"Oh, I am, Mrs. Jennings," he said, and Octavia heard the implied meaning in his words, even if Mrs. Jennings did not.

And felt her body shiver in anticipation.

Perhaps they would learn new things together. Perhaps she'd return to London a much more informed woman who could—

Who could what? Who could take a lover, now that she knew her own pleasure more intimately? Her own body?

But she didn't want that. She didn't want anybody else. She wanted *him*, with his whisky eyes, and his broad shoulders, and his delicious arse, and how thoughtful and kind he was, while also demanding she be the best possible version of herself she could manage.

Not to mention how his clever fingers and mouth could make her feel. And from what he'd said earlier that day, there was more to be explored. Namely, his tongue and her cunny. She wriggled just thinking about it, startling him.

But he didn't drop her. He'd never drop her. She knew that, as surely as she knew she seldom planned ahead for anything, that Cerberus was the best dog ever—no offense to Nyx—and that Mrs. Jennings was likely the nicest person she'd ever met.

"Well, I'll just let you get on with it," Mrs. Jennings said blithely. "I am on my way to the kitchen for a cup of tea."

"Shall we get on with it, then?" Octavia couldn't resist asking, looking up at his face. At his strong jaw, which had the shadow of the day's stubble. At his cheekbones, which defined his handsome face, a perfect underpinning for those beautiful eyes. At his mouth, which could say the loveliest things and do the wickedest.

He met her eyes, the heat in his gaze nearly undoing her.

"Hurry up," she murmured.

HE WALKED INTO his bedroom, somehow slamming the door behind him before tossing her onto his bed.

"There," he said, looking down at her, pinning her with his hungry stare. "That is what I want to see."

She raised herself up on her elbows as she lifted her chin. "What about what I want to see?"

"And what do you want to see, Octavia?" he breathed, planting his hands on the bed next to her, making it shake.

"You," she replied simply. "I want to see you."

Gabriel's breath caught at her words. At the moment. At the sight of her on his bed, her expression both wary and welcoming. Her body spread out on top of his coverlet like an offering.

That he would take.

If she would let him.

For the next week.

"You can see all of me, if you like," he replied. He straightened, quickly yanking his shirt out from his trousers and pulling it over his head, tossing it onto her face. She sputtered, and plucked it off, then raised the fabric to her nose and gave a delicate sniff. "Mmm," she said, meeting his gaze. "I like how you smell."

"How I smell?" Gabriel said, surprised.

She nodded. "You smell like grass and the pond and books."

"Because I walk in the grass, bathe in the pond— late at night when everybody is abed, mind you— and read books," he replied with a grin.

She rolled her eyes. "It's not as simple as that."

"Nothing ever is," he murmured.

She continued. "It's who you are, the person who would scythe grass and swim about in a pond and read musty books. And be excited about them!" As though it was the most outlandish concept she'd ever heard. She gestured toward him. "Stop distracting me, though, and give me what I want."

"And what is it you want?" Gabriel asked, wanting to hear her say the words.

"I want you to do what you promised," she replied. She didn't sound shy or embarrassed or any of the things Gabriel would have expected the usual woman to sound like. Because this was Octavia the Brave, who took what she wanted, and damn the consequences.

Likely because she didn't think of the consequences.

"Which is?" he prompted.

Instead of answering, she grabbed hold of the bottom of her gown and began to drag it up her body. Gabriel held his breath as it traveled shins, then knees, then thighs, until she'd pulled it up to her waist. And then she put her hand on herself and met his gaze. "I want you to kiss my cunny."

His cock throbbed in his trousers, which made him realize he was still wearing trousers. He removed them quickly, then shed his smallclothes, and went to the end of the bed, advancing toward her with a predatory speed.

Stopping when his mouth was at her knees. Kissing first one knee, then the other, as she made an encouraging noise in her throat. Her fingers were busy touching herself, and the scent of her arousal flooded his nostrils, made him hunger to taste for himself.

But he wanted to be patient. Not because that's what she wanted—in fact, if her noises were any indication, she wanted him to hurry the hell up—but because he wanted to savor every moment of this, now that he could see to the end. After the Big Event, when she'd either gotten enough money to pay her debt or she hadn't. Either way, she'd be headed back to London.

His thumbs were on her inner thighs, and he began to spread her legs wider, hitching forward on his elbows so he could reach her.

He glanced up to meet her gaze. Her eyes were dark, heavy with passion, and she was biting her lip as though impatient.

"You want me to kiss you?" he asked in a silky tone.

"You know I do," she replied, her voice strained.

"Right here?" he teased, blowing out a breath onto her nub. Her fingers were still on herself, and he reached up to twine his fingers with hers, moving them away. She made a noise of disappointment that changed to a gasp when he put his mouth where her fingers had been. Resting gently on that tiny nub for a moment before licking her, his thumb plucking where his mouth was.

She immediately began to thrash on the bed, and he leaned onto her leg to hold her still so he could taste her. He began to swipe her slowly, long licks that made her tremble.

Her legs were shaking.

He was subsumed in her scent, in the wantonness of her gown hiked up to her waist, in her cries of passion and frustration as he edged her closer to her peak.

He plunged a finger inside her, feeling her muscles grip him as she careened toward an orgasm. He increased the speed and pressure of his mouth on her, listening to her shifts in breath to gauge when to adjust.

And then—she screamed as she came, arching her body off the bed, her hands fisting his coverlet.

He reached down to touch his aching cock, pressed it against his bed in a fruitless attempt to assuage the roaring sexual hunger inside him.

Waiting as her climax peaked and then slowed, her breathing slowing, too.

And then he lifted his head and met her gaze. "Was that nice?" he asked, a smirk on his Octavia-drenched mouth.

She offered him a deep, satisfied smile, for once

not rolling her eyes or responding flippantly. "Very," she replied. Her fingers fluttered in the air, beckoning him. "And now let me take care of you."

He rose up on his elbows, then shifted higher on the bed so they lay side by side. His cock waved in the air, catching her eye, and she grinned as she saw it, her expression lighting up. How fortunate was he that she didn't feel ashamed or embarrassed about any of this?

But she wouldn't be Octavia if she was ashamed or embarrassed. Instead, she saw what she wanted, and she took it.

Just as she'd see what she didn't want and leave it.

Stop that, he chided himself. *This is now, and then is then, and there is nothing you can do to alter that.*

And then he wasn't able to think anything at all as she reached down and grasped his erection, twisting so she was on her side, facing him.

She leaned forward to kiss him, immediately sliding her tongue into his mouth as she began to slide her hand up and down, giving it a twist at the end that made him shudder.

He groaned low, deep in the back of his throat, his hand clutching her arm as her fingers held him. She continued her movement, a slow, steady, and intense motion that made him focus entirely there, on what she was doing, on her mouth actively engaged in kissing him.

Taking ownership of his pleasure.

He reached behind her to grasp her arse, that delicious round softness, rubbing his palm over her skin, then raising his hand for a moment and slapping her lightly on the cheek of her buttock.

She yelped, breaking the kiss, regarding him with eyes dark with passion. "Have I done something wrong that I should be punished?" she asked, her voice low and husky.

He shook his head slowly. "You're doing everything right. I thought you might enjoy that."

She dragged her lower lip between her teeth, nodding. "I do," she replied. "I like the mixture of pleasure and pain. Not that it hurts very much," she added. "But it feels so real. Not that that makes any sense," she said, shaking her head.

He wished he could ask her more about it, about all of it, but her hand was still continuing its delicious movement, her grip tightening, her speed increasing.

She seemed to know exactly what to do. Competent Octavia, absorbing things as quickly as they were shown to her.

As if she'd read his mind, she offered a wicked smile as she twisted her hand more forcefully at the top, making him groan.

"Like this?" she said, knowing full well that yes, indeed, like this.

"Mmf," Gabriel managed to get out before the climax began, before he was churning up that hill of ultimate pleasure, propelled by her hand and her wit, and intelligence and perseverance, and everything that made her her, and made him love her.

He groaned as he came, shuddering, collapsing

to the bed next to her, her hand slowing its rhythm and then stopping. But still holding him. And then she released him, turning to lie on her back again.

He lay there, breathing hard, never wanting to have to get up, wishing they could stay in that bed forever.

"I told you it would be nice for both of us," she said in a wry tone after a few minutes.

He laughed, muffled because his face was buried in his coverlet. How had he never even imagined he could have deliriously amazing sex in one moment, and then be laughing the next? When he'd thought about it at all—which he had not, not really—he'd assumed a satisfactory sexual relationship would be separate from laughter. That had been his experience in the past, at least.

But the past hadn't included Octavia.

Nor did his future.

OCTAVIA ALLOWED HERSELF to remain still for a few moments. On his bed, with him entirely unclothed beside her, the reality of his naked form far surpassing whatever she'd imagined after seeing him in that pond for the first time.

Her mind wandered as she stared at the ceiling— at the various marks and splotches indicating a leak, or a smoker, or just plain bad housekeeping. Similar to her own ceiling, albeit with a different configuration of marks and splotches.

She never thought, when she'd pushed those

rusting gates open, that she would be finding this. And more than this—a family, as she'd said to Gabriel that day.

And when she left, she'd just be . . . leaving?

But what was the alternative?

There was none. She needed to just enjoy every moment she had here, then return to London and never look back. Pay off her debt, and resume her life as it had been before. Before Gabriel, before their bargain, before the realization that you could open your heart to someone else and not always be hurt.

Before, when Ivy had been her only care and worry. When she hadn't given a thought to whether someone else's feelings would be hurt if she didn't like their food, or care if her reputation—such as it was—would suffer.

When she didn't care or believe that anyone besides Ivy might miss her when she was gone.

She didn't dare ask, though. Which was another enormous change—when was Octavia anything but daring? Bursting in when other, more reasonable people would demur?

But nothing had mattered as much before. Not even the club, where she thought she'd found a home.

She had, of sorts. But here, with him, and with them—this was a home.

A home she would not be living in, not after the Big Event.

She pushed that thought away and leaped off the bed, startling Gabriel, who jerked upright.

She shoved her skirts back down and tried to smooth her hair, which she knew must be a riotous mess.

"Since we're here," she said in an abrupt tone of voice, "we should look for my father's papers. You said we could."

She turned away before she could see how her words made him react. She didn't want to know if she'd hurt him. She definitely didn't want to know if she hadn't hurt him.

What if this was all mere nothingness to him? What if he saw it as just a bargain, a mutual exchange of pleasure, as she'd said before?

Not that she wanted him to profess his undying love or anything—there was no future in that—but she wanted to know she had affected him nearly as profoundly as he'd affected her.

But she also didn't want to know. Because then she'd have the Before Knowing time and the After Knowing time, and she didn't think her heart could take the After part.

She heard the rustle of clothing behind her, and took a deep breath. She could do this. She could protect her heart while still enjoying all of it. He'd never have to know this meant more to her than she'd admitted.

Because she didn't want to know if this meant more to him than—well, he'd never said much about it, had he? Just agreed to her bargain, and then given her moments of sheer, unadulterated pleasure, all without risking an unplanned consequence.

Ha! she thought. He was planning again, while she—she had stumbled into the whole thing like a drunken sailor, intoxicated by his appearance, and his mind, and how he made her feel.

But she'd known—if she'd thought about it at all, which she had not—that he would have everything well in hand, so to speak. She smirked as she looked down at her right hand, which still bore the evidence of what they'd just done. She withdrew a handkerchief from the pocket of her gown and wiped her fingers.

He understood what she hadn't said, what she hadn't thought to say.

The words were drifting by, how she felt about him, but she did not, she would not allow herself to admit them, even within the confines of her own head. Because if she did that, then every action after would be predicated on that truth, since it was not possible for her to know something and not to do anything about it.

She couldn't think on it. Because she was going to return to Before. She had no other choice.

Thank goodness she had a task ahead of her— searching for the will, the books, anything of value—or she'd be forced to confront her feelings.

Chapter Twenty

"The King of Corinth was a good king," Gabriel began. His usual audience was in attendance, some of them looking sleepier than usual—Mary and Mrs. Wycoff had collaborated on a truly delicious dinner, a beef stew that had wiped all memory of Mrs. Packham's monstrosity of the same name. Everyone had eaten more dinner, and the heaviness of the meal plus the warmth of the day combined for a multitude of yawns.

Gabriel hoped he could keep his audience from falling asleep. A small goal, but one he knew might be difficult—he himself was tired. After pleasuring Octavia, they'd spent a few hours searching through his bedroom, then back to the library. Still finding nothing, but having an enjoyable time doing it.

It was the kind of day he would eventually look back at and miss.

"Was he as good a king as our queen is a good queen?" Charlie asked.

Gabriel nodded. "Yes, though he faced different problems than Queen Victoria does. She doesn't have to find her citizens water, for example, which is what the King of Corinth had to do."

"Find water!" Mrs. Jennings exclaimed. "They didn't just have a stream? Or a nearby river?"

Gabriel shook his head. "Not for the purpose of this story, no."

He met Octavia's gaze, and the two shared a quick, conspiratorial smile. For no other reason, he surmised, than that they'd been naked with one another a few hours ago.

It was a good reason to smile.

"And he was trying to figure out a good source of water when he spotted the river god, Asopus, flying by."

"As often happens," Octavia remarked dryly.

"Of course," Gabriel replied matter-of-factly. "Asopus wanted to know if the King of Corinth had seen Zeus. You remember who Zeus was?" he asked Charlie.

"The king of the gods," Charlie replied in an enthusiastic voice. "He could do whatever he wanted."

"And he did," Octavia murmured. Gabriel shot her a sharp glance, and she stuck her tongue out at him.

"Well, the King of Corinth had just seen Zeus flying by with a river spirit in his arms. And Asopus asked the king if he knew where Zeus was, since Zeus had been with Asopus's daughter. The King of Corinth told Asopus he would tell him where Zeus went if Asopus would give his kingdom a source for fresh water."

"The King of Corinth likes to bargain, it seems," Octavia said, her tone deceptively mild. "I like a good bargain myself," she continued, laughter dancing in her eyes.

Gabriel shook his head in mock aggravation.

"And then what happened?" Charlie asked, sounding impatient.

"Then Asopus gave the King of Corinth a fresh water source, and the king told Asopus where he'd seen Zeus. And then—"

They were interrupted by the sound of the front door opening. Gabriel gave Octavia a questioning look, and she responded with a gesture indicating she didn't know.

"Octavia!" a voice called, before the door slammed closed.

Octavia's eyes widened, and she half rose from her chair, an expression of panicked surprise on her face.

"Octavia!" the voice said again. "I know you're here. There are candles, and the lawn has been cut recently."

Octavia glared at him, as though the cut grass was to blame for her being found out.

He rolled his eyes before gesturing toward the door. "Perhaps you should go see to—"

"To my sister, Ivy," she replied. "Coming!" she called.

She walked quickly out of the room, and the rest of the group rose, chatter bursting out as they wondered why Miss Holton's sister was here, and why Miss Holton hadn't known about her visit.

Gabriel raked a hand through his hair, hoping—selfishly—that this didn't mean their bargain was concluded even earlier than he'd thought it would be.

And then he walked out to the hallway, where Octavia and two other people stood.

"Ivy, Sebastian," Octavia said, gesturing toward Gabriel, "I would like you to meet Mr. Fallon."

A woman with dark brown eyes and hair stepped forward, holding her hand out. "Mr. Fallon!" she exclaimed. "You're the son of—"

Gabriel felt as though his chest was being constricted. He had managed not to think about his father for almost the entirety of his stay here, but now here he was being confronted with one of the most heinous gambles his father had ever undertaken—the literal wagering of someone's life. Their future.

"Yes, I am," he said, taking the other woman's hand in his and shaking it. He dropped it almost immediately after, turning to the gentleman.

"Mr. de Silva," the other man said, shaking Gabriel's hand. "I am Ivy's husband, and Octavia's brother-in-law." He shot a grin toward Octavia, who replied with a warm smile.

The heat of jealousy burned through Gabriel, even though he knew he was being ridiculous. Because she wasn't his to be jealous about, and the gentleman was married to her sister anyway.

But still. He was jealous.

"Can I fetch some tea, Miss Holton?" Mary said from behind them.

Octavia turned, relief flooding her expression. "Yes, please. Could you—would you mind bringing it to the library?"

"Of course," Mary said.

She bustled away toward the kitchen, and Octavia held her hand toward the library. "We can go in there."

Ivy nodded, her expression determined. Fierce. "I am eager to hear why you are living in our father's house, and how you've managed to hire servants. And for what purpose."

Octavia opened her mouth to reply, then shut it again, shaking her head.

The four of them walked into the library, Gabriel the last to enter, and he shut the door behind them as Octavia busied herself adjusting chairs and moving books.

When everyone was settled, Ivy folded her hands in her lap and addressed Octavia. "Would you be so kind, Octavia, to tell me just what is going on here?"

JUST WHAT IS going on here? For the first time in her life, Octavia was at a loss. Not just about what to say, but about what was going on here.

To begin from the beginning, she knew, would be difficult, what with Ivy interjecting every few seconds to exclaim at Octavia's foolish impulsiveness. And it would be hard to explain the later part, specifically the fake engagement bit, without letting Ivy know that Octavia had hopes of selling their father's house. Ivy would want to know why Octavia needed the money so badly, and why she hadn't followed the proper channels of writing to discover if there was a will, and if so, if she and Octavia were mentioned in it.

"I don't know," she said, after a long moment of silence.

"You don't know." Ivy's tone was so familiar in its disapproval.

"Your sister," Gabriel began, making Octavia's eyes snap to his face—what was he doing?—"is hosting an event here while we discuss who owns this property." He shot her a sly look. "Me, to be clear."

"Absolutely not," she shot back. No, she hadn't found proof yet, but that just meant finding proof would be closer at hand. Didn't it? It had to be. Otherwise—

"How did you come to own this house?" Ivy began, then sighed. "Never mind. I can guess. He lost it in a wager against your father."

"Got it in one," Octavia said. "Though I believe he won it back, because you know Gabr—that is, Mr. Fallon's father could never win against ours."

"Except that one time he *did* win, and I had to play against him myself," Ivy retorted.

"Using me as a stake," Octavia shot back. If she could just get Ivy to focus more on the past than on the present, she might not have to explain everything about why she was here. Why she'd stayed.

But Ivy was not so easily dissuaded. As Octavia should have predicted.

"That is not what we are discussing now," Ivy said in a haughty voice. "I want to know why you left London, leaving the club, leaving me, without a word for weeks. Until I received this letter," she said, waving it in the air, "that said vaguely that you were fine, and had no return address. Thankfully I ran into Lady Montague, who inquired if you had reached your destination." She glared at Octavia. "I managed to get your location from Lady Montague without her realizing I had no idea where you were. But," she continued, rising from her seat, still shaking the letter in anger, *"I had no idea where you were."*

Octavia stared at her sister, her heart racing as her mind ran frantically through any answer that would tamp down Ivy's fury.

Unlikely.

"She has been here this whole time," Gabriel said, his tone mild. "And suitably chaperoned, as Mrs. Jennings will attest." He put his hands behind his back as he spoke. "We met one another, and discovered we could not agree on the rightful owner of this house. But since we are both reasonable people—"

Which made Ivy snort as she glared at Octavia.

"—we decided to make a bargain."

Octavia felt her cheeks heat at his using that

language for their first agreement when she thought of their second agreement as a bargain far more often.

"We'd work together to get this house up to a state of proper cleanliness while searching for the proof your sister insists is here." He shrugged, as though what he was saying was a perfectly normal sequence of events. She admired his aplomb. "In the course of our work, we've found some treasures."

"Books," Octavia said flatly.

"Your father, it turns out," he continued, "owned some rare books, and I wanted you and your sister to have them. It has just taken us a while to unearth all the volumes. She has been kind enough to let me have them for a while. She recognized that we could help one another even if we were on opposing sides." He turned to give her a warm smile, and she felt herself marveling at his quick explanation. There had to be some spontaneity lurking within him, if he could come up with something that was so close to the truth and yet wasn't quite so quickly.

She found herself admiring him even more. In fact—

No, no, no. She couldn't. She wouldn't.

She nearly clamped her hands over her ears to drown out the words, but the words were inside her head, arriving at the worst possible moment.

She was in love with him.

She loved his patience, his intelligence, his wit,

his strength, and his kindness. She also loved his dog, his clever fingers, his wicked mouth, and that taut arse.

So much to love. So little future.

She needed to push that aside, because it hurt too much to think about. Never seeing him when she returned to London? Reclaimed her life there? Never feeling his breath on her skin, or seeing his playful smile as they teased one another?

Never, never, never.

She wouldn't survive this. But she had to.

"Octavia." Ivy's stern tone broke through her thoughts.

"What?" she snapped, then covered her mouth. "Oh. I'm sorry."

Just then, Mary and Mrs. Jennings entered the room, Mary carrying the tea tray and Mrs. Jennings trailing behind, holding a basket.

Mary set the tray down on Gabriel's desk, and Mrs. Jennings glanced around, avid curiosity writ large in her expression.

"Ivy, Sebastian, may I introduce Mary, the cook, and Mrs. Jennings, the—"

"The chaperone," Gabriel supplied easily.

"It is a pleasure to meet you," Mrs. Jennings said. "That is, I knew of you before, but we hadn't ever met. I've lived in Greensett my whole life, I saw your father frequently, and you a few times." She emphasized her words with several short, quick nods of her head as Ivy rose to walk to Mrs. Jennings, her hand outstretched.

"Thank you for taking care of my sister," she said in a warm tone. "And Mary, thank you as well. Octavia looks well taken care of, I assume your food is responsible for some of that."

Mary directed a slight smile toward Octavia. "It is not my food, I assure you," she said. "I can't cook worth a lick, but nobody here has told me that." She paused, her smile growing broader. "Everyone here is so kind."

Octavia was stunned into silence, trying to form words that would adequately respond to Mary's words.

"You don't need to deny it, Miss Holton, I know the truth," Mary said. "But Mrs. Wycoff is helping me, and I am improving. And I am handy with a needle, that much is true, so I'll be able to alter your gown for the Big Event."

"The Big Event?" Ivy echoed.

"That's what we're calling it," Gabriel explained. "It will occur here in less than a week. Miss Holton is inviting her most exclusive clients, the people who are rich as Croesus who won't miss losing a few hundred pounds."

"Is she." Ivy glared at Octavia, who pointedly ignored her.

Then realized she couldn't spend the rest of her life ignoring her sister, so she turned to meet Ivy's angry gaze.

"Mary, Miss Jennings, Mr. Fallon, and Sebastian," Octavia said, keeping her eyes locked with her sister's, "could you excuse us? Ivy and I would like to take tea together. Alone."

Sebastian opened his mouth to argue, but Ivy made a slight shooing gesture, and he left, followed by Gabriel, who gave Octavia an encouraging look as he shut the door behind them.

"Well, Octavia," Ivy said, putting her hands on her hips, "can you tell me what this is really about?"

GABRIEL EXHALED AS they left the room, relieved he didn't immediately hear yelling.

"You and Octavia seem to be on good terms," Mr. de Silva said. He looked like the kind of gentleman Gabriel's father usually took pleasure in fleecing—handsome, polished, and mannered. But if Octavia's sister was married to this man, it was unlikely that he was fleeceable.

"They're engaged!" Mrs. Jennings said, as Gabriel winced.

"Engaged?" Sebastian said, stopping to look at Gabriel.

Gabriel met the other man's eyes, his mind racing with what to say.

Thankfully, Mrs. Jennings was there to explain. Or perhaps not thankfully, since Gabriel really wished the whole thing needed no explanation.

"Engaged, years after they were supposed to be married because of that bet," Mrs. Jennings said in a dreamy tone of voice. "It's so romantic. Mr. Fallon was my student when he was younger." She let out a wistful sigh. "He was so intelligent, even when he was little. There was one time when I had to—"

"I want to hear about that, of course, but can we return to this engagement?" Sebastian said, his voice betraying a tinge of impatience.

"Well, Mr. Fallon will have to tell you about that. I wasn't there when he proposed. I did see them just after, when they came into town. Miss Holton didn't have a chaperone or anybody to help her, and so we came here."

"I see," Mr. de Silva said, looking as though he did not.

"And Mrs. Hall sent Mary, who is a terrible cook, though she is improving, as she said. And then Old Joe came, and I brought my daughter and my grandson. Together we're all working on the Big Event so Miss Holton can pay her debts."

Goddamn it. Gabriel should have known the household would have figured out why that moneylender and his henchmen had come. What's more, he should have figured out something to explain it all away long before this so Mrs. Jennings wouldn't have just—blurted it out.

"Pay her debts?" Mr. de Silva echoed, his gaze sharpening.

"Mr. de Silva," Gabriel began, speaking hastily, "I could use something to drink. Would you want to walk into town with me? It's just a mile or so."

Mr. de Silva looked narrowly at Gabriel, who braced for—for something. For the other man to take a swing at him, or demand to know what the hell was happening here, in front of Mrs. Jennings, who would share everything she heard, even if she didn't *mean* to ruin everything.

And the Big Event would be canceled, Mr. Higgins would come to claim the payment Gabriel had promised him, and Gabriel would be left alone for the rest of his life. Because even if she did care for him, once the truth came out, she would be livid.

And he knew she would be so stubborn she would refuse to compromise, because she'd already told him as much. She'd gone to a moneylender rather than turning to her own sister and her sister's husband. She even counted a duchess among her friends, and she hadn't gone to her. How would she possibly accept help from someone she had met a mere month before?

This whole situation, he realized, was happening because Octavia found herself so unable and unwilling to ask for help that she went to someone who would then have a hold over her rather than asking a friend or relative.

What kind of woman had he fallen in love with?

Well, he knew that already—a woman who was proud, stubborn, intelligent, determined, and spontaneous. A woman who would turn eagerly to lovemaking after being hoisted over a shoulder like a bag of potatoes, as Mrs. Jennings had said. A woman who was so unable or unwilling to make plans that it took the promise of a reward—a very satisfactory reward, as it turned out—to get her to put pen to paper.

So yes, he could see her refusing to ask anyone

she knew and cared for to help her. She was that stubborn.

The question was, was there any way to help her that wouldn't reveal what he'd done so there was a chance for them?

That he wanted to continue to help her, despite what he'd just realized, was the truth of it. He'd fallen in love with her, with *all* of her, and that included the parts that made bad decisions.

Because her bad decisions—such as arriving at her late father's house with no way to return home—had resulted in some very good outcomes. Because without her engaging in such risky behavior, they wouldn't currently be exploring their mutual bargain. Because if she hadn't made any number of bad decisions, he wouldn't have fallen in love with her, and wouldn't currently be anticipating having his heart broken when she left.

"Mr. Fallon?"

Mr. de Silva was using that impatient tone now directed at him—apparently he'd been lost in thought for too long.

"Yes, apologies. Town?"

Mr. de Silva gave a short nod. "Yes. I want to hear about this engagement and the debts my sister-in-law owes." It sounded as though Mr. de Silva wasn't surprised by any sort of Octavia news—she likely had been causing trouble for a lot longer than the past month or so.

Perhaps because he hadn't punched Gabriel in

the jaw at the end of their conversation, Gabriel could ask his advice for how to manage her. Though it didn't seem anyone was able to manage her, not even her sister.

"Come along, Nyx," he said, the little dog barreling down the hall, Cerberus following after. "You, too," he murmured at Cerberus.

He hoped Octavia was all right, though he knew she would be—she was a survivor, she would do what was necessary, as she'd proved many times over.

He just hoped she hadn't done irreparable damage to her relationship with her sister.

Chapter Twenty-One

"Where should I begin?" Octavia said, pacing around the room.

Ivy sat in the chair facing the desk—Gabriel's desk—a cup of tea in her hand.

The library wasn't a refuge from reality now—a place where she could feast her eyes on Gabriel's splendid form while looking for whatever inheritance her father might have left.

Now it was the place where she'd be judged, and found wanting.

The weather didn't seem to want to indulge Octavia's mood, however; the day was warm, and the doors that led to the outside, the one through which Cerberus had escaped that first day, were flung open, letting in a tiny bit of a breeze. It wasn't much, as relief from the heat went, but it was something.

"You should begin at the beginning," Ivy said dryly.

Octavia rolled her eyes. Of course she should. But did that mean she would?

"And in case you are thinking of trying to

obfuscate the truth, may I remind you I am your older sister, and I have known you your entire life? I know when you're lying."

"Good thing you said the last part, since I have no idea what *obfuscate* means," Octavia muttered. Ivy and Gabriel should get in a room together and practice their exceptional language skills.

Only perhaps not. She didn't want Gabriel in a room alone with anybody else, even her sister, who was happily married to Sebastian.

She wished she hadn't had her whole *I'm in love with him* revelation just now. It would make everything so much harder.

Though did she really? She wanted to revel in it, to shout it from the rooftops.

Or from the front lawn. She didn't really relish climbing up onto the roof. It would be dangerous, and it would also be possible for people to look up her skirts, which she didn't want.

Unless it was Gabriel, who she wanted to look up her skirts for the rest of her life.

"Octavia." Ivy's tone was sharp.

"Yes, of course," Octavia replied. She went and plopped herself down in the chair next to Ivy's, leaning forward to make herself a cup of tea. "I know you are going to be mad at me," she said.

"I'm already mad at you, so there's less to worry about," Ivy said, but at least her voice was a bit softer.

Octavia snorted in reply, then sat back in the chair, taking a sip of the tea.

"I'm not sure which is the worst part," she said,

darting a quick glance at Ivy. "Borrowing money without telling you, coming here without telling you, or entering into a fake engagement with Mr. Fallon."

Ivy blinked as her mouth opened and closed a few times.

Should Octavia be proud she'd stunned her sister into silence?

Likely not, and yet here she was. Proud.

"Begin at the beginning," Ivy said at last.

So Octavia did.

"And Mr. Fallon supported you when Mr. Higgins arrived to threaten you?"

Octavia nodded. She had shared all of it—or almost all of it—with Ivy. She'd left out the more salacious parts of the narrative. It wasn't that she was ashamed or embarrassed—Octavia never was either ashamed or embarrassed—but it wasn't her sister's business. It would all be over soon enough anyway. There was no point in going over it.

Her sister hadn't said much during the recitation, just murmured a few words of surprise as Octavia spoke, given her a few disapproving glares, but eventually her expression had softened.

"I don't understand," Ivy said, shaking her head. The two had finished off all the tea, and Octavia had discovered a dusty bottle of . . . something in the bottom drawer of the desk, which she was now drinking from a teacup. It was fruity, and sweet, and burned a little going down. Ivy had taken a sip, but had refused any more than that. "Why did you have to say you were engaged?"

Octavia shrugged as she took another sip of the liquor, whatever it was. "It wasn't my idea."

"But you went along with it," Ivy persisted. "I've never known you to go along with something if you didn't want to."

Octavia met her sister's gaze, giving her a rueful smile. "I'm fairly certain you could stop speaking after saying 'I've never known you to go along.'" She gazed out of the doors toward the pond, but what she saw wasn't water and summer grass, but him, rising out of the water like a Greek god. How appropriate, she thought with a chuckle.

"You don't. And I understand why you wouldn't come to any of us to ask for money, especially if you thought to make improvements to the club by yourself. But why wouldn't you come when the moneylender threatened you?"

Octavia shrugged again, staring down at her hands, which were clasping the teacup. Her thumb ran along its edge. "I suppose—" she began, then looked up at Ivy, taking a deep breath as she did. "I suppose I was wrong. I was stubborn, I thought I could handle it myself, and I didn't want you to think I'd messed up again."

Ivy placed her hand on Octavia's arm, giving it a gentle squeeze. "You did mess up," she said, her words at odds with her soft tone. "But things are not permanently damaged. We're here, and we can help you with whatever it is you've planned. It seems that there is more at stake now than just you paying off a debt."

Octavia nodded, feeling her eyes prickle with unshed tears. "These people who live here with Gabr—with Mr. Fallon, they care about us and each other. They're going to help, because helping means they help me, they help Mr. Fallon, and they help each other." She exhaled. "It is wondrous to see, truly."

Ivy gave her arm one last squeeze, then released it and leaned back, jerking her chin toward the bottle on the desk. "Have some more of that, and then we'll work on your Big Event."

Octavia laughed, reaching for the bottle and pouring herself a generous splash. She held her teacup up to Ivy, who clinked her own empty teacup against it. "This is to sisterhood and friendship, both of which I have with you." She hesitated, then said, "Thank you."

"You are welcome," Ivy replied, her brown eyes warm with emotion.

"ANOTHER," GABRIEL SAID, gesturing to Mrs. Packham. Her beef stew might be terrible, a blight upon nature, but the ale was fine. He would have gone to the tea shop he and Octavia had patronized before, but Gabriel didn't want to sit in the blazing sun in the garden. It would be far better to tuck into the Packhams' establishment, which had only a few windows and was usually dark, even in the daytime.

He and Mr. de Silva and the dogs had arrived in Greensett in the midafternoon, when the heat had peaked to an absolute boiling point and everyone looked wilted and tired.

Mr. de Silva, Gabriel noted, looked neither. If the other man hadn't talked so earnestly and besottedly about his wife, Octavia's sister, as they walked into town, Gabriel might have continued being jealous of the other man.

"It's cursed hot," Mr. de Silva remarked, pushing a strand of hair away from his forehead.

They sat at the bar, elbows up, manners be damned. Gabriel had rolled his shirtsleeves up halfway, and even that small change helped cool him a bit. And the ale helped, of course. The dogs were at their feet, lying on the cool floor.

Mrs. Packham set two more glasses in front of them, the condensation already sliding down. Gabriel picked his up and drank half of it in one long refreshing swallow.

Mr. de Silva picked up his glass, holding it aloft toward Gabriel. "To my sister-in-law, who is both the most aggravating and wonderful person I know. Her sister excepted, of course," he added with a wink.

Gabriel chuckled, raising his glass to tap it against Mr. de Silva's.

"So tell me," Mr. de Silva began, "when did you realize you'd fallen in love with her?"

Gabriel choked on his ale.

Mr. de Silva laughed, slapping Gabriel hard on the back. "It is obvious. At least, to anyone who's fallen in love with a Holton sister. Tell me about it."

Gabriel wiped his mouth with the back of his hand, taking a deep breath as he did. "I can, but I'm not sure if you'll want to drink more with me or knock me to the ground once I tell you," he said.

Mr. de Silva shrugged, giving Gabriel a jaunty smile. "Why not both?"

Gabriel snorted, picking up his glass and draining the rest of it. It was already going to his head—a combination of the heat, and dehydration, and the strength of the ale. It felt, he realized, similar to when he was with her, albeit with far less passion.

But it had that same loss of control, that spontaneity. The same freedom to just be who he was without worrying about judgment.

Not that he was judged, especially not since his father had died. But he often felt on display—the scholar whose father was a scoundrel, the man who'd gone to a school with wealthy aristocrats when he was neither.

And now the man who was engaged to the woman his father had tried to get for him seven years ago. It would be ironic if it were an actual engagement. If it were real.

"I'm waiting," Mr. de Silva said, his expression haughty, the effect of which he ruined immediately when he grinned. "Will I have to defend my sister-in-law's honor?"

Gabriel felt himself start to blush—blush!—as the other man began to howl in laughter.

This was not going at all as he'd expected.

"We're respectable." He leaned sideways, lowering his voice to a whisper. "We're engaged, after all."

Mr. de Silva snorted. "I heard that, and I don't believe you."

"Shh," Gabriel replied, glancing around. Nobody else sat at the bar, and there were only a few patrons scattered in the dining area, so it was unlikely anybody had heard.

"Why don't you believe me? I mean, you're correct, it's not true, but how did you know?"

Mr. de Silva shrugged as he set his glass back down. It was empty, and he gestured to Mrs. Packham, who raised her eyebrow, but brought two more. "Because if Octavia was truly engaged, she would be fighting against it more." He gave a pointed look at Gabriel. "She looks at you like she's dying of thirst and you're this ale here." He picked up the glass and took a sip. "Octavia is nothing if not contrary," he said.

Oh, but she is so much more, Gabriel thought. *Yes, she is contrary. But she is contrary for a reason— because she believes so profoundly in something that she will fight to the end to have it. She is passionate, and strong, and witty, and brave, and adventurous. She is beautiful, and clever, and—*

"You're lost," Mr. de Silva said, interrupting Gabriel's thoughts. "I can see it on your face. I am so sorry," he said with a cheeky expression. "Though I can sympathize. I feel the same way about her sister." He paused, his voice getting more serious. "Have you told her?"

Gabriel shook his head. "I've only just realized it myself," he replied. "If she knew, she would—"

"Bolt," Mr. de Silva supplied. "Octavia isn't accustomed to having many people care for her. It's been Ivy, and a few friends here and there." He nodded toward the ground. "And Cerberus, of course." He tilted his head in thought. "I don't think she's ever seriously contemplated marriage, or anything close to it, with anyone before." He shot another wink toward Gabriel. "Though there have been a few gentlemen who've tried."

Gabriel's throat immediately tightened at the thought of those other gentlemen.

"Oh, calm down," Mr. de Silva said. "She's here with you now, and from the way she looked at you, I'd say she hasn't thought about any of those gentlemen more than a few times." He spoke with laughter in his tone, and Gabriel tried to recognize the other man was poking him, but it was hard to unclench his jaw nonetheless.

"So, what is this thing you and she are collaborating on?" Mr. de Silva asked.

Gabriel struggled to turn his mind from the image of Octavia with anybody else to the relatively mild topic of the Big Event.

Except they were also collaborating—some might say mutually bargaining—on something else.

Mr. de Silva seemed to have already guessed that, but it didn't stop Gabriel from thinking about it.

Actually, nothing seemed able to keep Gabriel from thinking about it.

Which just meant he was, as Mr. de Silva had surmised, hopelessly and totally in love with her.

And with the moment of truth coming in just a few days, that meant she would be leaving. Either she would prove she owned the house and go off to find a buyer for it, or she wouldn't, and she'd have to rely on whatever she made from the Big Event to pay off what she owed. If she didn't make enough, then Mr. Higgins would own the house, since Gabriel had staked it against her debt. And then she would be furious.

But that wouldn't matter, would it, because they didn't plan to see one another after this interlude was over.

Which only pressed home the point further that he would not tell her how he felt—he couldn't bear to see the look on her face as she told him their arrangement wasn't supposed to last, she had a life and a business in London, and he wasn't a part of any of that.

Mr. de Silva nudged him in the side. Again. "Stop thinking about it," he said, sounding as though he knew precisely what was in Gabriel's mind. "It'll only make you do something rash."

Like storm into her room and offer her his heart?

Gabriel snorted at the image. Especially since he imagined determinedly blunt Octavia would have no patience for anything as mawkish as *offering his heart*. She'd prefer if he offered up a more useful piece of himself—his brain, so she could learn what he knew. His chest, since she seemed to admire it so much.

His cock.

That was something she might even accept, though he couldn't tell her why he was offering it.

Gabriel shook his head, trying to clear it of all his tangled thoughts. "We should get back," he said, standing as he spoke.

The room was pleasantly fuzzy now, the result of the ales and the surprisingly convivial—and not punching—company.

"My wife will be worried about me," Mr. de Silva said, getting up as well.

Gabriel looked at him, his eyebrows raised in an unspoken question.

Mr. de Silva snorted. "No, she won't be." He folded his arms over his chest. "I like to think that, but Ivy is no doubt too busy prying every bit of information out of Octavia to even spare me a thought."

Gabriel froze, while Mr. de Silva howled in laughter at his expression. "You have been taking advantage of the engagement ruse, haven't you? You don't need to tell me. I can see it on your face."

Gabriel took his new friend's arm, propelling him out the door. He hoped they could get home before Octavia told her sister *everything*.

Chapter Twenty-Two

"No more, please," Octavia said, holding her hand toward her sister.

They'd finished the mysterious liquor, and had gotten the idea to go up to the attic to look at the items Octavia had unearthed when she'd been searching for proof that might help her cause.

Back in the library when Octavia had mentioned finding some of her and Ivy's things from before, it had seemed like an excellent idea to venture up and see for themselves. They were getting along, somewhat, though Ivy kept biting her lip, Octavia noticed, likely to keep herself from lecturing Octavia.

But now that they were actually looking at the things—seeing the detritus of their lives here, before their father upended everything, it *hurt*. Octavia didn't want to remember that time before, when she believed a parent was supposed to care for you, not gamble you away. When she thought she'd stay in Greensett until she married, which she presumed would be when she was seventeen or eighteen.

She was three years older than that now in actual years, and about a decade older in experience.

She had never looked back, she realized. She had come to this house with the determination to sell it, to pretend it had never mattered to her, that her life before didn't matter to her.

But she was wrong.

"Do you remember this?" Ivy said, ignoring her sister's plea to stop. Ivy knew why Octavia was so reluctant. She was always trying to get Octavia to face her weaknesses, and Octavia made it one of her strengths, ironically enough, to refuse.

But it felt as though there was a reckoning coming. That Octavia would have to reconcile herself to what her life had been before and what it was to be in the future. What would it look like?

She couldn't just saunter through life as though her decisions didn't have a real, significant impact on people. That was proved wrong plenty of times before, but more profoundly now that Ivy and Sebastian had arrived, concerned about her. Not to mention her new . . . family, she supposed, the people who were willing to pitch in to help a relatively new acquaintance.

That kind of goodness made her feel as though there was hope in the world. She'd lost hope when she and Ivy had left here before—when she'd understood what their father had done. And that wasn't even the worst of it, which she'd learned years later—that Ivy herself had risked the wager, gambling that she would prevail in a bet against Gabriel's father.

Thank God she had won. But if she hadn't, the sisters would still have left, but would have had to go further than just London. Perhaps to Scotland, or the Americas. They would have used more of their money to get them somewhere safe, and Ivy would likely not have opened a gambling club. They would have had to find employment, though neither of them had the skills to be a governess, and they were too aristocratic in appearance and manners to be offered anything else—they would have been viewed with suspicion whatever they chose to do.

That Ivy had had the foresight and resolve to open her own club was something Octavia had taken for granted. Had she ever thanked her sister?

"Did I ever thank you?" she said abruptly, turning to Ivy, who sat cross-legged in front of a trunk filled with papers and toys.

Ivy looked up, a confused expression on her face. "Thank me for what?" She held her hand palm up. "If you mean to thank me for tracking you down here, it is the least I could do. I was frantic with worry, Octavia."

Octavia swallowed, her throat suddenly thick. "I know. I am so sorry I wasn't more forthcoming."

Ivy snorted. "Not forthcoming? If that's how you want to put it."

Octavia drew a deep breath. "I mean to thank you for coming here, but more than that, for taking care of us so many years ago. When Father was actively not taking care of us."

"Oh," Ivy said softly. "That."

"Yes, that," Octavia replied. She went to sit beside her sister, mimicking her cross-legged seat. She wrapped her arm around Ivy's shoulders and drew her in close. "You must have been terrified, but I never saw it. I just saw an adventure. I mean, I knew that Father had done something terrible with his gambling habits, but I didn't understand the extent of it until later. But you took care of us, you started Miss Ivy's, and you gave me a purpose."

She squeezed Ivy's shoulder as she leaned her head against her sister's. They sat there still for a moment, Octavia feeling an unfamiliar rush of emotion.

Though she'd have to revise that thought—her emotions had become familiar; chagrin at realizing she couldn't just sweep into her old house and find precisely what she was looking for, though what she found was far more than she could have expected.

She'd found him. She'd found him, and had fallen in love with him. And all she could do with that was sit with the knowledge, because she would never put him under more of an obligation than he was already. He was allowing her to turn this home into a gambling den, for goodness' sake! A pastime that he abhorred, that his father engaged in and therefore didn't engage with Gabriel.

He was too thoughtful not to respond as he believed he should, and if she told him she loved him, he would do something about that, even if it altered his plans for his own future. Which of course it would—what other response would he have except to ask her to marry him?

"Are you all right?" Ivy asked.

"Why?" Octavia said, sounding more like her usual self.

"Because your breathing changed, and then you sighed, and shook your head as though you're disappointed in something. I've never known you to sigh or be disappointed."

Octavia gave a rueful laugh, untangling herself from her sister. "I think I've changed since I've been here," she admitted.

Ivy tilted her head to look at her. "Changed how?"

Octavia took another deep breath, on the verge of telling Ivy everything, but drew back at the last moment. Yes, it might make Octavia feel better—for the moment—but having her sister know how she felt about him would make it worse. Or Ivy would encourage her to say something to him, and Octavia knew she couldn't— Ivy wouldn't understand what a fundamentally good person he was, that he wouldn't deny her if he thought it would hurt her.

She couldn't do that to him. So she shrugged, pulled Ivy in for another hug, and said, "I'm able to say thank you for something, and to admit I needed a plan. I think that is a fairly big change, don't you?"

Ivy laughed, as Octavia meant her to, and she pushed all those thoughts away, not daring to let them emerge lest they ruin his life.

She really had changed, hadn't she?

Now she just had to keep reminding herself that saying what she felt would be an irrevocable action she could never take back.

GABRIEL ONLY SAW Octavia in passing over the next few days. She and her sister threw themselves into the planning, Octavia proudly demonstrating her organizational work to Ivy, who looked suitably shocked.

Octavia and Ivy had walked to Greensett to mail off the invitations, sent to their patrons who were most likely to want to attend. Gabriel listened to them discussing it, and was gratified that they did not invite those whom the two deemed to have gambling problems—from what he gathered, they truly did watch out for their patrons, all of them, keenly aware that one bad night at the tables could mean disaster for a family.

He also listened as they talked about the patrons they particularly liked—Lady Montague, whom Octavia had asked to drop her here, and others, making it clear that their club was not just a business, but a community of sorts.

Of course the event Octavia planned to host

here was mostly business, but it was business engaged with reliable people.

All of his thoughts, however, were tinged by the awareness that each day was one day closer to her departure.

Until it was the day before. The house was as sparkling clean as it was going to get. Furniture had been unearthed from God knew where and placed at strategic intervals in the downstairs rooms. The kitchen had been in full use for days now, enticing aromas coming through the hallways both day and night.

It was the height of summer, and the day had been hot and still, no breeze to relieve the stifling heat. Gabriel lay in his bed, the sheets a mere suggestion on his lower legs, Nyx eschewing her normal place against his side in favor of a cooler spot.

It was too hot to sleep. Too hot to do anything except lie still and hope for blissful unconsciousness.

Gabriel's mind kept circling the same ideas—she would be leaving soon, he loved her, he couldn't tell her, but she was leaving, and he would never see her again.

Was this how Hades had felt when he'd found out his bride Persephone would be departing his hellish home? Hades likely felt as warm, that was for certain. Gabriel gave a rueful snort at the similarity in their situations. But Hades, at least, knew he would see his wife again, even if it wasn't for six months. Gabriel was unlikely ever to see Octavia again—once she returned to London, she would be there, and he would be here. He never went to the city, and it was clear how seldom she'd ventured into the country, unless by necessity.

Necessity being hiding away from a moneylender until she'd been able to get enough to pay him back.

Either way, she'd be done.

Gabriel pushed the sheets off his legs, getting up out of bed. Nyx made a snuffling noise, but didn't move.

He slid on his dressing gown, but didn't bother putting anything on underneath. It was close to two in the morning. Everyone else would be abed.

He walked carefully and quietly down to the library, opening the doors that led outside.

The water gleamed in the moonlight, as though it was beckoning him.

It would feel so good just to relieve some of the heat.

He draped the dressing gown over his desk chair, then strode outside in his bare feet. In his bare everything.

And walked into the water, the cool shock a welcome relief.

He slid under the water, immersing himself in it, then rose up, flinging his hair away from his face.

"Too hot to sleep?"

Her voice came from behind him, and he

snapped around, his eyes greedily drinking her in. She wore a dressing gown, but her feet were bare, the fabric of the gown swirling around her legs.

As he watched, she shrugged her shoulders, letting the dressing gown fall off her body, leaving her gloriously and totally naked.

She grinned at his expression, then began to walk into the water.

"You didn't think you were the only one to have this idea, did you?" she asked. "It's so hot, and I'm already nervous about tomorrow."

He snorted. "You? Nervous?"

She splashed him in reply.

"I do have concerns," she said, coming to his side. She'd wrapped her hair up in a loose twist, and a few strands dangled on her shoulders. Her skin gleamed, her nipples dark in the dim light. "What if the pasties are inedible? What if Lady Montague wins for once? What if nobody comes?"

"You know well enough that things will turn out all right." He jerked his chin toward the house. "Your sister will ensure you are fine."

Her expression grew mulish. "I don't want to have to rely on Ivy to rescue me. She did that when she took me away from here. She shouldn't have to keep doing it so many years later."

He stepped toward her, wrapping his arm around her waist. "It is just because she cares for you," he said, lowering his mouth to kiss her shoulder.

She glanced up at him. "I know. I should be grateful, and I am. I just wish I could have done all of this by myself."

"You can depend on other people, you know," he pointed out dryly.

"I can, but I don't wish to," she shot back.

She shook her head. "Though that's not true anymore," she said in a much milder tone. "I am not the same person who arrived here a month ago." She took a deep breath as she sank lower into the water, forcing him to let go of her.

As if he wasn't already aware he'd have to do that soon enough.

"I've always had Ivy, but I never had family like you do."

"Like I do?" he said, puzzled.

She tilted her head back toward the house. "Everyone there. They are your family. They care about you."

"They care about you, too," he replied.

She nodded. "They do," she said quietly.

Some of her hair had fallen loose and floated in the water. She looked like a mermaid, or a ghost. Nothing stirred around them, and for a moment, it felt as though they were in a dream, that he'd conjured her because of the heat and the night and the stillness.

Until she grabbed his arm and yanked him down into the water, accompanied by her gleeful giggle.

"Octavia!" he said, remembering at the last minute to keep his voice low. He definitely did not want anyone from the house coming to investigate the noise.

"Gabriel!" she said, imitating his tone.

She leaped up, then sank below the water, popping up again within seconds, still smiling. "It is so blasted hot, but this is wonderful." She went onto her back and floated, her hands making little swimming motions alongside her body.

He watched her in the moonlight, her gleaming pale body, how comfortable she looked to be.

He marveled at how she was able to adjust to nearly any situation, or at least make it appear that she'd adjusted. Be the fiancée he claimed she was, or launch into a story when called upon, or learn how to care for others.

"What is it?" she said. Her eyes were closed as she floated on the water.

"What is what?" he asked.

"I can hear you thinking. You should stop that. It's not healthy to think all the time."

He snorted, then propelled himself toward her, scooping her up in his arms and tossing her back into the water, jumping after her as she splashed down.

She emerged from the water, sputtering as she grinned at him. "See? That is what I meant," she said, smacking her hands on the water to create a splash.

He pushed all his thoughts away, staying here, with her, now. Enjoying how the water felt, how she looked magical in the moonlight, how comfortingly bizarre this interlude was.

Tomorrow would come, as it always did, and he could return to his usual mode of thinking.

But right now, he was here with her, and that was enough.

He reached for her, drawing her into his arms for a quick kiss.

She responded with alacrity, wrapping her arms around his neck and pressing her body against his. The warmth of her skin contrasted with the coolness of the water, with the heat of her mouth against his.

"Perfect," he murmured as he kissed her.

"Yes," she agreed.

AND THEN IT was the morning of the Big Event. He and Octavia had snuck back to their respective rooms a few hours earlier, sharing one last kiss in the hallway.

He'd gone to sleep at last, not thinking about anything beyond how refreshing the water was, deliberately avoiding anything that might keep sleep away. It helped that they'd kissed; he felt as though a part of him was complete, because they'd shared that simple moment in the water. It wouldn't be enough to last the rest of his life, but he could deal with that later.

Chapter Twenty-Three

"Lady Montague sent word that—" Ivy prompted, as she, Octavia, and Sebastian walked out of the house.

They'd spent the morning putting the finishing touches on the house. There wasn't much they could do with the worn furniture, but they'd unearthed some forgotten rugs in the cellar and placed them throughout the house, making sure to put chairs and a table atop each one.

The result looked just as Octavia had pictured it when she'd first thought of it—warm, cozy, familial. As though the gambling was merely another activity in a delightful house party. As though the money the players lost was nothing more than would be gone during a friendly evening of cards.

She hoped for much more, of course. But she wanted to give the appearance that it was nothing. She wouldn't allow any players to wager beyond their means, but beyond their wants? Certainly.

"Oh yes," she said, realizing Ivy and Sebastian

were waiting for a reply. "Lady Montague sent word that not only is she coming today, but she is bringing a variety of cousins. It seems all the older ladies of the family spend their summers together in Lady Montague's country house, and it sounds as though they are in search of diversion beyond knitting and gossiping."

"Excellent!" Ivy said, clapping her hands. "Did she say when they would arrive?"

Octavia nodded. "She and her cousins are taking three coaches, and they said they would be in Greensett in the afternoon. It seems that Lady Montague is the ringleader among her cousins, and she has been distraught at not having enough to entertain them all properly." She grinned as she finished speaking.

"And here you are with your gambling lures!" Ivy said admiringly.

At least her sister wasn't furious with her about the debt—at least not at the moment. Soon enough, Octavia knew, she'd be given a lecture about responsibility, and planning, and asking others for help. The usual type of thing she heard from Ivy.

But this time, perhaps she'd actually listen.

Because she'd realized that the way she'd always done things was not the way things should always be done.

"Mr. Fallon—how is he going to explain the broken engagement when you leave?" Ivy continued.

Octavia took a deep breath as her heart started

to race. Leave. She would be leaving. Not just Greensett, not just the house, not just the people she'd come to—to care for, but she'd be leaving him.

"We haven't discussed it," she said in a bright tone that she hoped would close the question.

"But you have to," Ivy replied, undeterred by Octavia's determined tone of voice. "He'll be left here when we go back to London. We're leaving soon. We'll stay long enough to clear anything up after this evening, but we can't stay away from the dogs for so long." She offered a warm look toward her husband. "And we miss our home as well."

The love they shared was so palpable it made Octavia's heart hurt. It was like the love she bore for Gabriel, only she was going to leave him to return to the life she'd made.

What if she was to tell him how she felt? She'd considered it before, then tossed the idea away. He was too wonderful, too much the man she'd fallen in love with, for her to tell him.

Ironic, if it also wasn't lacerating her heart.

He'd do . . . something to placate her, to compromise his future because of what she'd said. He'd never get the chance to make his own decisions about his life because she would have forced something on him.

Ironic again that they would already be married, would already have been together for years now, if neither of them had a choice about their futures. If the gamble his father and her sister had risked had turned out differently. Just a different shake of the dice, or a play of the cards. She wouldn't have gone to London, wouldn't have tasted the freedom of being her own woman. Wouldn't have discovered how satisfying it was to run her own business.

She'd be here, with him, likely with a few children by now. Children who sat at their father's knee as he told them sanitized stories of Greek gods and goddesses whose desires often overcame their common sense.

"We agree on that, then," she muttered.

"What?" Sebastian asked.

"Uh—nothing," Octavia said, shaking her head firmly. "I wasn't saying anything."

Because I can't say anything. Because if I say something, I'll ruin his life.

"I NEED TO make certain everything is in order, and I need to change, and I need—"

"We're all helping you, Octavia. You don't have to handle it all yourself," Gabriel said, laughter in his voice. But reassurance, too, and she forced herself to relax, knowing what he'd said was true. They were helping her. She could not have done all of this completely by herself.

And she would lean on them until it was time for her to leave.

A day from now.

And then she'd be on her own again. Completely in charge.

Why didn't that sound as appealing as staying here and letting other people help her out?

She truly had changed.

But she was still going back to London.

GABRIEL RUMMAGED THROUGH his clothing, hoping to find something that wasn't completely worn and ragged. He had forgotten that if he was going to see strangers that he would be . . . seeing strangers, and they likely wouldn't trust him if he wore what he usually did: trousers softened by age, shirts that he'd outgrown but wore with the sleeves rolled up, and jackets that—well, he only had one jacket. So that would have to do.

He found a less-worn pair of trousers that he'd stuffed in a drawer and forgotten about, then drew a shirt from a different drawer, peering closely at it.

It was worn in the elbows, but could pass muster—if his jacket wasn't in far worse shape.

He let out a breath, shaking his head as he drew his shirt off. He wished he had thought about it before—wished he had *planned*, as he'd demanded Octavia did.

The irony did not escape him.

He was just finishing putting on his boots when he heard a soft knock at the door. He strode over to it and opened it wide, only to be struck dumb.

She stood in the doorway.

She wore a gown—the gown she'd arrived in—but it had been altered and draped and changed so much he would not have recognized it if not for its distinctive color, and its clear quality, quite different from what she'd been wearing since her second day.

Before it had been an elegant, if entirely impractical, traveling costume.

Now it was a gown fit for a queen.

Instead of the voluminous sleeves it had before, it had tiny puffs of fabric right at her shoulders, leaving her arms bare. The cavalcade of buttons had been replaced with a similar line of colorless gems, glinting in the early evening light. The neckline—which had gone up to her throat before—had been lowered. And lowered more, revealing the creamy swell of her breasts.

The huge skirts remained, but an additional layer of fabric had been put on top, a sheer gauzy thing that sparkled with gems even smaller than the ones on top.

Her hair was pulled back and coiled into a complicated mass on her head, while she wore simple sparkling earrings with the same colorless gems. She wore white evening gloves, a bracelet of light blue stones circling her wrist.

Nothing at her neck; nothing to distract from the beauty of her revealed skin, the delicate collarbones, the gentle rise and fall of her breasts.

"Octavia," he said in a ragged voice.

"You think I look good?" she said, turning in a circle before him, holding her skirts out wide. "It turns out that although Mary lacks much in the culinary arts, her dressmaking arts are incredible." She cocked a brow. "It does seem odd that

Mrs. Wycoff was the good cook in the house and Mary is the seamstress. But I am grateful both have found their respective callings. Mary truly did a wonderful job." She gave him an apprehensive look. "But you do think I look good, don't you? You haven't said."

Because you've been talking all this time.

He lowered his gaze, noting all the new elements, then raising his eyes slowly until he met hers. "You look good enough to eat," he said in a growl. He stepped toward her, but she held her hand up. It trembled slightly.

"You can't," she said. "Not now. But—" Then she bit her lip, glancing away to the corner of his room. "Later, I wanted to ask if I could come to you. If I could—"

"You can come," he replied, emphasizing the innuendo of his words. "Gladly."

Thank God, he thought. She still wanted him. He would get to taste her again, at least one more time. More than once if he had his way.

She exhaled, as though she hadn't been certain of his reply. How could she not know?

But if she knew, she would have to tell him no. She would have to remind him how different they were, how little he belonged in her world, and how she could not belong in his.

So it was just as well she was uncertain. He didn't want her to have to suffer the pain he was going through. He wanted her to return to London without feeling as though she'd left something—someone—behind she would have to worry about.

Not that he could see her worrying about anybody for long—she'd just solve the problem and move on to the next.

He didn't want that either.

"But you can come with me now," she said, her lips curling into a wicked smile.

"Don't you have to be downstairs?" he asked, though the thought of her in that gown, on his bed, right now was intoxicating.

She rolled her eyes. "Come with me to one of the spare bedrooms. I've found something I think you could use."

"Oh." When had he become someone who heard sexual suggestions in seemingly innocuous words?

Oh yes. When he'd met her. When he'd had her in his bed, splayed out for his pleasure. For hers as well.

He felt his cock begin to harden in his trousers, and he forced himself to take a few relaxing breaths. It would not be at all comfortable to work as a dealer all evening with a cockstand.

She extended her hand to him, and he took it, feeling the soft fabric of her gloves rather than what he'd like to feel—her softer skin.

They walked across and down the hall to one of the smaller bedrooms, and she twisted the doorknob to reveal a bare bed, a wardrobe, and a washstand set atop a table. She moved swiftly through the room, her skirts making a rustling noise as she walked. She opened the wardrobe, revealing a row of garments.

She took one out, turning toward him as she held it up.

It was a gentleman's jacket, an evening jacket, if he wasn't mistaken. It appeared to be far finer than anything he'd ever worn himself.

She thrust it toward him. "Try it on. I think it will fit you. It's got very broad shoulders." Her eyes held a look of appreciation, and he tried not to preen.

He took the jacket from her, slipping it off its hanger, which he tossed onto the bare mattress. Up close, he could see a few holes where intrepid moths had feasted, but not many people would be near enough to see them.

The jacket fit perfectly, even accommodating his shoulders, and he adjusted the fabric, flicking a few bits of dust from the lapels and smoothing the tails down.

"Where did this come from?" he asked, lifting his gaze to her.

She shrugged. "I was searching for table linens, and I found this instead. I figured you might not have something appropriate for tonight, and I thought it would fit. I see I estimated correctly."

He nodded. "You did. You must have made a thorough study of my body."

She waggled her eyebrows. "Not enough study, I promise you that," she said.

He chuckled, then extended his hand to her.

"We should go downstairs to greet your guests. I hope you fleece them for all that they're worth."

"Mr. Fallon!" she exclaimed in mock horror. "Don't tell me you are encouraging this kind of behavior!"

He grimaced, and her expression fell.

"I've gone too far," she said in a quiet voice. "I apologize. I know you are only doing this for me. Because then I will be gone from here."

"That's not—" he began.

"Did we just hear Miss Octavia Holton apologize?" a voice said from the doorway.

Gabriel and Octavia turned to see Octavia's sister and Mr. de Silva standing there, both dressed in evening wear.

Mrs. de Silva wore a dark red gown with ruffles at the hem, an alluring color with her dark hair and lush curves. Her husband, handsome no matter what, looked positively godlike in his evening attire.

"The guests are arriving, Octavia," Mrs. de Silva said. "I think you might want to greet them, don't you? This is your evening, after all."

Octavia gave a hasty nod, then dashed past Gabriel, touching his arm briefly as she went by. "I was just finding Mr. Fallon a proper jacket. Doesn't he look splendid?"

The other two both assessed him, Mr. de Silva with a knowing twist of his lips.

Gabriel shifted under the scrutiny, feeling awkward.

"You look more than splendid, Mr. Fallon,"

Mrs. de Silva said at last. "I believe you should deal at Lady Montague's table. She will be happy to lose all her coin."

"And all her cousins' coin, too," Octavia added. She gave a frantic wave. "Come downstairs. There's no time to waste. The Big Event is about to begin!"

Chapter Twenty-Four

$\mathcal{M}$r. Fallon," Lady Montague said, "can you please blow on my cards? For luck?"

She gave him a coy look, but was so earnestly and honestly appreciative, he couldn't be uncomfortable.

She had arrived with her cousins in tow, each of a certain age, ranging from clearly very wealthy—Lady Montague being the most opulent one—to ladies' companion poor. All the ladies, however, shared a giddy glee on entering the house, looking around avidly at all the furnishings, the food, and the staff. There was a cacophony of giggling as they assessed the variety of games provided for their pleasure.

Old Joe had found himself an evening jacket of sorts—clearly at least fifty years old, its cut was from Gabriel's parents' time, but Old Joe wore it with pride. He had wrapped a cloth around his neck to serve as a cravat, and his trousers clung to his thin legs, a slimmer silhouette than was in fashion now.

He beamed from his table, handling the cards

with dexterous ease. More than half of the chairs in front of him were full, and the people there looked as though they were enjoying themselves.

Gabriel's table had been full right away, a combination of Octavia pointing him out to Lady Montague and the latter lady insisting several of her cousins accompany her, more than the table could accommodate.

They were in the dining room. They had cleared the big dining table and brought in small tables and chairs, creating pockets of gambling intimacy.

In addition to piquet, which Gabriel's table was playing, there were tables dedicated to faro, baccarat, vingt-et-un, and hazard. There was even a whist table for the older people who preferred a more stately historic game. The stakes at the whist table were accordingly low. It wouldn't be where Octavia made much money, but it was a satisfactory way to keep her customers placated if they'd lost too much at the main tables.

Thus far, only a few of Greensett's most prosperous citizens had taken part, but Gabriel suspected some of Lady Montague's cousins would end up there by the end of the evening.

Octavia herself was in charge of everything, and seemed to be everywhere—flitting from table to table checking on her guests, summoning more food from the kitchen when the tables were half-empty, settling accounts and making change, and ensuring her guests were both well-fed and well-hydrated.

Gabriel watched her with a mixture of awe and horror, the latter because she was so good at what she did, it wouldn't be surprising to hear fortunes had been lost under her roof. But he had her assurance that wasn't the case, though to see her work was a thing of beauty.

The candlelight caught the dark red of her hair, the ivory glow of her skin, and her dancing dark eyes. She looked like a goddess come to earth to tease mere mortals with her presence.

But she was no tease. Gabriel knew that. What she offered, she gave.

It was difficult—some punster might say *hard*— to concentrate on his tasks now when he had the promise of her in the future.

"Mr. Fallon?" Lady Montague said, now sounding concerned.

Wonderful. He'd been thinking so much about later he was forgetting about now, shirking his responsibilities.

Before this summer, he was the most responsible man alive. Reliable, conscientious, scholarly. Now he was interested in her story much more than history, and was regaling children and old people with sanitized stories of gods and goddesses.

There were worse ways to change, he supposed.

And it seemed he'd found a family, too.

What would happen to all of them when it was over? If she didn't get enough money, or if she found proof at last, this house would not become the home he kept envisioning.

He wanted this family to stay and grow with one another—to allow Mrs. Jennings to manage everything and everybody. To nurture Mary's skill with a needle and Mrs. Wycoff's skill with a spoon. To give Old Joe more work, perhaps some accounts to balance, to make him an essential member of the household. To give Charlie more time with Pegasus, perhaps seeing if his childhood adoration of horses was something that could become a job when he was old enough.

But meanwhile, Lady Montague and the Montague cousins were waiting.

"Does everyone have their bets in?" he asked as he shuffled the deck. He'd watched as Lady Montague converted more and more of her pound notes into chips, and he wondered if just her losses would cover Octavia's debt.

He dealt the cards, waiting as the ladies considered their bets.

"It looks as though you are doing well," Mr. de Silva said in a quiet voice. He held an empty tray, as though he'd delivered something and was now on his way back. "I think Octavia is actually going to pull this off."

Gabriel felt himself bristle at the idea that she wouldn't, then immediately wanted to box his own ears.

"A good thing, since I can tell you we have little to spare," Mr. de Silva continued. "We can always borrow, but I know Octavia would hate that."

"Yes, I would imagine so," Gabriel replied. He already knew how much she'd hate it if the only recourse was for him to give Mr. Higgins the house.

The ladies were settled with their bets, and he dealt some more cards, waiting as they assessed their play.

"We'll be leaving tomorrow," Mr. de Silva said, his tone somber as though he knew what his words would do to Gabriel. "You might want to say—"

"Thank you," Gabriel said, cutting him off. He couldn't say anything to her. Not without obliging her to explicitly break his heart. Better for them to part as . . . as people who'd shared a summer with no expectations. Better for her not to know how thinking about losing her made his chest ache.

"It's your choice, you know," Mr. de Silva said quietly.

Gabriel forced his attention back to the cards, quickly raking in the chips that belonged to the house.

"Thank you," he said again, his tone one of clear dismissal.

Mr. de Silva hesitated, as though he was about to say something more, but then shook his head, walking toward the door to the kitchen.

Gabriel focused on his work, pushing all thoughts of her and what she wanted later aside. He would do his best to make this evening work for her, not mess it up because he was distractedly in love with her.

That would be his final gift to her.

OCTAVIA COLLAPSED INTO one of the chairs in front of the whist table. The whist players had left earlier than the other gamblers, and she'd been using it as a place to set things that needed to go somewhere but she didn't have time to take care of them.

Glasses, plates, and a few worn packs of cards were strewn across the tabletop.

She leaned back, closing her eyes and taking a few deep breaths.

She'd done it. She hadn't done the final count—Old Joe was currently toting all the cash—but she could estimate that she had enough to pay Mr. Higgins and perhaps make some of the improvements she'd wanted to make before. Not all of them—she could admit she had been far too ambitious—but enough to make a difference.

"There you are," her sister said. Octavia opened her eyes, seeing Ivy and Sebastian standing in front of her.

"I've been here," Octavia said in a grumpy voice. "Where have you b— Never mind," she said hastily. She'd asked the question one too many times, and Ivy had threatened to tell her, in exhaustive detail, just where they had been and what they had been doing. She did not want to know about her sister and her friend like that.

Sebastian chuckled at her response.

"I just wanted to tell you Mr. Joe finished his counting, and Sebastian and I have taken the cash for safekeeping."

Octavia frowned as Ivy held up her hand.

"Because I want to be certain you can sleep well tonight. You've worked so hard, and having all that money—even if you do have Cerberus— would likely make you nervous. So I've taken care of that."

"Of course you have," Octavia muttered, but she was secretly grateful. She didn't want to just leave the money in her room while she indulged her pleasure with Gabriel. Neither did she want to wander the halls carrying a trove of cash, especially since she was on her way to a forbidden tryst.

"We've arranged for a carriage to take us back to London tomorrow," Ivy continued. "You, me, Sebastian, and of course Cerberus."

"So soon." Octavia couldn't help the note of dismay in her voice.

Ivy nodded firmly. "Yes, the club has been without its leader for too long, sister." She put a hand on Octavia's shoulder. "You are its leader now," she said in a softer voice.

It had been understood, of course. But Ivy had never said it explicitly, even though Octavia had behaved as if she had.

Until now.

"Is this because I planned tonight?" Octavia blurted.

Ivy laughed, squeezing Octavia's shoulder. "No. Though it does make me more confident it's the right course. You'll have to take care of things by yourself in a few months," she added, putting her hand to her belly.

Octavia's eyes widened. Then she leaped up to embrace her sister, grabbing Sebastian by the shoulder to pull him in.

"I'm going to be an aunt!" she exclaimed, her eyes welling up with tears.

"And a very successful businesswoman," Ivy said, drawing back from Octavia's embrace.

Octavia waved her hand. "I'm already that."

Ivy just rolled her eyes.

"But I don't want her away from London for too long," Sebastian explained. "It was important we come see if we could help, but now we have to go back. There are so many things to do. To plan," he added, a twinkle in his eye.

Octavia nudged him on the shoulder. "I can plan," she said defensively.

He held his hands up in surrender. "I know, I know." He jerked his chin toward Ivy. "She is proud of you, even though she was furious you borrowed money."

Ivy wrapped her arms around Octavia. "I can be proud of you and be furious," she murmured.

Octavia patted Ivy's arm. It was unfamiliar to be on the receiving end of Ivy's approval. Ivy wasn't harsh in her judgment or anything, but she did have an older sister's tendency to worry and to lecture.

But perhaps, Octavia could admit, all that concern had borne fruit. Octavia was better than she was before, and she knew she had survived because of Ivy.

If Ivy hadn't intervened, it is likely that Gabriel's father would have eventually gambled for Octavia as his son's bride and won. Their father was not nearly as skilled in games of chance as Ivy was.

And she'd be married to Gabriel.

She gave a rueful snort.

"I need to take Ivy upstairs," Sebastian said. "She needs all the rest she can get."

"And more," Ivy added in a sleepy voice. "We'll see you in the morning."

"See you," Octavia replied. She watched them walk up the stairs to their room, realizing she was alone now.

The table had been cleared while she and Ivy were talking, and all the tables were bare, no indication of what had happened here earlier.

And she would be leaving tomorrow, leaving no mark of her presence either.

She felt a lump rise in her throat at the thought.

But tonight—tonight he'd agreed, he'd sounded eager to welcome her in his bed.

So she was going to do what she wanted with no plans for the future.

Because they had no future.

Chapter Twenty-Five

Gabriel leaped to his feet as he heard the soft knock at the door. It was well past two o'clock in the morning, and he'd been pacing the floor impatiently, waiting for her.

She had a multitude of responsibilities, however, and he knew not to expect her for some time.

It didn't keep him from pacing.

She still wore her evening gown, the glorious one he'd been surprised to hear that Mary had altered. But she'd uncoiled her hair and removed her gloves and jewelry, so she looked more as he was accustomed to.

Beautiful as she always did.

"Can I come in?" she asked, a sly smile on her lips.

He had been gawking. He swung the door open wide, and she stepped inside, waiting beside him as he shut it.

And when it was safely closed, she reached up to curl her fingers in his hair and yank him down to her.

Her mouth pressed against his, and he wrapped

his arms around her waist, the smooth fabric against his work-roughened hands. She opened her mouth and slid her tongue into his, an urgent moan coming from the back of her throat.

She kissed him feverishly, as though she had been waiting for hours. Like he had been.

Her tongue quested inside his mouth, licking and sucking as she leaned into him, molding her body to his, shifting so one of her legs was between both of his, his hardening cock making its presence known against her belly.

He felt the desire rush through him, the feeling that this—and only this—was all that mattered. That he could and should worship her body with his tongue, his mouth, his hands. His cock.

Meanwhile, her fingers tugged on his hair, then slid down his back, splayed, then reached his arse, squeezing as she kept kissing him. She ran her palms over the curves of his buttocks, grasping the muscles there.

She broke the kiss, just for a moment, to gasp, "Your arse is incredible."

He let out a surprised snort of laughter, then reached down to touch hers. Running his hands over the soft globes, the fabric making a silky noise against his palm. "Yours is pretty delicious also."

"Delicious?" she said, raising a brow.

"Mmm," he said, lowering his head to nuzzle her neck. "I'd like to bite that firm, juicy arse. Maybe smack it if you've been naughty."

"Ohhh," she moaned, then lifted her mouth to his again.

He gazed down at her, keeping his eyes locked with hers, then lowered himself to reach her legs, lifting her up suddenly and wrapping her legs around him. Her mound was pressed against his lower abdomen, and he could feel her reaction, shifting to press herself harder on him.

"Patience, love," he said, his hands holding her up just under that gorgeous arse. "I know you're eager to come, but we have all night." He paused, his breath catching in his throat. "We do, don't we?"

She flashed him a quick, wicked smile. "We do," she confirmed. She twisted her head to look toward the bed. His bed. "Are you going to carry me around all night, or are you going to take me over there?"

He stalked to the bed, holding her easily. "So bossy." He tossed her onto the bed, then swiftly followed, caging her with his arms. She looked up at him, face flushed, lips swollen from their kiss, eyes sparkling. He had never seen a more gorgeous thing in his life.

"What do you want, Octavia?" he asked. His voice was a low rumble.

She lifted her chin in classic Octavia fashion. "I want—I want," she began, her voice breathy. Sounding not at all like the bold Octavia he was accustomed to. "I want all of you," she said, glancing down to where his erection tented his trousers. "I want all of this."

He stilled. "You want—" He needed her to be absolutely clear, to say it so they both knew precisely what was going to happen. Not just because it would inflame him to hear her saying in precise detail what she wanted him to do to her, but because he wanted them to have the same expectations.

"I want you to fuck me."

The words hung in the air above them, and she kept her eyes locked with his, her steady gaze letting him know she was absolutely certain.

He couldn't speak for a moment. He lowered his head to her shoulder, sliding his mouth across her skin to her neck. Her pulse was fast, but strong. Like she was.

She arched her neck as she shifted underneath him. "Well?" she said at last, her voice husky with desire.

"Yes," he replied, speaking into her skin. He raised his head to meet her gaze. "I will fuck you."

OCTAVIA WASN'T SURE when she had made the decision. Just that it had felt right. That she wanted him, wanted all of him, this last night.

She wouldn't tell him it was their last night until later. Not just because it would tinge everything with a patina of sadness, but because she couldn't bear to acknowledge it herself.

So she would put it all aside and focus on what was happening now. That was her unique talent, wasn't it? Not to plan for the future at all, but to live out the moment as it was?

And right now, at this moment, she wanted to just be here in his bed.

I will fuck you.

The words echoed in her mind, and she slid into them, relishing his ragged voice, as though he was on the edge of losing control. She wanted both of them to lose control, to forget who they were and who they would be and only know who they were in relation to each other. Each other's wants and needs.

Speaking of which. "I need to get out of this gown," she said, struggling to raise herself up on her elbows. He drew back, holding his hand out for her, and she took it, getting into a sitting position, then off the bed to stand at its foot.

He put his hands behind his head, raising one eyebrow as his gaze raked over her. "I need you to get out of this gown, too," he replied.

She undid the buttons that ran down the front of her gown, grateful she didn't need any help to get out of it. She wriggled her shoulders out of the gown, then slid it down her arms and stepped out of it, clad only in her chemise.

She heard him draw in a breath, and she glanced back at him. His eyes were hooded, dark with desire, and his penis swelled the front of his trousers, making it appear as though the fabric was floating.

She laughed at the image, and he drew his eyebrows together.

"What is there to laugh about?" he asked.

She bit her lip to keep from laughing more. "I

was thinking about gravity," she said, gesturing to his erection.

He glanced down, his lips quirking. "It does seem ridiculous, doesn't it?"

She got onto her knees on the bed, spreading her legs wide so his were in between. Raising her chemise, she moved up on the bed until she was poised just below his cock. She lowered herself down onto his legs, then put her hands to his trousers, undoing the placket and reaching for him.

He groaned, arching his back as she took him in her hand. Hard, yet soft. She gripped it in one hand while her other hand drifted to her core. Right where her body ached for him.

"That's it, Octavia," he urged. "I want to see how you touch yourself."

Her fingers hovered above that bundle of nerves that was clamoring for attention. "Don't you want me to touch you?" she asked, holding him tighter.

He nodded slowly. "Yes. I want all of it. Isn't that what you said?"

"Yes," she breathed, her fingers making contact with herself.

"You're so beautiful," he said, watching her hand move. "But you need to take more clothing off," he said with a frown. "I want to see all of you."

She gave him a pointed look. "You need to do the same, Mr. Fallon."

"With pleasure, Miss Holton," he said. He gestured for her to rise up, and within a minute he was entirely naked. She felt an appreciative smile curl her mouth, and she let her eyes wander over him—from his strong, broad shoulders, to the planes of his chest, to the interesting ridges of his abdomen, the V that went down from his hip bones to there.

To *there*, which still waved proudly in the air.

"And you?" he said, sounding impatient.

She picked up the bottom of her chemise and drew it over her head, tossing it behind her without seeing where it would land.

There would be time for ironing and folding and taking care.

But that time was not now.

She held her hands out, still perched on his legs. "And now what?"

"Now this," he said, swooping up and flipping her onto her back.

She gasped in surprise, then let out a delighted laugh. "I like it when you toss me around," she said with a grin.

He caged her with his arms, his eyes intent on her mouth. She licked her lips, and his gaze darkened. "Are you going to kiss me?" she asked softly. She reached down as she spoke, taking hold of him and sliding her hand up and down.

He shuddered, and closed his eyes.

She chuckled, keeping up her rhythm.

Until he put his hand on her breast, palming its fullness. Squeezing the flesh as his fingers grazed her nipple. She yearned for more of that, for him to touch her there, touch her everywhere, and she was on the verge of saying so when he lowered his head and drew her nipple into his mouth, sucking it gently.

She inhaled sharply, arching her back to thrust more of her breast into his mouth. He murmured against her skin—saying what, she had no idea—and his fingers went to her core, beginning to rub. He didn't touch her precisely there yet, and she squirmed, desperate for him to move his fingers just a little bit—

"Ahh," she sighed, as his fingers finally found that little nub.

"So impatient," he said. "So greedy."

"I did say I want all of you, Mr. Fallon," she replied in an imperious tone. *"All."*

"And you'll have me, Octavia." His voice was full of dark promise, and she shivered.

"You're certain?" he said, keeping up his gentle rubbing. She stifled a moan as she felt the tension increase.

"I told you, didn't I?" She let out a soft snort. "Do you need me to write it out as proof?"

He shook his head, his hair falling on her skin. He was so hard in her hand, and she slid her grip up and down him, twisting a little bit at the top because he seemed to appreciate that.

If *appreciate that* meant groan and utter a stuttered breath.

He met her gaze, his fingers still working on

her. Still touching and petting and caressing. And then he slid one finger into her, and her eyes widened. Her channel immediately tightened, and he growled, his eyes intent on her face.

"You're so wet, Octavia. Do you feel ready for me?"

She slowed her movement on him, feeling hesitant for the first time. She knew the mechanics, of course, but he was *that* size, and she was *this* size, and she didn't see how it would work.

"If you're not ready—" he began, but she shook her head, drawing the head of his penis to her entrance.

"I want you," she said. "All of you."

And she tugged on him so he was touching her there, and then he moved his hand to her hip, holding her as his other hand guided himself in.

And then—

And then—

A feeling of stretching fullness, of his body resting on hers, of warmth and throbbing and ache and everything all jumbled up together in a delicious kind of mayhem.

"Are you all right?" he said, his voice hoarse. He hadn't moved.

"I'm fine," she said, reaching down to grasp that gorgeous arse again. "I want to feel all of it." And she pushed against him so he went further in, making her gasp.

So full, such an odd sensation that wasn't exactly wonderful, but wasn't horrible either.

He stilled, getting her accustomed to the feeling.

"What happens now?" she asked, squirming underneath him.

"Now we fuck," he replied simply, increasing his pace and thrust.

It felt good after a while, especially when his thrusts hit her in just that perfect spot, the one he'd been rubbing before. She angled her body to try to get more of that contact, and he adjusted them so she did.

Soon she had that rising feeling again, the increase in a pleasurable build that was leading inexorably to her climax.

He kept moving, his arse muscles flexing under her hand. That alone was bliss enough, but then there was the pressure, and the sensations flowing through her whole body.

And then he was pistoning into her, and she was holding on to him as he thrust in and out, his rhythm increasing as he panted above her.

"Aaagh," he cried as he withdrew, spilling his seed on her belly. He collapsed on top of her so they were a sweaty, sticky mess, and she loved it.

Even if that part of her still ached for release.

After a few minutes of inarticulate noises, he raised himself off of her and gave her a sly smile. "Now it's your turn," he said.

He hopped off the bed, yanking her feet and dragging her down so her lower legs dangled toward the floor.

He knelt in front of her, and she took a sharp breath, anticipating what he was about to do.

She made a noise of encouragement as he lowered his mouth to her bud, licking it as his finger entered where he had just been.

It felt tender, but satisfyingly so, and his mouth worked her, his tongue swirling around that bundle of nerves as his finger slid in and out.

He touched something inside, and she jerked, the rival streams of pleasure making her see stars. Was it possible to simultaneously climax in two different ways?

She didn't know, but it seemed like she might find out.

The pressure built, and built, his tongue licking her rhythmically as it felt as though she was going to burst from it. Every bit of her was focused on that area, his mouth, his fingers, his hair drifting over her belly.

Until she arched and spasmed, letting out a cry that came from deep inside as the pleasure washed over her.

He made a noise of satisfaction, then planted a final kiss before leaning back to meet her gaze. His mouth was wet. From her, she knew.

He still looked as though he wanted to devour her. Even after all of that.

But she couldn't blame him; she wanted more, too.

"Good?" he asked in a low voice.

"Good," she sighed, reaching down to grasp his shoulder and urge him up. He lay down beside her, flinging one leg over her and dragging the forgotten sheet over their bodies.

She had never felt so content. So relaxed. So happy.

She would not think about what would happen in a mere matter of hours.

This was enough. For now.

Chapter Twenty-Six

I have to go," she said.

The sun was just beginning to creep up into the sky, and the air was almost cool. They lay tangled together in his bed, her limbs entwined with his.

"Of course," he said, but then covered her mouth with his and grabbed hold of her hip, sliding his fingers down her leg.

She shifted away from him, sitting up in the bed. Her hair was gloriously askew, and she looked rumpled and sated. Certainly the most beautiful thing he'd ever seen.

"No, I—I have to go," she said, imbuing her tone with a finality that made his chest tighten.

"What do you mean?"

She flung the sheet off herself and walked to where her clothing lay in a heap, plucking her chemise from the pile and putting it on.

He heard her take a deep breath, then speak.

"It's time, Gabriel," she said, turning to face him. "We had an agreement, did we not?"

"Surely we can have a few more days," he said,

frantic. She couldn't be serious. "You haven't shown me your proof. Aren't gamblers supposed to put all their cards on the table?"

She bit her lip and walked back to perch on the mattress. "I can't put it off any longer. Ivy needs me at the club, and I have to concede defeat. I haven't found anything that would indicate I own the house. You own it." Her eyes grew soft. "I want you to have it, anyway. Even if I found proof, I'd want you to have it. That is my card on the table, Gabriel. You're making a home here, and I don't belong. Not anymore."

His throat closed, and he found it difficult to speak.

"Here is where you taunt me with giving in," she prodded. Her eyes were moist with unshed tears.

"You can't give in. You never give in." *Don't give in to this, Octavia*, he pleaded. *Fight for it. Fight for us.*

She would have to be the one to say something, though. But she already had, hadn't she?

I don't belong.

"I have grown since my arrival," she replied, sounding thoughtful. She wasn't looking at him any longer, her gaze unfocused as if she was recalling something. "I've realized that compromising is not always a terrible thing." She shrugged, then offered him a slight smile. "And I've also realized that doing things on your own isn't always the best way." Her smile widened. "Especially when you're doing—" She gestured to the bed.

"You made enough to pay off your debt." He wouldn't even have the opportunity for her to be livid at him for what he'd done. She'd repay Mr. Higgins, and she'd never know he was going to offer up the house in exchange for forgiving the loan.

He'd never see her again.

"I did," she said, with some satisfaction. "My customers should be returning to London soon. I expect business will start improving."

She was a businesswoman. A London resident who didn't belong here. She'd said it herself. But a woman who was willing to give up something she'd fought so furiously for just a few weeks ago.

She had changed. And he had had something to do with that, but not enough. Not enough to make her think she could have a life here.

"Well, then," he said at last, the words feeling like he was choking on them, "I am glad things worked out all right."

"Yes," she said, her voice strained. "Yes, they did."

She gathered the clothing up in her arms and left his room without a backward glance.

"You're leaving now," he said, wishing it didn't hurt so much. He'd had a few hours to absorb it, to realize that last night was truly the last night, but that just made him ache all the more.

She glanced away from him for a moment, biting her lip. That lip that he'd kissed so thoroughly only a few hours before.

"Yes." She raised her voice out of deference to the household members who were nearby. Mary and Mrs. Wycoff were straightening chairs, Charlie was playing fetch with the dogs, and Mrs. Jennings wasn't doing anything but standing there, eavesdropping.

Even Old Joe was there, apparently untangling a shoelace that had to be taken care of right there in the dining room.

"My sister wants me to review plans for the wedding, and she is needed back home." Her voice was forcedly cheerful, and Gabriel wondered if anyone would be fooled.

"Oh, that is splendid!" Mrs. Jennings said. Mrs. Jennings, then, was fooled. "When I got married, my sister was already a married woman herself, moved far away, and couldn't help me." She turned to look at Mr. and Mrs. de Silva, who hovered nearby. "That is, I know you are a married woman, too, but you are able to help your sister. That is the difference," she said, as if she had to explain.

"You'll be back for the wedding, though," Mrs. Wycoff said, glancing from Gabriel to Octavia and back again.

"Of course!" Octavia said, still using that forced tone. "I—I," she said, faltering.

Goddamn it.

"My fiancée is trying to say that she will miss you all, and she knows you only want the best for her," Gabriel said, his throat tight. Hopefully they would think he was merely upset she was leaving for a while, not that he was upset because she was leaving forever.

Forever.

Goddamn it.

"Yes, that is it." Octavia's expression was grateful. And there was something else there, something he couldn't identify. Something very different from what was usually in her expression.

But that didn't matter. None of it did. Because she was leaving, and she was leaving here, and most importantly, she was leaving him.

For a moment, he considered telling her. Just opening up his heart to share everything he felt about her—her wit, her intelligence, her bravery. How bold she was when she wanted something.

I want all of you.

But if she did truly want all of him, wouldn't she have said something last night? She was Octavia the Fearless. She wouldn't let anything stand in the way of her truth.

Would she?

But what would happen if—*when*—she responded, telling him her life was in London? That while she'd enjoyed their time together, she needed to put herself first? As she should.

That she could never stay here in Greensett. She was too much of a shooting star. A bouquet of wildflowers filled with competing chaotic colors.

"Well, do hurry back," Mrs. Jennings said, clasping Octavia on the shoulders. "You have become part of the family now." Her brows drew together. "That is, not that we are a family, since only my daughter and Charlie and I are related, but you know what I mean."

Octavia bit her lip again. She looked as though she was on the verge of crying.

Of course. She had a good heart, and she likely wasn't accustomed to people who weren't her sister caring for her. It didn't mean anything beyond that.

"I do know what you mean," Octavia said with a warm smile, before drawing Mrs. Jennings in for a hug.

Once she'd released Mrs. Jennings, it was everyone else's turn to get hugs. Cerberus and Nyx scampered around everyone's feet, snuffling at each other and the interesting-smelling people.

Gabriel looked down at Nyx, who'd miss her friend Cerberus nearly as much as he would miss Cerberus's owner.

And then it was his turn.

She approached him, a tentative smile on her lips. "I—" she began, but he shook his head. He didn't want to hear her say something to placate the people in the room who believed their lie. He didn't want to hear her say anything, since saying anything would mean saying goodbye.

Instead, he wrapped her in his arms, tucking her head under his chin. They clung together, her arms around his neck, his around her waist. Everyone around them had stilled, as though aware this was an important moment.

And then her sister spoke.

"Octavia, we should—" she said, her voice strained.

"We should get going," her husband finished. He met Gabriel's eyes, and the understanding and sympathy Gabriel saw in Mr. de Silva's eyes nearly undid him.

"Thank you," she said in a soft voice. He saw her throat work as she swallowed. She met his gaze again, and he saw something there that nearly made him say something, tell her—things, but then she snapped her head away, calling for her dog. "Cerberus!" she called, even though the dog in question was in the room, sitting next to Nyx.

"There you are," she said, her voice higher than usual. "Come, we have to go."

Gabriel folded his arms over his chest as the two sisters and Mr. de Silva walked out of the house. Everyone else followed them onto the front lawn, but he and Nyx stayed inside. He couldn't watch her go, not with everyone else there. Even if it seemed odd to everyone else.

"It's back to just us," he told Nyx, who regarded him with huge eyes.

He turned to walk down the hall to the library, though the prospect of working on his research wasn't the welcoming thought it usually was.

But it didn't matter what he thought about anything—this was now his life, and he would have to muddle through it as best he could without her. It was a sacrifice, but it was one he knew he had to make. He would never make her regret what had happened between them.

"ARE YOU ALL right?" Ivy asked as the carriage pulled away from the house.

Octavia sat opposite her sister and Sebastian, twisting her hands in her lap. Cerberus lay on the floor at their feet, occasionally looking up to give her a worried look.

At least, that's what she thought he was doing.

"I am fine," she said, even though she sounded exactly the opposite. "Fine, fine, fine."

Ivy rolled her eyes, while Sebastian raised a brow.

"You could have stayed, you know," Ivy said gently. "I know you well enough to understand that if you had wanted to stay, you would have found a way."

Octavia felt her face heat as emotion flooded her. She glanced down at her lap. Ivy had retrieved some of the items they'd unearthed in the attic, items that reminded them of their childhood together. She supposed it was good to remember, good to feel the ache and pain of losing that happiness. Because she and Ivy had created a new kind of happiness.

"I need to go to London to pay Mr. Higgins and to reopen Miss Ivy's," she said in a stubborn tone.

Ivy opened her mouth as though she was going to say something, but Sebastian took her hand as he gave a shake of his head. *Good*, Octavia thought. She didn't want them to try to tell her what she could or couldn't do. That was always true, but especially so now when it wasn't just her life, her future, that she would be risking. It was Gabriel's. Could she be the one responsible for obliging him to live in a place he didn't want to in a life he hadn't chosen?

No.

"You'll be busy, at least," Ivy continued after a moment.

"What?" Octavia asked.

"Busy. Everyone will be returning to town soon, and I won't be able to help as much."

Sebastian wrapped his arm around his wife's shoulders and drew her in to him. He placed a kiss on her head before looking at Octavia. "You should think about what it is you truly want, Octavia."

Octavia froze; she'd never heard Sebastian sound so serious before. He was her buddy, they shared commiserating glances when Ivy was being too bossy, and both of them loved their dogs. But they hadn't gotten much deeper than that, though she knew she could with him, if she wished.

It just hadn't come up.

Until now.

Was she a coward that she didn't want to have this conversation now? Mere minutes from leaving the house?

She was. But she'd never been a coward before, and she knew she had to change things about herself, so perhaps this was an improvement?

She gave a rueful snort at her own faulty logic.

"You do have enough, don't you?" Ivy asked.

"Enough?"

"Enough money. To pay the debt to the moneylender?" Ivy sounded irritated and judgmental again. At least some things were going back to normal.

"Oh. Yes, and there's even some left over. I could take you two to dine, if you like," she said, glancing from one to the other.

"I think I will wait until after," Ivy said, caressing her belly. "I haven't been ill, but food and I are less fond of one another than we used to be."

"That just means the dogs and I get all the nicest bits," Sebastian added with a wink.

Octavia smiled, relieved that she didn't have to think all the time about Gabriel. About his smile, the warmth of his voice, how he tried to protect and care for every person he encountered.

About how he made her feel.

Excellent work not thinking about him, a sarcastic voice said in her head.

But he belonged in Greensett, and she belonged in London.

She sighed, leaning down to pat Cerberus's head. There was room for only one gentleman in her life, and he was currently slobbering on her shoes.

She began to sort through the items in her lap, only half paying attention. The box she'd found in the attic before, the one she hadn't bothered to go through. Ivy must have pulled it out, and there wasn't enough room in the carriage for it to go anywhere but on Octavia's lap. A few drawings from childhood, some recipes that must have come from a long-ago ancestor, and—

The papers were on similarly sized pieces of paper, the penmanship varying depending on which man was writing.

Mr. Holton gives Mr. Fallon the right to marry his eldest daughter Ivy, dated seven years ago.

Mr. Fallon will allow Mr. Holton to name his prize pig Mr. Fallon in payment of a gambling debt, dated after that.

Mr. Holton will stand on one leg for ten minutes or he will have to pay Mr. Fallon the sum of twenty pounds.

Mr. Holton gives Mr. Fallon his house in lieu of cash, dated two months prior.

Mr. Fallon returns the house as forfeit for losing at cards, dated later that same night.

She blinked, then began to laugh uncontrollably. After looking for it all this time, here it just was. When she had resigned herself to the notion that she would never find it, what with having looked for it everywhere.

"What is it?" Ivy asked.

Octavia picked the paper up and waved it toward her sister. "It's the proof I was searching for," she replied. She put it back down and began to read, laughing even harder. "It says—I own the house, after all. Even though I told Gabr— Mr. Fallon—that I ceded it to him."

"Are you going to take it back?" Sebastian asked.

"No, of course not," she replied. "I mean, I didn't ask you what you want—"

"My home is in London," Ivy said, interrupting. "I was wondering if you might want to return for other reasons."

Octavia looked at Ivy, who was regarding her with soft eyes.

"He belongs there," she said simply. "I do not."

"I suppose not," her sister agreed. "It's hard, isn't it," Ivy added in a soft tone.

Octavia began to nod in agreement, then gave a vigorous shake of her head. "No. It's not. Because I have you, and Sebastian, and Cerberus. The staff at the club. You are my family, and I can take care of myself."

Ivy's mouth spread into a wide smile. "You are right." Her hand went to her belly again. "And there will be more family soon."

"And that is all the family I need," Octavia said, both to Ivy and to herself.

She folded her arms over her chest, leaned her head back against the cushion, and tried to go to sleep. Images of him distracted her, making her feel irritable. She needed to rest. She had so much to do when she returned.

And besides, there was only so much yearning and despairing she could do during that time.

Or so she hoped.

A WEEK SINCE she'd returned to London, and she'd discovered that one could, indeed, do quite a lot of yearning and despairing.

At first she'd been occupied with reopening Miss Ivy's, and of course paying Mr. Higgins what she owed. That gentleman had returned the Mytho-whatever book, along with his assurances that she could always borrow money from him if she ever needed to again.

He'd also told her that Gabriel had written a note promising to give him the house if Octavia couldn't pay her debt. She'd been furious for all of five minutes, until she realized that it was just something that Gabriel would do. She had grown enough when in Greensett not to get outraged over someone doing what they knew was best for her. And she had to admit that it *was* the best thing for her, and his offer to Mr. Higgins was its own kind of gamble: either she proved she owned the house, and then sold it, in which case she would never know that Gabriel had nearly given it away, or she would make enough at the Big Event to pay it off, in which case she would never know that Gabriel had nearly given it away, or she would have no money and no house, in which case she would have to turn to someone for help.

It was a risk he was apparently willing to take.

She thanked Mr. Higgins as politely as she could thank a man who'd threatened her limbs, while vowing to herself never to get into such difficulty again. If it meant she had to plan for the rest of her life, so be it.

To that end, she'd begun carrying a notebook

and pencil with her at all times. She discovered she had quite a few good ideas when she was walking around town, and before she used to just . . . forget them.

But now she took time to stop and write them down, finishing her evening by reviewing the day's notes.

"Ah," she said, running her finger down the page, "I see I thought that introducing pasties would be a good idea. What do you think?"

She posed the question to Cerberus, who lay snoozing at her feet. Perhaps it was her imagination, but it seemed as though he was less happy here. Missing the pond? The country air? Nyx? Or just everything?

"I suppose it is that time," she said in a resigned voice. "The time when I sit and think about what I am missing, and how much I love him, and why I can't possibly tell him." She shook her head. "I am as woebegone as one of the heroines in a Gothic novel, only those women get to land their brooding dark stranger by the end." She gave a snort. "My brooding dark stranger is neither brooding, nor dark, nor a stranger." Another pause. "Nor will I land him," she said.

Her gaze lit on the book, the one that Gabriel coveted. She rose, picked it up off its table, sat back down in her comfy chair by the fireplace—unlit since it was still summer—and opened it, touching the worn pages carefully.

The book was in Latin, so she couldn't read

it, but her eyes caught some familiar names—
Proserpina, which she thought might be Persephone. Pluto, which she knew was Hades.

She let her mind wander to that night when
he'd told the story. Gabriel had spun the tale so it
seemed as though Hades had truly loved Persephone, not just wanted her to belong to him. Charlie had demanded to know what a pomegranate
was—how she missed that inquisitive boy—and
Gabriel had presented all sides of the story so that
the result seemed reasonable. Six months below,
and six months above.

Six months below. Six months above.

Her eyes widened as she thought about what
that might mean now. What kind of compromise
she could come up with.

And snatched her pencil up and began scrib-
bling frantically in her notebook, so furiously
that Cerberus raised his head and glared at her
for disturbing him.

Chapter Twenty-Seven

That's the third time you've chopped the grass this week," Mrs. Jennings pointed out, as Gabriel finished a tremendous blow on a particularly stubborn blade of grass. Or he thought it was a particularly stubborn piece of grass; perhaps he'd just missed it the first two times he'd chopped.

He planted the scythe in the ground and turned to face her, raising his forearm to wipe the sweat from his brow. She stood just outside the front door, a book in her hand. Nyx lay in the closest thing she could find to shade, underneath a shrub at the side of the house.

"Grass does not grow that quickly," Mrs. Jennings added, nodding to the neatly cut lawn. She walked toward him, holding the book in front of her like an offering. "I found this in the back of one of the desk drawers. It looks old."

She held it toward him, and he took it, his breath hitching as he saw what it was—another volume of the *Mythologiae*. One step closer to the entire collection.

He hoped Octavia had gotten the book back from her moneylender.

She'd been gone for a week and six hours and fourteen minutes. Not that he was counting.

"I was thinking," Mrs. Jennings continued, "that you might want to take it to Miss Holton yourself." She jerked her chin toward the book. "It looks old," she said again, "and perhaps it is valuable. She should know immediately, since I understand from what I overheard"—at which point her cheeks turned pink, as she realized she was admitting to eavesdropping—"that some of Mr. Holton's books are quite valuable."

She looked at him expectantly, and he felt his chest constrict at the thought of it.

Go to London? On the flimsy excuse of having found another volume in a still incomplete set of ancient books that she'd already said she had no use for? That she had given him already, but then had to take back?

There were worse ideas.

And then the need to see her, even if it was just one more time, hit him like he was that stubborn blade of grass and the idea was his blade. It didn't matter that he had no reason to go. In fact, it was likely a terrible idea that he'd reject if he thought about it for too long, so it was best not to think about it for too long.

Mrs. Jennings kept her gaze on him, and she must have seen his decision, because her mouth curled into a warm, approving smile. "I knew you would. How can two people who are so much in love be separated for that long? I know her sister has a wedding to plan, and she is busy herself, I'm sure, but that doesn't mean she isn't longing to see you." She made a shooing gesture. "Go on. The grass will keep until you return. I'll just see about getting some things ready for your journey."

Gabriel stared at her for another moment as his mind whirled with all the reasons he shouldn't just take off for London: she wasn't expecting him, their affair was over, it was at least six hours away, who would take care of Nyx, he'd rarely been to London himself, and the grass—well, the grass would keep, as Mrs. Jennings had said.

He shrugged, deciding to ignore everything his logical brain was screaming at him, and walked back to the house, setting the scythe against the wall before entering.

He took the stairs two at a time, striding quickly down the hall to his room, where he shoved a few items of clothing and the book into his valise. Then he picked it up and went back downstairs.

"We'll have your pasties ready in a minute," Mrs. Wycoff called from the kitchen. Apparently Mrs. Jennings had already spread the word of his trip. The lady moved quickly, he could say that much.

Old Joe came in, nodding at Gabriel. "Pegasus is saddled up for you."

Did Mrs. Jennings have wings?

Nyx trotted up, twining herself around his

legs. He leaned down to pat her on the head, but she ran away as Mary emerged from the kitchen, a cloth bag in her hands.

"Mrs. Jennings said you were going on a trip, and Mrs. Wycoff and I just baked a new batch." Mrs. Hall had come to the Big Event, and while she hadn't gambled, she had partaken of quite a few of her cousin Mary's pasties, and had then asked her and Mrs. Wycoff if she could order pasties for Hall's Elaborate Emporium, to be sold at the counter. Thus far, they had done fairly well, and they were discussing if they should try to make it an actual business venture, combining it with a dress shop where Mary could ply her skills and the two could encourage one another.

Making a family. That was what she had said, wasn't it?

He took the bag, sliding a pasty out and giving it to Nyx, who gobbled it in one bite. Mary gave him an exaggeratedly disapproving look. "I was going to give her one anyway. Now you have one less."

"And since you already have her best interests at heart, could I ask you to take care of her while I am away? Perhaps Charlie would be able to help."

"Of course," Mary replied. "You should go. It's a long trip."

So not only were they all snapping to help him get ready, they were aware of his destination and who he was going to see.

It was a good thing he had so few secrets, because Mrs. Jennings would be certain to discover them.

The only one he had, in fact, was that he had fallen in love with Octavia. And he suspected that that wasn't much of a secret, judging by how everyone was behaving.

"Thank you," he said, nodding to Mary, Mrs. Jennings, and Old Joe in turn. He picked up his valise with one hand, holding the bag of pasties in the other, and strode outside.

Pegasus was there, all saddled, as Old Joe had promised.

He looked back at the house to see everyone—now including Mrs. Wycoff and Charlie—standing at the door, each wearing an iteration of what could be termed an encouraging smile.

He would bet—if he gambled, that is—that they all knew the truth about his and Octavia's engagement, and also knew how he felt.

He would tell *her* how he felt. If she felt the same? Oh God, was it possible?

Then they would discuss it like intelligent people. Find some solution that wouldn't compromise either of their wants and needs.

Why hadn't he thought of that before?

Because he had assumed she wouldn't want him permanently. He'd assumed she thought of being in Greensett as a temporary pleasant respite from her engaging, exciting life.

He shook his head at himself, mounting Pegasus before he could use his excellent brain for more doubts.

There was a time for thinking, and a time for feeling, and now was his time to feel.

He hoped she felt the same way.

OCTAVIA FROWNED AT the door. Not that it was the door's fault someone was knocking on it; but since she couldn't see through to the other side, frowning at the door would have to do.

It was an hour after closing, about three o'clock in the morning, and she had sent the staff home twenty minutes earlier. Business had slowed around one o'clock, thanks to a thunderous rainstorm that continued to beat against the roof and windows. She was grateful her living quarters were at the back of the club so she didn't have to venture outside.

But someone, it seemed, wanted to venture in.

Cerberus was with her, but the wretch was sleeping. As usual.

She approached the door, glancing around for a weapon in case she needed it. Her brother-in-law, Sebastian, had used a cribbage board to thwart a would-be thief, but she didn't think she would be effective in wielding one herself.

"Who is it?" she said, lowering her voice in a fruitless attempt to sound more dangerous.

"Gabriel."

Her heart clenched, and she undid the locks with trembling fingers, flinging the door wide open when she was done.

He stood at her doorway, somehow looking bigger and more handsome than before.

And wet. As wet as the first time she'd seen him, emerging dripping from the pond.

But more clothed, unfortunately.

"Can I come in?" he said in a ragged voice.

"Yes," she said.

He stopped just inside the door, looking down at himself. "I don't want to drip all over your floor," he said.

"It doesn't matter," she replied, taking his hand and walking him through the main floor of the club to the door that led to her rooms.

"Take that off," she said, gesturing to his coat.

"Already asking me to remove clothing, and I've just arrived," he said, a wry tone in his voice.

She gave him a pointed look as she took his hat and hung his coat next to the door. "Your boots, too," she said, pointing at them.

He bent down and took each boot off, placing them to the side.

"Aren't you going to ask me what I'm doing here?" he said, when he was standing in his stocking feet.

She bit her lip. "I suppose that you are here for the same reason I've hired a horse and carriage." She lifted her chin. "I was going to return to Greensett tomorrow morning." She beckoned him down the hall.

"You were?" he said as he followed her. "Why?"

She whirled around to face him. "It's not just because I discovered that you and Mr. Higgins had spoken about my debt," she said, waggling her fingers in the air.

He winced.

"You likely didn't think I would find out about it." She stepped closer to him. Goodness, she'd forgotten how beautiful he was. *Do not get distracted, Octavia*, she warned herself sternly. "But I did. If I was the Octavia from before, I might not ever forgive you." She took a deep breath. "But I am not. I am the Octavia who has learned how to compromise, and that it is possible to depend on other people without being weak."

"Is that why you were coming to Greensett?" he asked in a low voice.

"No, it is not. It is because, Mr. Fallon, I have a plan," she said haughtily.

He blinked in surprise.

Not unexpected, since Not Planning Octavia had been her style heretofore.

"Come in," she said, leading him into the small room she used as a sitting room. "Sit there," she indicated, pointing to the least fragile of the chairs in the room. Hopefully it wouldn't collapse under his power.

Though she might, she thought in hopeful anticipation.

Patience, Octavia, she reminded herself. He might not want to, after all.

He sat gingerly, as though aware of where her thoughts had gone, planting his stocking feet on the carpet. His hair was wet, clinging to the sharp angles of his face. His eyes tracked her every movement, and she felt as though he was looking at her hungrily.

Or perhaps that was her.

"I need to get something from the kitchen. Wait here," she commanded.

She practically ran to fetch it, then scurried back, holding her breath as she moved, wondering if his presence here was just a figment of her imagination.

But no. There he sat, drops of rain clinging to his face, dampening his shirt, his size making everything else in the room seem to shrink.

"Here," she said, flourishing the fruit.

"YOU ARE SHOWING me . . . a pomegranate?" Gabriel asked, puzzled.

She looked as beautiful as he remembered. More beautiful, truth be told. It was clear returning to London had been good for her—her eyes were sharp and focused, she moved with more purpose than he'd seen her move in Greensett, and her life seemed tidy. Did she need him adding the element of him to her life?

Though that was *her* decision, not his. *His* decision was that he was going to tell her how he felt, ensure she knew she had options and choice, and then negotiate.

It sounded very dull, but love wasn't all sparkle and kisses. Sometimes it was communication and negotiation and reconciliation. *Compromise.*

"A pomegranate, yes," she said, nodding as though the fruit was significant somehow. "It took quite a lot of doing to obtain one. They are not a popular item. At least not from the merchants I purchase from."

"I am so glad you were able to acquire one, then," he said, sounding confused.

She rolled her eyes as though what she meant was obvious.

"Look," she said, waving her notebook in the air, "I've thought it all out. I've planned. The pomegranate—the pomegranate is just the representation of all that thinking and planning."

"Perhaps you'd better explain how an exotic fruit might serve as a plan," he said.

She sat down in the chair beside his with an audible harrumph. "It is so obvious, I can't believe you didn't think of it. Unless you did? And that's why you're here?"

He shook his head slowly. "No, I'm—I'm here because I love you."

There. It was out. He'd said it.

Her face lit up as though a thousand candles flickered within her. "You do?" He nodded. "Well, that will make all of this much easier, then."

"What will make this easier?" he said, his tone impatient. "I love you, but that doesn't mean you're not aggravatingly obtuse."

She beamed. "I am, aren't I?" She handed him the pomegranate, then lowered her gaze to her notebook. "I was thinking about the story you told. About Persephone and Hades, though in the Mytho-thing it's Proserpina and Pluto." She looked up at him. "The names were about all

I could read, since it's in Latin. You'll have to translate it for me later."

Later. So there was to be a later. Now he could not wait for her to get to the point.

"Anyway," she continued, consulting her notebook again, "I thought that the way you told the story, it made it seem as though those two might actually be in love. Like us."

He blinked. "You—you're in love with me, too?"

She huffed out an exasperated breath. "Yes, of course I am. It's all that," she said, gesturing toward him, "with the shoulders and the face and that arse. And how kind you are, and intelligent, and you understand me when I'm difficult, and refuse to let me mow you down."

"You love me."

"Yes. I've said that."

He gave her a puzzled look. "Shouldn't we be kissing frantically about now?"

"After I explain." She cleared her throat. "Hades and Persephone were separated because of where they had to live. It doesn't matter that their situation was different than ours. The reality is the same. I need to be in London for my business, and I know you don't want to live here all the time, so I thought we could work out a compromise." She gave him an anxious look, as though worried how her words would be received. How could she doubt his answer?

"We live here in London together for six months, and then we live together in Greensett—in our house—for six months. I can keep an eye on my business, and train someone to take my place when I am away. You can go to the libraries and museums here for your research, and then you can review your notes and do your academic things when we're back home." She tilted her head in thought. "You can share more of your stories with everyone both here and in Greensett, and perhaps collect them all together for publication."

Silence as he let her words fill his mind with possibility.

And then— "Is this the part where we kiss?" he asked hopefully.

She rolled her eyes, but her mouth had curled into a smile. She rose, moving to him and sitting on his lap, wrapping her arms around his neck as she placed her lips on his. "This is the part where we kiss," she murmured. Then she sprang back, her eyes wide. "If you agree to my plan?"

"It's a wonderful plan," he replied, at which she sighed in relief before returning her mouth to his.

Chapter Twenty-Eight

$\mathcal{S}$he had missed this so much. Missed him.

It had only been a week, but it had felt like a lifetime. How could she have gone for so long without feeling the strength of his arms around her, his mouth pressed against hers, his—

Well, it seemed he had missed her, too, because she could feel him hardening underneath her bottom already, and they had just begun to kiss.

She liked how that felt. She wriggled, and he groaned, kissing her more ravenously. His hands were on her arse, cupping her buttocks, and she slid her hands to his shoulders, then lower so they pressed against his chest.

She was able to undo the buttons of his shirt, putting her fingers inside to stroke his warm skin. She broke the kiss for a second, saying, "You should get out of these wet clothes," before returning to his delicious lips, his tongue sliding into her mouth to stroke and tease her.

His cock was a hard length underneath her, and she shifted again, wanting to press its hardness against the part of her that was aching for him.

This was what life would be like now—them negotiating their way through their respective lives, coming together to . . . come together, respecting one another while also supporting one another. Compromising with blissful abandon.

Glorious. Perfect. He would never question why she was the way she was, though he would question how she did things. As he should. She would bring spontaneity, and passion, and friendship into his life, and he would be able to receive joy and pleasure as well as give it.

"What are you thinking about?" he said in a growl as he moved from her mouth to her neck, sucking the skin gently. It sent a skittering arc of pleasure through her, and she arched her neck to give him more access.

"You and us," she admitted. "Mostly you." She tugged on his shirt, pulling it out of his trousers. "I want this off you, for example."

He withdrew his hands from her arse, shifting her so he could better reach his clothing. He yanked the shirt up and over his head in one smooth motion, tossing it past her ear.

He jerked his chin toward her breasts. "I want to see you, too. It's been too long."

She leaped off his lap to stand, undoing the buttons of her gown as she kept her gaze locked with his. Then she began to pull her gown and chemise up, up over her ankles, her shins, her knees, until she had bunched up fabric in her hands and her entire lower half was exposed.

His eyes looked like whisky set ablaze, and she

could have sworn his gaze was heating her skin if she didn't feel so warm already.

He rose, his hands going to the placket of his trousers, and then he was naked except for his stockings. She glanced down, admiring the fully erect penis that waved gently in the air, then down more to his feet, uttering a snort of laughter at the sight.

"Do you need help?" he asked, reaching for her gown. She surrendered it to him, and he drew it up over her head, pausing as her face was covered. He pulled her arms up, shoving the fabric into her hands. Then she felt him lower himself to the ground, and then his mouth was on her, on that aching part. Her knees buckled, and he wrapped his arms around her to hold her upright, his lips and tongue going to work on her as she stood, still unable to see anything, just feeling everything he was doing.

"I've missed the taste of you so much," he said, his strong fingers gripping her arse.

She flung the gown up and over her head, then looked down to see him at the juncture of her thighs, the sight of which made her swallow. "Dear God, you're gorgeous," she said, reaching down to tug on his honey-colored hair. He looked up at her, his mouth wet, his eyes dark with passion.

"No more than you are." He licked his lips, and she exhaled. He was licking the taste of her. "What do you want, Octavia?"

"You," she said simply. "I want all of you."

Like she'd said that night just over a week ago. Only now she meant *I want all of you for all of the time*, and he had to know that. But just in case he didn't, she said, "I want all of you forever."

His mouth curled into a smile. "And I want all of you forever. But right now, if it's all the same to you, I want to fuck you."

"Yes, please," she breathed. He tugged her down onto the floor, and she lay with her back on the carpet, her legs splayed out in a wanton display.

His eyes traveled over her face, down her chest, to where she wanted him the most, then back again. His hand went to her belly, stroking the soft skin there. And then his fingers dipped lower, and he was stroking her as he raised himself onto his elbows, positioning himself atop her. He reached down to guide himself in, and she gasped at the intrusion, the delicious stretched-tight feeling overwhelming her senses.

And then he was thrusting, hard. There was no finesse now, not like before; he was fucking her, and she wanted it, wanted all of it, wanted to feel those urgent thrusts as he slammed in and out of her. She wrapped her legs around his hips and grabbed his arse, feeling the flex of his muscles as he pushed in and out, unrelenting.

Until he gasped and shouted, and she felt his release inside as he collapsed on top of her, panting.

"I missed you," he said at last.

She chuckled, her fingers drifting up his back.

"I can tell. I missed you, too. I love you," she said. "My Hades."

He raised his head to look her in the eyes. "I think in this scenario, you are Hades, and I am Persephone."

She considered it for a moment, then gave a slight nod. "I suppose so." She made a noise of contentment. "I hope you like pomegranates. I bought a dozen."

He shook his head, laughing against her skin.

Epilogue

$\mathcal{G}$abriel looked down at her as they approached the house.

She wore a gown as impractical and fashionable as the one she'd worn when she'd first arrived. This time, however, it was a creamy white, rows and rows of ribbons and flounces and frills spilling down the bottom half. A bit of lace was atop her head, while she wore a string of pearls—loaned to her by Mrs. Jennings—at her throat.

"Are you ready?" he asked. She nodded, and he leaned down to sweep her up into his arms, fabric spilling everywhere as he grasped her under the knees and back.

She wrapped her arms around his neck, giving him a warm smile. "Take me inside," she commanded, and he stifled a laugh at how she was unable to resist giving him orders.

Until it was time for him to tell her what to do, at which point she obeyed with alacrity.

He nudged the door open with his shoulder, then swung her inside the house. Cerberus and

Nyx were already there, greeting them with leaps and barks and wagging tails.

He lowered her to the floor, keeping his gaze locked with hers. "Welcome to the Underworld," he said.

"Oh, my goodness," she said, her eyes wide.

Everyone had worked so hard to make the house sparkle. To make it into a *home*. There were fresh coats of paint on the walls, new fixtures purchased from Hall's Emporium, window hangings that Mary had cleverly fashioned out of scraps of fabric. The floors gleamed. The chandelier glittered above, free of all spiderwebs.

It was the home he'd never even imagined, since he couldn't have imagined such beauty.

"Oh, Gabriel," she said on a sigh. And then she drew her brows together. "I thought we agreed that London was the Underworld and this is aboveground. Because if this is the Underworld, I don't know why Persephone would have ever left."

He shrugged. "I don't care what we call it, as long as we are together. Mrs. Fallon."

"On that we are agreed, Mr. Fallon," she said, raising her mouth for a kiss.

He pressed his lips against hers, and then stepped back as they heard the door open to let their guests in: her sister, Mr. de Silva, all the house's residents, as well as a few of his friends and acquaintances from Greensett.

They were swarmed immediately, Mrs. Jennings

beaming and talking nonstop, Mrs. Wycoff distributing pasties as Old Joe held court in a corner of the room, apparently discussing his plans to expand the stables in order to teach Charlie and possibly some of Greensett's children how to ride.

Mary was receiving compliments on Octavia's gown, which she'd sewn in a matter of weeks. She and Mrs. Wycoff were in the midst of their plans to open Desserts and Dresses, a shop that would spotlight both of their respective skills. The ladies of Greensett were already clamoring to purchase gowns that would make them look as lovely as Octavia.

Not that anyone could look as beautiful as Octavia; she shone like a star, her eyes glinting with joy.

They'd agreed to the Pomegranate Compromise, as Octavia had dubbed it, and they'd also agreed that they wanted the same people to continue living at the house, even though the need for chaperonage was past. Mrs. Jennings had made a half-hearted try at saying they would leave, but was quickly persuaded otherwise. Someone needed to listen to Gabriel's stories, after all.

Mrs. Jennings and Charlie had found volumes five, six, and nine of the *Mythologiae*, leaving only three, eight, and ten. Octavia and Gabriel had promised to continue exploring the house for them, which probably meant exploring one another's bodies as much as hunting for ancient books in Latin.

It was a house full of joy and love—a home created by the people who lived there, by the friendship and connections that had been forged there.

Gabriel had never thought, when he'd gone to take a dip in the pond those months ago, that he would now have a wife, a family, and a home.

It was a gamble he was pleased to make. It would pay off. He knew that. Just as he knew he would love Octavia, and she would love him, no matter what the odds.

Keep an eye out for the next captivating
romance from Megan Frampton

HER LESSONS IN PERSUASION

Coming soon from Avon Books